28 DAY BOOK

3/13 Po. 7/06 24+12   ©1990

BOOKS BY LAURIE COLWIN

Passion and Affect
Shine On, Bright and Dangerous Object
Happy All the Time
The Lone Pilgrim
Family Happiness
Another Marvelous Thing
Home Cooking
Goodbye Without Leaving

GOODBYE
Without
Leaving

•

LAURIE
COLWIN

•

POSEIDON PRESS

New York London Toronto Sydney Tokyo Singapore

POSEIDON PRESS
Simon & Schuster Building
Rockefeller Center
1230 Avenue of the Americas
New York, New York 10020

Designed by Karolina Harris
Manufactured in the United States of America

1   3   5   7   9   10   8   6   4   2

Library of Congress Cataloging in Publication Data
Colwin, Laurie.
Goodbye without leaving/Laurie Colwin.
p.   cm.
I. Title.
PS3553.O4783G6   1990
813'.54—dc20   90-6797
CIP
ISBN 0-671-70706-X

We are grateful for permission to quote from the following:

"Underneath the Harlem Moon" (Mack Gordon, Harry Revel) © 1932 Chappell &
Co. All Rights Reserved. Used by Permission.

"Hi-Heel Sneakers," words and music by Robert Higgenbotham © 1964 Lily Pond
Music. International Copyright Secured. All Rights Reserved.

"I've Got What It Takes But It Breaks My Heart to Give It Away," words and music
by Hezekiah Jenkins and Clarence Williams. © 1929 by MCA Music Publishing,
A Division of MCA Inc., New York, NY 10019. Copyright renewed. Used by
Permission. All Rights Reserved.

"I've Sold My Heart To the Junkman." Leon Rene & Otis Rene. Copyright © 1935
Mills Music, Inc. Copyright renewed. International Copyright Secured.
All Rights Reserved. Used by Permission.

To Juris and Rosa
and in memory of
Leo Frischauer

Americans leave without saying goodbye,
Refugees say goodbye without leaving.

Oh, such a tidy world.
Seeing the April blossoms, my eyes water
Just for the sake of anything that works.

from *Walking Home*
BY JONATHAN ALDRICH

PART ONE

*I've Got What It Takes
But It Breaks My Heart
to Give It Away*

1

During my career as a backup singer with Vernon and Ruby Shakely and the Shakettes, it often occurred to me that this was not a lifetime occupation and that someday I would have to figure out my rightful place in society.

I did not want to think about these things: I wanted to get out on stage and dance. The Shakelys thought it was cool to hire a white Shakette every once in a while, and for a while I was it. Previous to that I had been a graduate student, sitting in the library at the University of Chicago getting older and older, trying to think of a topic for my doctoral dissertation and, once having found the topic, trying to write about it. I was an English major and I intended to write something that would turn into a book entitled *Jane Austen and the War of the Sexes.* Another thing I did not like to think about was how much I did not want to write about this or any other thing.

Once in a while I would take a part-time job to see if some other calling was calling to me, but I did not enjoy work in a bookshop or a restaurant. I did not want to put on adult clothes and go into the Loop and get a job in advertising. Actually, I was and had always been a rock and roll addict. You can hardly admit this to the college adviser of your high school, but what led me to the University of Chicago in the first place was the large number of local blues and jazz clubs as well as a substantial rock and roll scene. I spent my undergraduate years in and out of these clubs, and in the privacy of my room I practiced routines in front of the mirror. At the drop of a hat I could have stood in for a Chiffon, Shirelle, or Marvelette, and I could do a fine imitation of Brenda and the Tabulations.

It is painful to think about those days. It is like yearning for a lover you will never see again and to whom you never got to say goodbye.

Everyone was either startled or horrified when I decided on this line of work. Wasn't I supposed to spend the golden years of my youth in Regenstein Library like the rest of my friends? To be a Shakette had in fact been the burning desire of my heart since puberty, but I had shared this secret with only one person in the world, my college roommate Mary Abbott. She was a sober, contemplative person—a Catholic from Connecticut who leaned more toward Jerry "The Ice Man" Butler and Jackie "Lonely Teardrops" Wilson.

She had been assigned as my freshman roommate and I loved her at once. She had lugged from Connecticut to Chicago a large wooden box containing over seven hundred and fifty choice and vintage 45's. Second of all, her new wardrobe hung in the closet week after week with the price tags still on, while Mary wore her real clothes—the ones she had rolled up in a duffel bag—day after day. To go to church she wore the things her mother had bought her, with the price tags tucked into the sleeves.

It did not take us long to discover that what we liked to do best was to sit endlessly talking and listening to the same record over and over again. One particularly grim winter weekend, we played "I Love You Eddie" (the flip side of the Crystals' major hit "He's a Rebel") all weekend until our dorm-mates felt we had wigged out.

Mary admired the early Ruby whose hits included "Jump for Cover," "Man He's Mine," "Shake and Boogie" and the immortal "Love Me All Night Long." When the time came for me to go on the road, Mary did not entirely approve of my decision, which she felt was my way of staving off real life. While this was true, it was also true that never again in my life would someone say, "Hey, Geraldine, wanna wear a Day-Glo dress with fringe, smoke a lot of reefer and dance as a backup to a rock and roll star?"

Mary was my closest friend and in fact my favorite person. I deeply admired her devotion to religion and, when she took me to church with her, I found myself close to tears. I come from a family of relentlessly assimilated Jews and my experience of ritual and observance was minimal. It was Mary who dragged me to ecumenical meetings at Friendship House in which Christians and Jews discussed their similarities. How I wished I had it in me to believe! But just as I had not fit in in high school, and just as I was a misfit as a graduate student in the English department, I felt I also did not have an allotted place in the angelic order.

But these issues were temporarily swept away when I got my big break, which came, in fact, after the High Holy Days. In a fit of longing, I had gotten dressed up and crept into the back of a Conservative synagogue, where I sat and stood, prayer book in hand, not understanding most of what was said, and staring at the Hebrew I could not read. To ease my soul, I went on a kind of rock and roll binge and, finally, my dream came true.

It happened this way. For more years than I cared to think about, I had been a regular at any number of clubs: Billy's Blues Box, the Rib Cage, Bob Hayes' Trapp Club and Pete's Sweet Potato. I had seen just about every bluesman alive, and by the time I joined Ruby a lot of them were dead. I liked sitting in a dark place blue with smoke, drinking a warm beer and watching Mississippi Fred McDowell singing "Good Morning Little Schoolgirl." It was not unusual for the stray white rhythm-and-blues addict to find his or her lonely way to these places, but it was unusual for them to hang around for so many years. At first I was known by face and then I was known by name, and finally I became accustomed to sitting at the owner's table.

My favorite was the Rock and Roll Pavillion, an enormous place where fledgling acts got their start and then came back to pay their respects after they had made it in the big time. I was very tight with the owner, since I used to drop by in the afternoon and watch rehearsals. One day I was told that Marvin Delton was in town but that one of the Deltrons was sick. I did not even have to offer myself. I was offered personally to Marvin Delton by Mack Witherspoon, the Pavillion's owner, who said, in my very presence, "Here's a boss white chick who knows all your routines and she can *move.*"

Marvin looked me up and down, giving me an insight into the feelings of female slaves about to be auctioned. Apparently he found this idea very wiggy. He hauled out the sick Deltron's dance dress and told me to go put it on. I looked it over and knew it would fit. It was a *sign*.

Mack threw on an old Deltron hit, "Bad Baby Mine." I got out on the dance floor and did my thing and was hired on the spot. I was not a bit afraid, except of how much I loved what I was doing. The other Deltrons were not thrilled to see me but I was only hired for a couple of nights.

Then Mack told me that the Shakelys were coming to town. His brother was their drummer and he said that their white Shakette had been fired and they were looking around for someone to replace her. A quick audition was arranged at the Pavillion and I was instantly taken on. I replaced someone called Pixie Lehar who danced under the name of Venus Cupid and was said to be a junkie.

I had one week to sublet my apartment, tell my department chairman and fly east to break the news to my parents. No one took it very well.

2

My mother was a portrait painter—portraits of children—and an occasional children's book illustrator, Gertrude Coleshares. Locally, she was famous: head of the county art center, sponsor and star of its annual show, creator of "Portrait Art in School," a project for ten-year-olds. Each year the art center had a show of my mother's work, and it was years before strangers stopped accosting me at the town grocery and telling me how familiar I looked: as a child, I was my mother's favorite model.

Deep in her heart, and evident in her work, my mother believed that children should look and behave as they had in Victorian England. Her work was full of long-legged little girls wearing black or white stockings, hair ribbons and white pinafores. She did not, of course, dress me this way, but she came close. She kept a tight rein on what I did wear. People like Mary Abbott, my contemplative roommate, believed that part of my decision to run off and join Ruby was my long-cherished desire to wear something in public my mother would truly hate. This may be true, but it hardly matters.

My father was like a cloud, a fog, a mist. He ran an import and export business and thus had good times and bad, but the household power was held by my mother, who ruled majestically. My constant memory is of her wearing a majestic violet and black tweed suit and carrying an alligator bag.

My mother had high hopes for me: I disappointed her daily. I suffered at ballet class, and after a few years my teacher threw up her hands and told my mother to take me off to a modern dance class. This, to my mother, was like being told that I was mentally retarded. My mother had never seen a performance of modern dance and did not like it when she finally did. I liked it quite well and it stood me in good stead when I went to work for Ruby.

My mother hoped I might have some artistic talent. In fact, I had not a scrap. I could draw boxes in three dimensions, and a thing that looked like a person—sticks and circles. Generally, I was hopeless. I did not have an art gene. This confounded my mother, who could not believe that the rich blood of her talent did not flow in my veins. She thought I might be a writer, but I gave no promise of that. Actually, I was crazy about music, but my mother knew nothing at all about it and therefore never gave it a thought. She went to the opera with my father as a social event unconnected to the music, through which she sat thinking her own thoughts or sketching the costumes with her little gold pencil.

Against this family tapestry I stood foursquare to announce my plans.

"Who are these people?" my mother demanded.

"There's no point discussing it," I said. "They are rock and roll performers. They have made a lot of records. I have been dying to do this. It was my childhood dream."

"It was *not!*" shouted my mother. "This is the first I have heard of this."

"You think this music is the raving of crazed jigaboos!" I screamed. My father sat in a chair. He looked like a pillow with the stuffing half out. It was clear he was very tired. Any minute one or the other of them would tell me that this ridiculous plan of mine would kill one or the other of them. I said: "I am an over-the-hill graduate student. I am not going to write my dissertation. I have studied and I have even taught. This is what I really want to do. I have given it a lot of thought. If I don't do it now, I never will. I am not doing this to hurt you."

When it was clear that I would never have their blessing—how could I have been so dim?—I called the suburban cab service, rode to the airport and flew back to my Chicago apartment to get my life in order. I said goodbye to that fine, fine, superfine (as the song goes), intellectually challenging university. I had lunch with all my friends and arranged with Mary Abbott, who was going to New York to do her doctoral work, that she would move my things with hers. She was my best friend, and since I did not have a home, she would be my home. Then I flew to New Orleans, the Shakely group's headquarters. Ruby's brother, Fordyce, who drove the tour bus and carried a gun, met me at the airport and took me to the Mille Fleur Motel, where I joined my future dance mates, Grace Bettes and Ivy Vines (not her real name).

Within three days I had claimed the dream of my childhood.

3

Vernon and Ruby were the color of café au lait. Vernon was lean, mean and dirty-looking, with an evil little line for a moustache and that soft, poreless skin that looks like glove leather. Ruby looked very much like him, with high cheekbones and slightly slanted eyes. She wore a series of elaborate and expensive wigs. Her own hair was done in the kind of little braids very young black girls often wear. Many people believed that she and Vernon were brother and sister. It was hard to tell how old they were, but their son was twenty-three and their daughter was twenty-one. It was also said that Ruby had had her first child at twelve.

In the tour bus, on which we all spent a lot of time, Vernon and Ruby sat up front with their accountant or Ike Miles, their musical director. We sat in the back of the bus, blowing reefer and playing cards.

We liked reefer and the band liked speed. Vernon himself took a very hard line against heroin, which he pronounced "hair-oyne," but he did not mind reefer or bennies, without which no one would have set foot on his bus. His hatred of smack and alcohol was made clear to me when I was hired. Vernon said he treated his people like family and encouraged us all to drink iced tea and ginger ale, which he called "Virginia ale."

Our end of the bus—mine and Ivy's and Grace's—was a haze of cigarette and reefer smoke and nail polish remover. My thrall to rock and roll made it possible for me to endure the sort of tedium that might otherwise have driven me insane.

We practiced our routines over and over and over, and then we learned new ones. We rubbed each other's feet, or soaked them in portable bidets on the bus. We read fashion and romance magazines which featured such articles as "Color: What Speaks for You?" or "What I Found in My Husband's Pocket Made Our Marriage a Nightmare." Every now and again, to entertain Grace and Ivy, I would read one of these features in the voice of Dame Edith Sitwell. This was a big hit and proved to them, as nothing else, how wiggy college girls could be.

My university years had taught me nothing whatsoever about manicuring but, because of the fabulous shock absorbers on Ruby's bus, it was possible to gloss one's nails with sparkling Merry Berry or Poison Grape. Oh, the hours of boredom! The inferior reefer!

A backup singer's life was not an easy one, what with trying to find entertaining and not terribly toxic ways of passing the time on that humid bus. We spent hours listening to Vernon on the issues of the day, and there were certainly a lot of these. For example, civil rights. Ruby's husband opined, "It is my civil right to make a lot of bread and I intend to." And of the war in Vietnam he said, "The white honky devil is practicing on them before starting on us." Vernon was no friend of the white man, but I was so marginal a person that I hardly counted and was the white Shakette in the way of, say, an odd purple sock. Besides, I felt he was right.

However, no one gave these things all that much thought. Our destination was not some town or city but always "the Auditorium."

Being on stage made up for everything: the exhaustion, the greasy food, the boredom. It was an addiction. I loved it. I loved our dance dresses and our luminescent shoes. I loved to shake and sweat in front of those gigantic speakers. At concerts the audiences—black, white and mixed—threw us flowers, beads, gumdrops. When Ruby sang "Let Us Be Joined," which was taken for a song about integration when it was in fact a song about sex, the audience screamed, cheered and threw confetti made out of their shredded Ruby Shakely Souvenir Programs. It is hard to recapture the hokey fervor of those times.

It seemed to me like a fever dream, or even better, one of those sweet dreams from which you wake up and find that it was real. After years of being a sullen, uncooperative ballet student, of not truly un-

derstanding deconstructionist criticism, of living with the constant sus-
picion that I was not in fact a graduate student but an indeterminate
person walking around a university campus *dressed* as a graduate student, I was suddenly an authentic thing.

To be effortlessly yourself is a blessing, an ambrosia. It is like a few
tiny little puffs of opium which lift you ever so slightly off the hard
surface of the world.

Yes, I was myself. I was not black, I was not from the South, I was
not funky and I was not engaged to my high school boyfriend, who
was now in the Marine Corps. I was not a Ph.D. candidate and I didn't
care. I was a Shakette, and I knew my time had come.

4

Every week, in order to perform my imitation of a good daughter, I wrote my parents a respectful, generally untruthful letter from wherever we happened to be: Demopolis, Alabama. Dear Mother and Daddy. What an *interesting* part of the world this is. Last night the band was invited to an authentic barbecue. I noticed squirrel on the menu of the local restaurant, with eggs and grits. A journalist from some national magazine is traveling with us, but don't worry—he did not bring a photographer. I am very happy and very well. I do love traveling and I do miss you.

In reality, traveling involved looking out the window at a thruway, and these are all the same, probably the world over. I was happy and well, and a guy from a magazine had been on the bus one day but it was unclear if he was going to write about Ruby or go off with Martha and the Vandellas, who were enjoying a string of hits. I did not miss my parents one whit.

Once a month I called my father at his office to check in. A normal person would do this, I felt.

"Hi, Daddy! I'm in Lansing, Michigan."

"Your mother is very worried about you."

"I'm fine, Daddy, I'm having a lovely time."

"She worries about drugs."

"Oh, drugs," I said. "There's nothing to worry about. Vernon doesn't allow them. Besides, these people are straight as arrows. They go to church every Sunday."

Strangely enough, this was not a lie. Every Sunday morning Ruby, Vernon, Grace, Ivy and some of the band went to the local Baptist church, wherever that happened to be. Donald "Doo-Wah" Banks, the band's saxophonist, was an Episcopalian, and said his mother was very High Church—she was from Trinidad and liked a good deal of incense in her service.

Once in a while out of sheer loneliness I went along, and in many of these places I was the only white face. It never failed but that hymn singing brought tears to my eyes.

My parents were relentlessly secular. They believed that to be American was quite enough. Ethnic identity was slightly vulgar in my mother's eyes, or, at best, a kind of colorful peasant tradition.

I had no church to go to. My father's mother had been a Jew from an old family that had intermarried until there was nothing much of anything left except a tree at Christmas time. We had some aunts on my mother's side—this side was of a Judaism so reformed that it was indistinguishable from, say, the Girl Scouts—who held the traditional Passover meal, but no one in living memory celebrated anything silly like Hanukkah. On the High Holy Days my mother dragged my father off to the local reformed synagogue, where the rabbi had a phony English accent and repeatedly intoned in his sermons that Jews were really nothing more than good Americans.

I was sent to Sunday school at this place, where I learned to shoot spitballs and crack gum. I also learned how to make the bus transfer machine go berserk and spew transfers out all over the place. The real purpose of my attending Sunday school was that it made me eligible to attend the Inter-Suburban Dance Society, to which all really nice girls and boys from cultivated Jewish families belonged. Here we were taught the ballroom dancing thought to be useful for our future, since, it was believed, we would attend thousands of weddings, tea dances, and balls when we grew up. At these dances the boys went out and planted cherry bombs in mailboxes and the girls talked about what animals the boys were. As for me, I was usually in love with some gangly misfit or other with whom I discussed such works as *No Exit* by Jean Paul Sartre. There were a few girls who really liked to kiss boys. I was one of them, although I only kissed those boys who agreed with Jean Paul Sartre that hell was other people.

The first time I heard "Amazing Grace," in a sweaty little chapel outside of Gainesville, Florida, I began to cry. I found I could not stop crying, on and off, all day.

"Poor little white girl has flipped out," said Vernon.

I had a healthy, upright hatred for Vernon. Everyone did. He was the sort of person who, it would not have surprised you to learn, had sex with lizards and embezzled funds from handicapped widows. Ruby may have hated him too, but he was her engine; he was everyone's engine. He had come up from the most dire poverty in which ten children slept in a shack and were probably molested by their relatives. He had discovered Ruby and, by dint of being able to pluck the strings of a secondhand guitar and possessing an ambition that made forest fires look like birthday candles, he claimed Ruby—who could sing— and went out to set the world on fire. He had come a long way. At home in New Orleans, he and Ruby lived in a big pink house with a pink piano in the living room and a pink piano in the music room. He drove an elongated black Cadillac and had a collection of Civil War pistols. Ruby had her own masseuse, her own hairdresser and, when she finally hit the big big time (by which time I was long gone, as the song says), she even had her own designer and nutritionist.

Ruby was not interested in the private lives of her staff. The people who worked for her—musicians and dancers—were just so many crabs or spiders. She did not like the sight of anyone having trouble. The only reason she and Vernon saw me crying was because I burst into tears inside the church.

"Today is the anniversary of my grandmother's death," I lied. This made them all feel better.

I was taken for a little walk by Doo-Wah Banks, on whom I had a useless crush. Doo-Wah was a dense, middle-sized man with short hair and the kind of eyes that take in everything—like a cop's. He had actually graduated from Juilliard—I alone knew this—and he was having himself a little fun by traveling with Ruby. Since he was divorced and had to send money to his wife and two boys, being on the road prevented him from running up expenses. He had big shoulders and was shiny black. His affect was an irresistible combination of fatherly and sexual.

"Now, now, now, little chicken," he said as he walked me into the countryside. "Now, stop crying, you poor little thing. Are you lonely for your own people?"

"I don't have any own people," I said. "I think I'd feel a lot better if I could get in bed with you, Wah."

"Oh, no, honey-babe. We'd get lynched for it. Besides, I don't sleep with colleagues, that's my rule."

"Well, listen," I said. "How about just letting me put my arms around you."

He led me behind a large tree and allowed me to hug him. He was an excellent person, a truly good man, kind to girls and women, a teacher and friend to children, and he kept his mouth shut when it was wise to. A person could learn a lot from a guy like Wah. I held him tight. He smelled of spicy aftershave. I really believed that if I could just curl up with him everything would be fine. He put his arms around me and I began to cry again.

"Poor lonely girl," he said. "Why don't you get a boyfriend?"

"I have no faith," I sobbed.

Doo-Wah, who believed in self-improvement, thought I meant that I lacked faith in myself. While that may have been true, it was not what I meant.

"I mean religious faith," I said. "I'm nothing. I'm a lapsed Jew from an assimilated family. I don't belong anywhere. I'm alone in the middle of the universe."

This caused Doo-Wah actually to kiss my nose.

"Oh, come *on*, little girl," he said consolingly. "We *all* that."

5

My earliest memories were musical. My mother, for whom music was background noise, painted on Saturday afternoons while listening to the Metropolitan Opera broadcasts on the radio. I hung out in the kitchen, where whatever housekeeper we had, kept the kitchen radio on. The first time I heard Chuck Berry sing "Roll Over Beethoven" I was dazzled. I stood in the kitchen in a perfectly rapt state. I took money out of my piggy bank to get this record. I played it on a child-size phonograph in my own room every minute that I was alone.

This room was done after my mother's style. On the wall were framed watercolors of me at various stages: in a straw hat eating a watermelon, playing with someone else's Persian cat (we did not have pets), at the piano, and so forth. My bedspread was a pink and yellow quilt. My curtains were a faded rose-infested chintz, and on the floor I had an old Persian rug.

Eventually I dismantled this room. The watercolors came down and were stacked in my closet. The quilt, which had always daunted me by its being old and expensive, was changed to an Indian print bedspread. The children's books were banished to the cellar and my teenage books were settled on the shelves. And while I sought to keep my mother out, she got in anyway and edited me. I found certain books vanished—my mother thought they were seditious or too sex-soaked for a young thing like myself. Gradually, I learned what every upright teen with a snooping mother learns: to hide everything, and I was good at it. I could hardly wait for the wonderful day when I would graduate from high school and go away to embrace my own destiny with no one around to tell me what to do.

At college I passionately wished I were either very tall or quite short, extremely beautiful or terribly ugly. I wished I had a long funny nose, pierced ears and lots of shiny black curly hair. Or that I were oversized, like an equestrian statue, or had some odd quirk in my background, like having grown up in Cambodia or Hong Kong or on a sheep ranch in Montana. Of course, my mother was a portrait painter, but that did not seem as glamorous as having a father who had been blacklisted or a mother who studied primitive tribes in Africa and South America.

As I learned from the thousands of women's magazines I read on the road with Ruby, people, especially women, never see what is actually in the mirror. Once in a while, lifted on a pleasant little cloud of marijuana, I liked to lean back in my extra-padded Strat-o-cruiser seat, look out the window and wonder: can you see what is in the mirror? How much does a mirror distort? Was it not a terrible ironic joke that, of all the people in the world you need to see clearly, the one person you can never clearly see is your own self? Was this not in fact a tragedy? Then as I began slowly to come down and was left with that unpleasant little buzz you get from inferior reefer, the plain truth would emerge: people never like themselves anyway. Was that not the truth? Were there actually people who looked in the mirror and broke into a contented smile of acceptance?

My hair was neither blond nor brown, although as a child I had the loveliest mop of ringlets, according to my mother's portraits and the seven thousand photographs she and my father took of me. As I got older, my hair got darker—what a slump for my artistic mother! I was five foot four. My legs were neither long nor short. I was not short- or long-waisted. In fact, I was a fairly regular-looking person, easily pretty enough but not enough for my physically snobbish mom, who felt that being beautiful was the Big Thing.

Therefore she was very involved in the way I looked and I am sure that I have repressed the memory of fights we must have had about clothes when I was little. We certainly had them when I was older and confronted with an adolescent's perpetual dilemma: do I please myself or my mother? If I please myself, how much will I hurt her?

It was far easier, I realized, simply to hide. I kept a set of clothes in my bookbag. In the mornings I dressed to my mother's specifications, and changed my clothes in the bathroom at school. I did not reveal that on Friday nights, when she thought I and my little friends sat playing Scrabble or were practicing ballroom dancing, I was listening to rock and roll and necking with the brother of one of my little friends.

I cannot describe the sacred feeling of liberation that saturated my very bones as I got on the airplane to go to college. My first week there, I was picked up by an unsavory-looking person who was said to be a genius. He was a senior and lived in a grotty hovel off campus. He was a major in theoretical physics but I glommed on to him at once because he knew who John Lee Hooker was. We went to his nasty flat and listened to John Lee Hooker records for an hour or so. Then he played me Blind Willie McTell doing "Statesboro Blues." I fell in love with him that instant and decided that if anyone was going to be my first lover, it would be this person. He seemed to be a little nutty and he certainly was a slob, but he looked so pretty with his clothes off. Besides, I had never been to bed with anyone in my life and I found, after an hour or so, that it was perfect heaven. He told me he thought I was beautiful, which sent me into a kind of erotic rapture.

Several weeks later he passed me on the street and said hello as if he had met me years before at, perhaps, his little sister's sweet sixteen party. My heart was broken but, after all, he had introduced me to Willie McTell, and I was no longer an innocent girl. I knew that I was on my way

6

My diary, had I ever bothered to keep one, would have been littered with the names of boys (later men) I loved who did not want me. The boys who found me fetching, I found twinky and wimplike. When some unsuitable wild person with a bad reputation actually fell for me, I experienced bliss of short duration followed by desolation. Love was like that, I thought.

Of course, the music of the day did much to back me up. "You Don't Love Me," "Why Don't You Love Me?" "Standing in the Shadows of Love," "Wedding Bell Blues" and so forth, including Ruby's monster hit, "You Don't Love Me Like You Used to Do."

On the tour bus, I liked to let my eyes wander over the unattainable Doo-Wah, who was, he often said, no oil painting. It was his emanation I was after. When I was sad, which was as often as possible, he let me curl up in his arms if we knew we were alone.

"You oughtta quit this tour, girl," he said. "You been doing it two years now. This is a dead end."

"I don't care," I said. "I know it's a dead end. But I love it."

"Well, baby, the handwriting is on the wall," he said.

I looked over at the wall, which did in fact have handwriting on it. Most walls of the cheap motels we stayed at did.

"This one says 'Pat 'n' Bill 4ever,' " I said. "So what?"

"Honey-chile, Vernon has his eye on the *big* big time."

"Isn't this big time?"

"Shit, no," said Wah. "They want Vegas. Tahoe. Madison Square Garden. They don't want to mess around in these little shitty towns. And when they hit, baby-love, they will throw you out. You won't see any white faces when Ruby goes big time, unless it's her money manager."

I considered this.

"You living in a dream world," Wah said.

"What about you?" I said. "You're on this tour. What are you going to do?"

"I'm a black musician," Wah said.

"Me too!" I said.

"You better get yourself some nice white husband or go back to college, or you know how you'll end up, don't you?"

"Yes, Wah," I said. "I will be a hairoyne addict like my predecessor, Pixie Lehar."

"Exactly," Wah said. "Now, when I was coaching Little League . . ."

"Oh, shut up!" I said. "If you're so wholesome, what are you doing here? Why aren't you teaching at Juilliard or coaching some high school band?"

"I am making money," Wah said. "But *you* are having an experience. When I quit, I will still make money. But people don't pay for people to have experiences, not that Ruby pays all that well. This tour is not for you. You should quit. I would be proud and happy to escort you to your rightful place."

I looked at Doo-Wah mournfully. I hoped he would soon light a reefer and act more like a normal person.

"You find my rightful place, Wah," I said, "and I will be happy and proud to let you escort me to it."

7

I lived to be on stage. At the time there was nothing much else to live for. The food on tour was either wonderful (grits, collards, shoestring potatoes) or horrible (grits, hamburgers, antique fish cakes). Grace and I bought heads of cabbage and chopped them up for salad. We had a knife, a chopping block and a plastic bowl, and we made cabbage salad after the recipe of her sainted grandmother. The plastic bowl had a plastic top so that we could eat our cabbage on the bus. We carried a box of kosher salt and a box of black pepper, and left behind, in various motels around the country, empty bottles of cider vinegar and small vials of olive oil. God only knows what the management thought we had been doing.

Our longing for salad brought Grace and me together, and she confessed to me that she was sending all her money to her fiancé, Graham, and that in a year she would quit the tour. Graham, who worked for an accounting firm, would quit his job, too, and they were going to open a catering business together called Grahamgrace Delectable Foods.

Ivy's boyfriend, Bud, was in the Marines. When he got out he was going into auto-body work with his brother in Hartford, and Ivy was going to get married and have a large squad of kids.

And what was I going to do?

When they asked this question, a kind of whirring emptiness flapped in front of my eyes. Grace and Ivy assumed that if you had a college degree you could do anything. In their eyes it was like having a large inheritance. They couldn't imagine that you might have all the choices in the world but none of the skills.

I said, "I'm going to be a Shakette forever."

This caused Ivy and Grace to double up. The idea that anyone did this for fun after the first few months (much less two years) totally staggered them.

On Friday afternoons we washed our hair. Then we did our nails, and when they were dry we wrote letters. We sat there like three little schoolgirls using the arms of our chairs or stacks of magazines as writing surfaces. Grace wrote to Graham, Ivy wrote to Bud, and I wrote to Mary Abbott, my constant correspondent: Dear Mary, We are in Memphis for an oldies night. Fats will be on the bill. Next week, James Brown without the Famous Flames. Also Baby Jean and the Jerelles. The saxophonist says that Ruby wants to take this act to Las Vegas and, when she does, I will get the ax. Nothing good lasts, or so they say. I guess I should start thinking of what to do next in some structured way, right? It is hot here and cold where you are. In the meantime, sha la la la la la la la lala. All yours . . .

When we played Chicago I bunked with Mary, and when she moved to New York I stayed with her there. To wake up in a real bed in an apartment, with real oatmeal cooked on a real stove and drinkable coffee and lots of books and magazines around, made me feel as if I should never set foot out the door.

On the other hand, on stage I felt a way I had never felt before. I was an eagle, an angel. My body was made of some pure liquid substance and would do whatever I asked it to. I danced until I felt as smooth and effortless as an ice skater. I could fixate on one person in the audience and turn him into jelly. The big questions fell away. There were no questions—only answers. I was in the music. It wrapped around me. I was not lost in it, but found. The kind of ecstasy people found in religion, I found in being a Shakette. It was not an out-of-body experience, it was an *in*-body experience.

Grace, Ivy and I could have done our routines in our sleep. We wore little dance dresses with spaghetti straps. The dresses were made of layers of long fringe which shook when we shook. Each of us had three dresses: chartreuse, cerise and electric blue, with shoes to match. Sometimes we wore the same color. Sometimes, if Ruby felt it was the kind of crowd friendly to hallucinogens, we each wore a different color and covered ourselves with black-light makeup, so that when Vernon signaled the switch to black light, the three of us looked like three pairs of lips with polka-dotted arms. Sometimes we actually painted skeletons on ourselves, until one night in Memphis some kid on acid went totally berserk.

Once in a while, if a hall had very bad vibes, Ruby and Vernon and Ruby's brother, Fordyce, insisted on police protection and security guards. Young people were ingesting so many unique substances that it was hard to tell what anyone might do. The cheery ones threw jelly beans, which stung when thrown from the balcony and were banned after Grace suffered a minor eye injury. People were actually searched at the door for them and once a handgun turned up in the back pocket of some harmless-looking nut. It was quite a scene.

On bad days Grace suffered from sinus headaches, Ivy had terrible menstrual cramps, and I had constant hamstring pain. But then there were days when everything was right. Our rehearsals went as smooth as cream, and all of us felt fine. The ions in the air were charged with good things and our heads and hearts were light. There was no bad news, and nothing hurt. When the hall was filled up, we could feel that it was full of bighearted, innocent, friendly, rock-and-roll-hungry spirits who would tear themselves up with joy but never lay a hand on us. This sort of audience tossed us flowers. We tore off the petals and threw them back. Everyone screamed with happiness and Ruby ended these shows with "Jump for Joy," which made the audience leap to its feet and sing with her. Ivy, Grace and I stood in back in our chartreuse dresses, chanting, JUMP FOR JOY! JUMP FOR JOY! JUMP FOR JOY!

Ruby, like an angel, or a sprite or a devil from hell, took off her high-heeled dance shoes and jumped higher and higher until the final JOY! when she came down and the lights were cut and all was total darkness.

Eventually everyone I knew had given up on me. My parents could barely bring themselves to speak to me. When I called my father at his office, he told me I had broken my mother's heart and that she felt strongly that I was now on drugs.

"But I'm not, Daddy!" I said. "I drink milk all the time and I'm healthy as a horse. Besides, I'm being interviewed by a couple of magazines."

I heard a kind of gasp from the other end of the phone.

"This will kill her," he said.

"Kill her?" I said. "She ought to be thrilled! How many of her friends' daughters are interviewed for anything?"

"Priscilla Meyerhoff is a White House Fellow," my father said sadly.

"Gee, I'm really sorry," I said. "Okay, tell Ma I'm wallowing in sin."

"She'll be thrilled to hear it," said my father bitterly.

It was true my friends were forging ahead in life: getting married, having babies, being promoted, becoming White House Fellows or junior partners in their law firms. Even Mary Abbott had gotten a fellowship at Columbia, and on one of my two-week breaks I flew to New York and moved my things into a tiny room in her new apartment.

My actual home was our giant tour bus. I got into it in order to go somewhere in order to get out and into a motel room where I would put on a dress the size of a corset and get up on a stage to back up Ruby, and then, after losing four pounds in sweat, I would get back into the bus and go somewhere else.

After the Boston show I started noticing a person who sat in the second row wearing a tie and jacket—most uncool. He turned up in Providence, New London, Hartford, then Waterbury. It was hard to tell how old he was. He also had short hair.

He appeared at both the Apollo and Filmore shows, and it occurred to me that he might be some sex nut fixated on Ruby, who was one of the hotter acts around. I was glad my parents would never come to see me perform and therefore spare themselves the sight of Ruby wrapping herself around the microphone in numbers such as "Love Me All Night Long." She liked to break into a throaty monologue that began, "Darling, why don't you slide your big, strong arms around every part of me?" Naturally, creeps were inspired by this sort of thing and sent her dirty letters in care of Crackerjack Records.

It was after the Filmore show that the person with the jacket and tie came backstage. He caught me off guard. I was alone. There was a big party for Ruby uptown, but if I had gone I would have been the only white person there. Instead I sat in my damp dance dress, taking off my false eyelashes. When I looked up, there he was. It occurred to me that he might be dangerous.

"What are you?" I said into the mirror. "Some kind of Boy Scout from Mars?"

"I'm a journalist."

"Oh, yeah? Are you the guy from *Bop* Magazine?"

"Well, not exactly," he said. "I'm very interested in you as the white Shakette, and also interested in the Shakelys. I've been following them for years. Would you like to go out?"

"Are you kidding?" I said.

"No."

"Well, out where?" I said.

"Well, how about out to dinner?"

Up close this person seemed sort of cute, about my age or maybe older. He had blue eyes and curly brown hair, and nice white teeth. I hadn't been out with anyone for longer than I could remember.

"I guess I ought to change my clothes," I said. "What's your name, anyway?"

"Johnny Miller," he said. "I'm a lawyer."

"No kidding!" I said, trying to keep all this straight. "But I thought you said you were from *Bop* Magazine."

"No, *you* said you thought I was from *Bop* Magazine. I'm not a journalist. I lied to get backstage. I just wanted to meet you."

"Okay," I said. "I'm Geraldine Coleshares."

"I'm well aware," said Johnny Miller. "I know lots about you. I especially dig it when Ruby lets you have a little solo. You have a wonderful voice."

"Listen," I said. "I'm tired. I'm hungry. I just did a show. What's your story, anyway?"

"I love rock and roll with all my heart," he said solemnly. "I have every single record Ruby ever made, including the original pressings of 'Sugar Doll Man' and 'Boy Oh Bad' from when she was Ruby Martin and the Vonelles."

I took this in. Only a hard-core fan would know about Ruby Martin and the Vonelles, whose two records never went anywhere in particular. Then an idea struck me.

"Oh," I said. "I get it. You're one of those music industry lawyers." Around Ruby and Vernon, the term "music industry lawyer" was said as one might say "psychotic ax murderer who eats live babies."

"I am not," Johnny said. "I work for what you would call a prestige firm. I work very long hours and I feel entitled to a little entertainment once in a while. I've been watching you since you first started. What's *your* story, anyway?"

"I'm a failed graduate student and a successful Shakette. That's all there is."

"Why don't you get dressed," Johnny said. "You look like you're starving."

8

It turned out I was starving for everything. Lately we had eaten at some pretty terrible places. Most nights we were so tired that we didn't even have the energy to make our motel-room cabbage salad. Johnny took me to an expensive steak house and talked to me while I consumed a steak with *pommes soufflées*, buttered embryonic string beans and delicious bread. With this we had a bottle of red wine from California. The wine I was used to seeing was the mint-flavored kind that in many states can be bought in drugstores and is favored by young girls and skid row alcoholics.

I devoured everything with single-minded ravenousness. By the end of the meal, I wanted to devour Johnny, too. He was undeniably attractive and he knew more about rock and roll than most people.

He knew the B side of every record ever made, it seemed, including "Let Your Conscience Be Your Guide," the flip side of Jackie Lee's immortal "The Duck," and "Can't Stay Away" by Don Covay and the Goodtimers, the flip side of "Mercy, Mercy," a song that had caused some of my old friends to leave the room.

I looked into Johnny's nice blue eyes and saw myself married to him. It was clear I was what he was looking for. I sighed inwardly and thought to myself that here, doubtless, was one of my "own people," and that I ought to give up and surrender to my fate. But then what would happen to me? Being married to a lawyer and being a Shakette were mutually exclusive, as they say in college.

For dessert we had cherry tart. Johnny said, "Will you eventually go back to graduate school?"

"Never. I will always be a Shakette."

"Oh, yeah, really?" said Johnny. "Even when you're fifty?"

"I don't like to think about the future," I said. "I'm happy in my present."

"Yes, but soon your present will be your past, and your unused present *is* your future." I stared at him. This was the way people usually talked when they were stoned. I felt my heart open slightly, as when you play a weak note on an accordion. "But," he continued, "how about thinking about the next couple of hours? What would you like to do after dinner?"

Most of the time after a show there was no dinner. We flopped our exhausted selves into bed and lay like stones or zombies until the next morning. Curiously, with Johnny, I felt amazingly energetic, due, perhaps, to all that steak. I thought it was unwise to say to this person, whom I had just met, "I'd like to go to your house and take all our clothes off." I said nothing.

"Where do you stay in New York?" Johnny said. He looked as if he were paying a good deal of attention to tallying up the bill.

"I share an apartment with my old college roommate," I said. "Actually, last night was the first night I've spent in it in nearly a year."

"Is she expecting you?" Johnny said.

"Well, she's in Connecticut this weekend," I said. "So she's not expecting anything in that way."

"I have a very nice apartment," Johnny said. "Surprisingly enough for a straight guy who wears a suit, it's in this neighborhood. Shall we go there and hang out?"

I suddenly felt drunk and giddy. I felt I was losing my balance. "Let's go for a little walk," I said. "I need some air."

It was a wet spring night. The streets of Johnny's neighborhood were glazed with mist. We walked past shops full of Ukrainian blouses and Russian jam, and shops that sold books about nutrition and peace. Girls with long, flowing hair ambled next to skinny boys who wore blue jeans and patchouli oil. The air was full of the smell of exhaust, of rain, of that salty smell of the river that reminds you that Manhattan is an island.

"I believe I have to kiss you," Johnny said. He walked me over to a doorway, held me by the shoulders and kissed me on the lips.

I hadn't kissed anyone in years. I was mesmerized. My knees felt like syrup.

"Let's go to my house and take our clothes off," Johnny said.

"Then you won't have any respect for me," I said.

"To hell with that," Johnny said. "I'm going to marry you."

9

He followed me to Philadelphia, Wilmington and Baltimore. He booked us into a nice hotel in each place, stayed the night with me and insisted on my having a proper breakfast with hot cereal and an egg. He wrote letters and sent flowers. Ivy and Grace suggested that I marry him at once.

"You lucky duck," Ivy said. "Cute, good job."

I hung my head in shame. How could I be so ungrateful? Why did I not see that I was a lucky duck? Ivy and Grace waited for the day when their savings accounts hit a magic number and they could quit the tour, marry their boyfriends and begin their lives. I dreaded the day when I would have to leave Ruby and end mine. What was wrong with me?

Then it was summer. Ruby and Vernon went home to New Orleans —they did not tour in the summer. I flopped down in the tiny bedroom of the apartment I shared with Mary Abbott and did nothing. I was so tired my bones hurt. I tried to think of something to do but the only thing I could come up with was to introduce Johnny to my parents. After all, it was a done thing. The trap had been set and I was in it. It was only a question of time.

When they saw Johnny, all was forgiven. It no longer mattered that I had almost killed my mother by almost giving to a journalist from a national magazine an interview about traveling with an all-black act. It no longer mattered that I had left graduate school to run around the

United States of America with a bunch of colored people for two years. Of course, the final ignominy was that nothing *I* did made it better. It was simply Johnny who set things straight. My parents were delighted with him and, in the months to follow, did everything they could, short of tying me up with string and delivering me to a justice of the peace, to get me to marry him.

Everyone wanted me to get married, even Doo-Wah, whom I ran into at a dingy secondhand record store.

"You marry that guy," Wah said. "He's real smart. If I ever get into trouble, I'll hire him as my attorney."

"If *you* ever get in trouble, Wah, little fish will fall from the sky as rain."

"You listen to your old friend," Wah said. "Do it to it."

But I did not want to be in love with Johnny. I figured that when you fall in love with a lawyer, you end up marrying him. And is not being a Shakette an unseemly profession for a lawyer's wife? At the end of the summer Johnny proposed. I turned him down.

"Get realistic," he said. "You can't be a Shakette forever."

"You love me because I'm a Shakette," I said. "And I love me because I'm a Shakette."

There was nothing he could say to this. While not entirely true, it was not entirely untrue. Furthermore, I had not yet had enough.

I went back on tour in the autumn and Johnny pestered me by letter and telephone. There was no doubt about it: being with him was so much nicer than being a Shakette. We had spent the whole summer in each other's company and our weekends in bed. We ambled and strolled and ate dinner at ethnic restaurants. Late at night we listened to the sounds waft up from the street below: that evocative blend of arguing, Puerto Rican music, dogs, the occasional rooster. We listened to late-night jazz on the radio and went to jazz clubs, thick with smoke, and drank warm beer. In the daytime I lay on my own bed and read books. I kept a stack by my bed and read them off one by one till they dwindled like a pile of pancakes.

It was hard to give that up and go back on tour, but I was driven. Doo-Wah was sincerely disgusted to see me. He felt that I had been on the verge of a mature, adult decision. Also, he had bad news. Ivy and Grace were quitting and being replaced by two girls who were learning the routines—LaVonda and Denise. I burst into tears.

"Oh, poor you," Grace said. "We thought *you* were going to quit. It's the right time. If you have any sense, you'll get out, too. Ruby's going for a Vegas contract, girl, and you won't have a job."

LaVonda and Denise were highly polished. I was suddenly too short and too funky for Ruby's act. I knew the end was near but I could not give up.

I loved being on stage. I especially loved it when Ruby did an oldies show. I loved to hang out backstage sharing a reefer or a soda and shooting the breeze with the other acts. I watched Muddy Waters sing "Can't Be Satisfied." I watched Fats Domino push a piano across the stage with his stomach. What was married life compared to this?

Besides, an audience was more potent than any drug. It was pure thrill: the chance to make a large number of people *feel* something. What would I be without it?

Then Ruby cut her monster album *Joyjuice*. Instead of our one tour bus there were two, and a van for costumes. One bus was for the band and backups, and one bus for Ruby, Vernon, their astrologer, hairdresser and nutritionist. A designer from Hollywood was hired to do the costumes and Ruby was suddenly on the cover of every major magazine.

It was okay to have a white Shakette when you were playing Huntsville, Alabama, but not when you did Vegas, Lake Tahoe, the Palestra. The end had come. I would have to get my thing together, as one of Ruby's songs advised. I quit before I got fired.

I did not even tell Johnny. I crept home with my suitcase in my hand and lay down on the bed in the little bedroom at Mary Abbott's. I had a key to the apartment, a respectable amount of savings, a substantial past, and no future. The two people I had spent most of my time with —Ivy and Grace—had disappeared. Probably they had gotten married. The waters of their own lives had closed above their heads. For a week I was too depressed to do a thing. Finally, Mary called Johnny and one evening he burst into the apartment.

"You stupid little jerk!" he said. "I was worried sick about you."

"Oh, shove off," I said, and burst into tears. "I have nothing."

"You have me," he said.

I gave him a look. How wonderful to have that kind of confidence!

"Come on," he said. "Let's get married. I'll push a piano across the room with my stomach. We'll have fun."

I said I did not want to have fun. Johnny tried to wear me down. I said I needed a job. Johnny suggested I go to law school.

"You could be a lawyer in the music business."

I looked at him sadly. It was clear he didn't get it, but then he had never met a lawyer in the music business, of whom Vernon often said, "There is the scum of the earth, and what lives *under* the scum of the earth, and under this we have music lawyers."

I said I wanted a job that made me feel like a Shakette: marginal, hard-edged, and as if I hadn't given in. Obviously this was going to take quite a long time to find, as there certainly didn't seem to be much of that particular kind around.

10

Now that I was no longer a Shakette, my parents reappeared in my life as if nothing had happened. My two and a half years on the tour were like a tidily annulled marriage to some unsuitable lout. My mother's contempt for my past gave off a whiff, like expensive perfume, if the subject even threatened to come up.

She wondered, since I did not have a job and was not going back to graduate school, if I was sick, and she felt I ought to go see her doctor. She had changed her tack, by and large. She treaded around such issues as my awful wardrobe, my lack of ambition, my strange taste in occupations. She knew that within her grasp was the Big Picture: her daughter, married to John Franklin Miller.

My mother adored Johnny and set about to do a kind of genealogical number on him. She was passionately interested in people's forebears.

Johnny's paternal grandfather had been a federal court judge in Savannah, Georgia. Both his parents had been reared in the South, in the gentle, downplayed traditions, if they can so be called, of Reform Judaism. Johnny's father had come north to law school, where he met Johnny's mother, who had gone to Smith. They brought Johnny up in Philadelphia, amidst numerous relatives. When Johnny was six, they began to summer in Connecticut and, in a sweet rural town called Wickham, they built a house. What a lovely family!

As my mother worked on her most consoling fantasy—my wedding —I, jobless and depressed, lived in a state of chronic dread whose focal point was the fact that one of these days Johnny's mother and mine would meet each other for the first time.

11

They fell into each other's arms, full of smiles and recognition, not for one moment dropping their faintly suspicious regard. Our fathers were much more reserved, stood quietly chatting about the stock market or the World Series, while Johnny moved between them like a Ping-Pong ball, bringing clarity and merriment to the proceedings. I felt slightly sick at the sight of all this conviviality.

I really was in love with Johnny but I had to overcome quite a lot of resistance to cozy up to him. It had been my initial plan, on what might be called our first date, to spend the night with him and then disappear. That would show him! But I had not reckoned with his determination, which was ferocious and alarming. He had obviously made up his mind about me on the spot. A little flak from some directionless former Shakette was not going to stand in the way of his goal. He was going to wear me down. At the same time, he could not appear to be in collusion with my mother, although their Big Pictures were pretty much the same. As for me, my big fear was that I was losing, giving in, making the mature, sensible adult decision apparently everyone ardently prayed I would make.

My future husband, I realized as I watched him in action, was a master diplomat. He managed to make everyone feel exactly as they wanted to feel. My mother was free to feel that I would marry Johnny and he would whip me into shape, and I was allowed to feel that Johnny was on my side and loved me for myself. What his mother felt at the time was unknown. As far as I could tell, she felt that she was about to marry my mother. The fathers chatted and drank their drinks, and my mother showed Dolly and Herbert Miller her studio. Then we all sat down at the huge mahogany dining room table while Erna MacIlvaine, the lady who had been cleaning and cooking for my parents for years, served fried chicken, biscuits with honey, butternut squash puree and string beans with almonds.

Any normal person looking around that table would have had a heart full of pride. Two fine-looking sets of parents: my mother with her hair in a chignon and my father with his French half-glasses; Johnny's mother, whose hair was short and frisky, dressed in clothes that were chic and age-appropriate (as the women's magazines say), and his father, who wore a gold watch on a chain. My dearly beloved had taken off his shoe and was doing things to my foot with his foot under the table: a straight-arrow with some strange, lunatic glint in his eye. This should have made me happy as a fly, but I was not any normal person.

Each bite was as dust. I could not wait for dinner to be over. Minute by minute I felt there was less air in the room. If I were the sort of person who fainted, I would have swooned dead away, but I had never even come close in my life. Finally it was clear that our parents had no need of us at all. We were excused from the table like a pair of ten-year-olds and we sped into the night.

"Now wasn't that lovely, lovely, lovely!" said Johnny.

"Let's get high," I said.

"Now, now," Johnny said. "It's not often that two families come together in the spirit of perfect love and commitment."

"I want to go to my house," I said. "I want to be alone."

For the first time since I had known him, Johnny looked alarmed. He did not underestimate this part of what my mother called my rebellious streak. He knew if he let me go he would never get me back. He rolled up his figurative sleeves and set to work.

"Let's go to Chat's and have a drink. Sleepy Jim Pulver's in town. Maybe we could catch a set."

"I'm tired."

"Pulver comes to town once every ten years," Johnny said. "Pull up your socks, girl. I'll send him a note and ask him to sing 'Bad Money Blues.' Come on."

"I want to *stop* at my place."

"Don't be silly, Geraldine," Johnny said. "It'll take us an hour to get there and back downtown. By that time Pulver may have died. He's a very old man."

I yawned. Suddenly I felt a kind of warmth in my stomach and my limbs felt useless. Was this how people feel when they are about to die of hypothermia? Oh, why not, I said to myself sleepily. What the hell. We'll go have a beer. We'll hear Sleepy John Pulver. We'll go to Johnny's and smoke dope and take our clothes off. It'll be fun, fun, fun.

"Okay, okay," I said. "Let's go. It'll be fun, fun, fun."

"We don't sing that kind of trash, girl," Johnny said.

"I'm not dressed for this," I said. "I need my blue jeans and my high-heel sneakers."

" *'Put on your red dress, baby, 'cause we're goin' out tonight,'* " sang Johnny.

" *'And wear some boxing gloves,'* " I sang. " *'In case some fool might wanna fight.'* "

Oh, my sweet Johnny. He knew the words to all the best songs. As we walked hand in hand to the subway, I thought to myself that a wide knowledge of rock and roll lyrics certainly guaranteed protection of one sort or another.

12

Although cornered like a weasel, I took my stand. I told Johnny flatly that I would not get married until I had a job and that was that. Who knew how long it would take me to get one?

I was gigantically unskilled. I typed slowly and inaccurately with two fingers and could not take dictation—or maybe I could. Graduate students and rock and roll backups generally aren't asked to try. I did not have a degree in early childhood education, nor had I graduated from the business school. I knew nothing about art or museums, and since my math skills had never been sharp, to say the least, I could not really see myself working in a record store or museum gift shop and learning to make change. I was not going to go back to graduate school, not ever.

I sat at the tiny desk in the living room I shared with Mary Abbott and wondered which way to turn. Johnny had suggested I write a book.

"*I Was a White Shakette for the FBI,*" I said.

"No, seriously," said Johnny. "You have had a unique experience." This sentence made me wince. I would never have a unique experience again.

I dialed Chicago and called Mack Witherspoon, who was responsible, if anyone was, for my being a Shakette in the first place. I told him I was looking for a job. He suggested I tour with Ronnie and the Tramps, but I said I was looking for a desk job. Even I knew that the day of the girl group was coming to an end. Mack said I should call his friend Pee-Wee Russell, of Pee-Wee's *Lunchtime in Space* on radio station WIS (What I Say). Pee-Wee was a big fan of the Shakelys and he would know my name. Maybe he could find me something.

It turned out that black-owned radio stations don't usually hire white people, but Pee-Wee, who actually had been a fan of mine, took pity on me. He said he would call up a man he knew, the Reverend Arthur Willhall of the Race Music Foundation, and see if any research jobs were available. They didn't pay very well, was that all right?

I said it was.

Pee-Wee said that the Race Music Foundation was in Harlem. Was that all right?

I said it was fine. An hour later I was on the subway.

It was a cloudy autumn day. The sky was the color of pewter, against which the yellow leaves glowed. The sidewalks were the color of slate because they *were* slate. The Race Music Foundation was housed in an old brownstone on one of Harlem's nicer streets. The neighborhood surrounding it was somber and old-fashioned. The building itself, a slightly crumbling five-story house, looked mournful.

I walked up the stairs and rang the bell. The door was answered by a tall, grim, skinny man wearing a dog collar. This was the Reverend Willhall himself, who led me into what had once been a parlor but was now sectioned into an office. On the wall in back of a large desk was a looming poster of Mississippi Fred McDowell which read I DO NOT PLAY NO ROCK AND ROLL. I had been warned by Pee-Wee that the Reverend was no fan of rock and roll, which he felt was black music polluted by commercialism.

I sat down in a camp chair and he sat at the desk. Outside, the light lowered. It looked as if it might storm. A London plane tree out in front let down large yellow leaves. The Reverend sat with his elbows on the desk, his fingertips pressed together.

"The Race Music Foundation has as its purpose"—the Reverend intoned in a deep, rich voice—"the preservation of the music indigenous to the black man. Gospel, blues, rhythm and blues. We do not believe that society as a whole is interested in this music except to plagiarize, or bastardize, or use it as fodder for its own commercial purposes."

He did not appear to be speaking to me, and I was tempted to look behind me to see if there was an audience he was, in fact, addressing.

I said, "You mean that white society is just going to rip it off unless you save it."

The Reverend looked at me as if I were a worm. He closed his eyes and opened them again, giving himself the aspect of a lizard.

"Quite," he said.

I heard myself sigh heavily.

"In this very house," the Reverend continued, "in this very house, ninety years ago, was born Mother Clara Hart, the foundress of the Hart African Gospel School. It is her generous heirs who have given us this building for our work."

He fell silent and closed his eyes. I began to shift uneasily in my chair. I felt I ought to do something, so I coughed. The Reverend Willhall opened his eyes again.

"We have organized an international network of researchers—a kind of living archive. These researchers send us endless material which must be meticulously catalogued and preserved. On this floor we house the library and reception room. On the second floor, our audio department and research rooms. On the third and fourth floors are the audio library, print, and copying facilities. My wife works here, as does my daughter."

He stopped again and was silent. Oh, well, I said to myself, when you have nothing, you have nothing to lose.

"Reverend Willhall," I said, "is there a job here?"

He sat back for a moment without speaking. "We need someone to catalogue female blues singers of the twenties and thirties."

"I want it," I said.

Reverend Willhall peered at me over his glasses. It occurred to me that I was a tiny bit overexcited.

"I mean, I love female blues singers of the twenties and thirties," I said. "I've studied them. I used to . . . um . . . sing myself."

"Yes," said the Reverend Willhall. "I understand that you were in popular music."

"I was."

"We don't have that here," Reverend Willhall said.

"I understand."

"We operate on a shoestring. The pay is minimal."

"I understand."

"I cannot give you any guarantees that once you have done this job there will be another project here for you."

"I understand."

"We have no benefits of any kind."

"I understand."

"And we need you only three days a week."

"I understand."

"Come with me and I'll show you around," said the Reverend Will-hall. "You can start tomorrow."

13

I could not believe my enormous good luck! I felt like dancing down the street, until it occurred to me that now I had a job and I had promised to get married when I got one. Fortunately, this job caused another round of squealing and disapproval. My socially conscious and enlightened sweetheart did not feel it was safe for me to walk around in a black neighborhood.

"I'm invisible," I said. "On the tour they used to call me Casper the Friendly Ghost."

"I don't like it."

"Tough," I said. "It's my job."

"Your parents are going to freak," Johnny said.

I looked at my beloved in a way that made him nervous.

"But you haven't even looked around," Johnny said.

"This is the opportunity of a lifetime, buddy," I said. "You go off and do your law work and let me do my thing. *'Where do you highbrows find the kind of love that satisfies?'* " I sang. " *'Underneath the Harlem moon.'* "

The next day I began my tasks. I sat in a large room on the second floor and began to go through a mountain of cartons containing 78 rpm records and taped interviews with old singers, the children of old singers, the musicians who had worked with these old singers. I found handbills, sheet music, handwritten songs, photographs and other artifacts. All these had to be catalogued and filed. I sat at a console wearing a pair of headphones and listened to old records. Through the scratching and static came the pure strong voices of Bessie Smith, Gertrude Perkins, Mrs. Eartha Parks and dozens of others. Above my desk was a reproduction of a poster (the foundation had the original) of Bessie Smith and Clara Smith (no relation). It said: MY, BUT THESE GIRLS DO SING BLUEFULLY.

The old records, lent to us by a network of collectors, were processed, through the miracle of modern science, into almost perfect recordings. The foundation covered its costs by leasing these to record companies and clearing the rights with the singers or their survivors.

I sat alone in an office while across the hall the sound engineer, the pop-eyed, silent but hyper James Hill, worked behind a heavy wooden door lined with what looked like foam-rubber waffles.

On the third floor worked two young women called Maryanne Thomson and Ava Brent, who ran the audio library and print room.

Downstairs was the domain of the Willhall family. Mrs. Willhall, whose first name was Queenie, answered the telephone and bossed around the porter, an old soul saved by Reverend Willhall in his preaching days. The porter was known only as Moby, a small, dense black man of about fifty, who carried cartons, hauled equipment and drove the foundation's battered van. He lived in the basement and used the enormous, ornamental bathroom to wash in. Formerly he had lived on the street, and was now paid just enough to keep him in tobacco and off drink.

Then there was Desdemona, the Reverend Willhall's daughter. She was fiery and beautiful. Looking at her solemn father and her placid mother, it was hard to tell where she had come from. She wore her glossy hair in a crown of braids on top of her head. Her clothes were suitable for the daughter of a clergyman, except that she liked skirts with slits to show off her legs. She wore gold earrings and her perfect nails were painted with a shade I recognized from my tour days as Frosted African Pumpkin. Desdemona did not speak much, at least not at the foundation. She sat in her office and worked the telephone, and she traveled frequently to raise money.

Mrs. Willhall believed that it was her duty to see that the foundation staff was properly fed. Each morning she started a large pot of vegetable soup on the stove in the huge old kitchen. At lunchtime we sat at a tin-top table eating vegetable soup, cornbread and applesauce. The

Reverend Willhall did not believe in conversation with food. We gathered at the table and waited while steaming bowls of soup were placed before us. The Reverend extended his long skinny arms out over the table and intoned; "O Lord, for the food which we are about to eat, we thank you! We thank you! We thank you!"

It often seemed to me unfair that he did not thank his wife, but there you are. We ate in silence, which was just as well, since it was at mealtimes that I felt most alien—the lone white face. Would I ever find some fellow humans to be at peace with?

Upstairs I sat at my console and stared out the window. Dark autumn rain fell steadily. I switched on a record and positioned the needle. That powerful clear voice of Bessie Smith almost knocked me backward. As I listened I realized how very dirty those old dirty songs were, like "I'm Wild About That Thing" and "You've Got to Give Me Some." It turned out they were written under a pseudonym by a nephew of the Madagascar royal family—the world of music was full of such anomalies. Sunshine suddenly flooded me. I was an anomaly, too. It was all okay.

" *'You can see my bankbook,'* " I sang along. " *'But don't you feel my purse.'* " I happily sipped my coffee. There was no one to hear me, so I was free to sing as loud as I liked: " *'I've got what it takes but it breaks my heart to give it away.'* " It seemed to me to be my personal anthem.

14

It didn't take me long to love my job at the Race Music Foundation. It was rather like being on tour except more restful, and the food was better. I was sincerely interested in women singers of the twenties and thirties. In two weeks I had settled in. I did my work, which required familiarity and devotion—I had plenty of those—and did not call for any special skills, of which I had none.

Considering the nature of the music we were working with—dirty blues, songs about money, praises of God and what-all—the mood at the foundation was solemn. No matter what the weather, the building itself gave off a kind of serious, gray aura I found very consoling. The Reverend Willhall was supernaturally grave. He was especially disturbed when popular groups—by which he meant white acts—remade some classic blues number and turned it into a hit. He would then pick up the phone and put in a sorrowful telephone call to the foundation's lawyer and set him on the case to see if any money could be liberated for the songwriter, or the heirs if the songwriter was dead, as was often the case.

"Those English boys stole 'Little Red Rooster,'" he would say mournfully. "When will this ever stop?"

I always wanted to say, "Cheer up, Reverend Willhall. No white girl group is ever going to remake Gertrude Perkins' 'Black Snake Moan' with violins."

No one else, however, was very happy about my job.

"I worry about your welfare," Johnny said.

"For a guy who likes rock and roll," I said, "you sure are funny about spades."

"I love spades," Johnny said. "I just don't like my woman hanging around spade-infested areas in the late afternoon."

Of course, this job was more than just the job of a lifetime. It was a loaded gun and it kept everyone off me, no matter how they nagged. One false move about this, the terrible look in my eye said, and there will be NO WEDDING. My mother knew it, and Johnny knew it. For the first time in my life I had some leverage.

It didn't take much to make me happy. I discovered a singer called Mrs. Verlie Waters, about whom little was known. She made three records, six sides in all: "Big Thumb Blues," "Empty Head Blues," "Bad Weather Blues," "Low Down Dirty Dog," "Under the Bed Blues" and "No One Can Sing It But Me." Her voice was sweeter than Bessie Smith's, but not as rich. For a blues singer it was almost girlish. I sat at my console listening to "No One Can Sing It But Me."

I looked her up in the library. She turned up in a discography which revealed that she had been one of the first female singers to write her own material. In a book entitled *Mama Do No Wrong: Black Lady Singers of the Twenties and Thirties* by Liam L. P. Hunt, I found a paragraph about her. Her parents had been teachers. She had graduated from a colored music academy and then ran off to New Orleans. Her career lasted six years and she died of tuberculosis at the age of twenty-eight. As the song said, *Life sure is rough, it sure is tough, but of that sweet sound I never get enough. No one can sing it but me.*

15

It turned out that unlike my fun-loving and gregarious lover, I was rather antisocial. I felt like a person who had been living on another planet, and who did not quite get how human beings connected in a social setting.

Johnny would come bounding over to my apartment and say, "Wash the blackface off, kiddo. We're invited to a dinner party."

"You go," I would invariably reply. "Tell them I have a disease."

"Come, come, my good woman," said Johnny. "We can't have this."

"Please, Johnny. I'm not good out."

In social situations I was hostile, defensive and shy, not a winning combination. If I was asked what I did, I would morosely answer that I was an ethno-musicologist. Or Johnny would say, "Geraldine used to dance with Vernon and Ruby Shakely."

"How neat! Are they classical or modern?" some nice host or hostess would politely ask.

"They used to be modern but now they're classical," I would respond.

Out on the street Johnny always pleaded, "Can't you make a little effort? These are *nice* people."

"I just don't *get* them."

"You don't have to get them. Just be nice to them."

Every invitation, of which there seemed to be hundreds, felt like a death threat. I looked at Johnny with envy. He was like a jigsaw piece that had found its happy little place and fit right in. His colleagues adored him. The senior partners adored him. Their wives doted on him. So why couldn't I sit by his side thinking my own thoughts and ruminating on my dinner like a cow?

These people were *sharp*. They knew their way around, and they all knew each other. Their fathers were partners or their mothers were cousins or had gone to school together, or were intermarried with people who had gone to school together. They wore snappy clothes and owned small European cars. They worked hard and took interesting vacations in wilderness areas. They were healthy and hale and red-cheeked and they had never spent a minute of their lives worried about the essentials. The essentials had all been taken care of. Instead they had worried about grades, getting into college, law school. They worried when their cars didn't work and when cholera broke out in some part of the world they had an impulse to go touring in. Later they had children and worried about early childhood development, what schools to send their children to. When they got together they talked about cooking equipment, and skiing, and gossiped about mutual friends. I was a total misfit.

The older set, the senior partners, lived not in one-bedroom apartments but in large spaces overlooking the park, or in brownstones and duplexes. These people had grown children, all full of accomplishment, and gave large multigenerational dinner parties. At these dinners the great issues of the day were debated. A successful dinner party to this group was one in which spirited discussion took place.

"If I hear one more conversation about social justice, as the colored maid serves me my leg of lamb, I'm going to faint," I said after one such event.

"How very noble you are," said Johnny.

"These people just feel they can say anything they want."

"Vernon Shakely said anything he wanted," Johnny pointed out. "It's all very well to talk about the white honky devil when your accountant is a white honky devil from the Wharton School of Business."

"Yes, but Vernon meant what he said," I countered.

"Well, so do these people," Johnny said. "And they treat you nicer."

"They don't treat me nicer. They're like my mother. They only like me because I'm appended to you."

"You don't give them a chance," Johnny sighed. "You've had an amazing career. You have lots of interesting things to say."

"I don't feel that these people are on my side."

"You're hopeless," Johnny said. "Life is not about who's on whose side."

I was incredulous. Could anybody actually believe that life was *not* about who was on whose side? I hung my head. How nice it would be, I thought, to withdraw from reality and spend the rest of my life dancing in front of the stereo in the privacy of my own warm home.

Not only was I shy, I could not cook. The only thing I could fix was red beans and cabbage salad, and neither Johnny nor I felt that this was appropriate for a dinner party.

"Gee," he said one day. "We can't feed Alice and Simon Crain red beans."

"I thought Simon used to work in the slums," I said. "Didn't Alice do some kind of field work in the Caribbean? Why can't we give them red beans?"

"We don't say 'slums,' " Johnny said. "We say 'inner city.' "

"We can order out," I said. "Besides, your kitchen isn't what I would call well equipped."

"We'll have to do something about this," Johnny said.

When Johnny said, "We'll have to do something about this," he wasn't kidding around. The next evening I ambled over to his apartment and found his kitchen full of important-looking boxes, inside of which was a battery of orange enamel French cooking ware: a soup pot, a frying pan, a family of saucepans and a flat pan with little ears.

"It's a gratin," Johnny said, reading the fancy brochure.

"Oh, yeah?"

"It's to make gratin in."

"Oh, yeah?"

"Well, yes. Look, here's a picture. It says here you scallop the potatoes and cook them in cream and cheese. Sounds swell."

I peered over his shoulder. "It says here *you* scallop the potatoes and cook them in cheese and cream."

"We both have to learn," he said.

I curled my eyebrow at him.

"Hey!" Johnny said. "We're supposed to be a team. Let's have a little cooperative spirit."

"Oh, take it to work," I said. "Walk the dog till you feel better."

"Don't be intractable. Eventually we're going to get married."

"I don't want to get married. I want things to be the way they are."

"Come over here." He put his arms around me. "You wanted to stay a Shakette. Now you want us to live like two graduate students going out on dates and living together on the weekends. Things change. You have to roll with the times."

"I don't want to roll with the times." Tears spurted out of my eyes. "Life is nice now. Can't we just groove with the now? Besides, why do you want to marry me? I can't cook. I'm not a social asset. I'm a drag at dinner parties."

"You're my soul and my inspiration," Johnny said.

"I never liked that song," I said.

"But it's true," Johnny said. " *'Without you, baby, what good am I?'* "

16

Because I loved him, I tried to get nicer. I read the newspaper every day and tried to figure out what my opinions were. Unfortunately, my opinions were almost identical to Vernon Shakely's, which was not much use if you happened to be a white middle-class person whose boyfriend was a lawyer.

Most intimidating to me was an invitation to the home of Bill and Betty Lister. Bill, a serene, gray-haired man, was Johnny's mentor at the firm. Betty was the administrator at a small foundation that gave away tons of money to worthy causes. They had two children: Penny, a filmmaker who had documented the plight of migrant workers and rural midwives, and Bill Jr., a journalist whose beat was city politics. They lived in a big, somewhat shabby house—after all, it was not material things that mattered—and their walls were decorated with the pickings from their extensive travels: Haitian folk quilts (sewn with tiny stuffed people riding on tiny stuffed buses pursued by trapunto alligators), a !Hmong wall hanging, a watercolor done by a sharecropper at a Freedom School in Mississippi. Their silverware, I noticed, was extremely heavy and old. I mentioned this to Johnny, who had spent a good deal of time telling me how much above such things Bill Lister was.

"Oh, come on," said Johnny. "People *have* things like that. They don't buy them."

Betty Lister did not cook but, as Johnny pointed out, this had never stood in her way.

"She has servants to cook for her while she's out doing good deeds," I said.

"She knows that you can always *hire* people to help you."

"How very upright of her," was all that I could say.

Friday night Betty Lister, who believed that a good hostess drew out her shy guests, decided to focus on me. She was a tall, wide-eyed woman, with the wondering gaze of a child. She wore long velvet skirts and what looked like an evening shirt tailored for a woman.

She sat next to me on a love seat in front of the wood-burning fireplace. We had been served our leg of lamb and were having coffee in the Listers' enormous living room.

"Now," she said, "Johnny tells me you work for a foundation. I do too! Which one do *you* work for?"

I said I worked for the Race Music Foundation.

"Really," Betty said. "I've never heard of it. Who does it give money to?"

"It takes money from," I said. "It isn't a foundation in your sense. It's an archive for the preservation of black music."

"How marvelous!" Betty said. This was the sort of thing *her* foundation funded. "And what is the guiding principle of the Race Music Foundation?"

"The Race Music Foundation believes that the white man is trying to eradicate black music from the face of the earth with incessant remakes by white performers."

Johnny gave me a look of pain.

"I'm afraid I don't understand what you mean," Betty said.

Bill emerged from the kitchen and put a tray of demitasse cups in front of us. Betty sipped at her coffee. Her hair was a kind of coppery color with streaks of gray. She wore it cut to her shoulders with a tortoiseshell clip on one side.

"Co-option is death," I said. "It's all in Dr. Willhall's pamphlet *Here's What I Believe.*"

"That sounds rather paranoid," Betty said. "I'm afraid I have trouble with organizations that seek to tear apart the fabric of our country rather than to mend it. Now our Crocket-Parker project, for instance, takes gifted children from the inner city and mainstreams them into some of our good private schools."

"How about if some of the gifted students from our good private schools were mainstreamed into the inner city?" I said. This was debate! Now I had the hang of it! Social life was a snap. I turned to beam at Johnny but I saw from his face that I had gotten it all wrong, so I drank my coffee and shut up.

Betty turned from me and to the company at large. They were on to a different topic: Nazis. Do neo-Nazis have the right to exist in a free and just society? On this subject everyone had a lengthy opinion.

17

At home I played a desultory round of a game I had invented called Who Likes Negroes Most? It had, at one time, amused my sweetheart endlessly.

"Who likes Negroes most?" I said. "Why, Bill Lister likes Negroes most. If a Negro were drowning in a lake of burning lighter fluid, Bill would take an ice cube from his own drink and float it out to the Negro so he could have an ice cube for *his* drink."

"We say 'black people,' " Johnny said.

"Vernon and Ruby found that demeaning," I said, and continued. "Who else likes Negroes most? Betty Lister does, because her foundation once gave fifty thousand dollars to a blond man from Yale who *said* he was a Negro."

"What makes you feel superior to these people?" Johnny said.

"Oh, nothing," I said. "I mean, I just used to live with black people. I worked for them. I sat and ate at the same table with them. During that big snowstorm in St. Paul two years ago, I actually slept in the same bed with one."

"Really?" said Johnny. "Which one?"

"The hotels were overbooked. It was a freak blizzard. Everybody doubled up. I slept with Grace, and Ivy slept with Ruby."

"What about old Vern?"

"He slept in a chair."

"And what about Doo-Wah?"

"He slept on the floor. These guys don't share beds with guys under any circumstances. It probably comes from not having gone to expensive sleep-over camps when they were little."

Johnny, who had gone to an expensive sleep-over camp when *he* was little, darkened. He looked at me glumly.

"Listen," he said. "Betty's foundation wrote the script for about a dozen of those inner-city schools for gifted children. There are hundreds of kids in Ivy League colleges now because of her. Bill oversees all the pro bono work at the firm. He is responsible for an immense amount of good. So what's your problem—that they don't regularly eat lunch with darkies?"

"I think they are morally bankrupt and out to lunch," I said. "They're like those debutantes who used to go into the slums and tell poor women how to raise their children. What makes you think it's so swell for some kid from the inner city to go to Yale and be surrounded by people who spend more on a pair of shoes than his mama does on food for a month and who have no idea where he's coming from?"

"I love you," said Johnny. "You're definitely right, and you're also wrong. You can be morally bankrupt and out to lunch and still do really good things for people. You don't see how well-meaning they are. You think they're full of shit because the only black people they know are servants."

That about wrapped it up.

"I can see both sides," Johnny said. "They're right, and you're right."

I merely looked at him. I felt a little as if I were drowning in a lake of burning lighter fluid.

"Speak," Johnny said.

"You'll get like them," I said. "Their values will cover you like slime. They'll get under your skin like chiggers and pour their attitudes into your blood. They'll invade your brain like tropical parasites and take you over."

"Aren't you *lurid!*"

"I'm so unhappy."

"Don't be," Johnny said. "You can go to a dinner party and not lose your essential self. You can be true to your school and still make normal conversation. You can act like a regular person and still boogie in your soul."

I listened earnestly but I felt that none of these things were true.

On the other hand, Johnny was my golden mean. He did boogie in his soul and I was deficient because I was too truculent to find any place for myself in what most people would call "the real world." Who else would ever have been so perfect for me? Johnny was a translator and I was a foreign language. Without him I would have been lost somewhere in outer space. Without me he would have adapted himself out of existence. We were made for each other. I told him so.

"I'm glad you feel that way," he said, kissing my ear. "Because next month the Listers are having a really big dinner party with caterers and everything, so start practicing now."

I did not look forward to this event but, on the other hand, fair was fair. Johnny came with me to the Newark Armory to catch a show of James Brown and the Famous Flames. He told me that, before he met me, he had gone to a dinner party at the Listers' and a large, drunken sportswriter named Adrien McWirter had slid a cornichon down the back of the wife of the dean of the law school. How I wished I had been there!

"Gee, does that guy get invited anymore?" I said, hopefully.

"Well, he made a lot of trouble. He stood up in the middle of a dinner party one night and said, 'Oh, how I adore neo-Nazi bikers. Those attractive leather uniforms and all.' And then he passed out on the couch."

He sounded like a man after my own heart, but Johnny told me that McWirter had been abandoned by all his friends, who could no longer stand to be around him. I sighed.

The week of the party I suggested to Johnny that I wear one of my old dance dresses since I could not go to a black-tie dinner in either of my two uniforms: blue jeans and turtleneck for home wear, black skirt and turtleneck for office. Johnny suggested that I go buy a dress and, on second thought, he'd go with me.

He sat in a chair like an elderly husband or sugar daddy and watched me try on things, and he made me buy a plain black dress which he said would look good with pearls. I said I had no pearls and two days later my enterprising swain was back with a string of pearls in a blue leather case. The enclosed card read: "For forays into the adult world."

I looked at the pearls. "Why don't you fuck off?" I suggested.

Johnny did not take this seriously. "See here, my good woman," he said. "I buy you a string of extremely good pearls and you tell me to fuck off. How about throwing your arms around me and saying thank you."

I threw my arms around him and said thank you. Then I said, "Why don't you marry Carol Adams?"

Carol Adams had been my predecessor.

"She's married," he said into my ear. "Now let's get dressed and get going."

At the Listers' our coats were taken by a handsome black man in a purple serving jacket. A handsome black butler served champagne and hors d'oeuvres from a silver tray. We were introduced to Mr. Something, a famous civil libertarian, and Mrs. Something Else, whose oversized black glazed pots were on view at the Hammerschuld Gallery. The enormous dining room table sat twenty. I found the sight of it depressing.

As we stood with our drinks, the door of the kitchen opened. A fine-looking black woman in a black taffeta dress and white apron stood at the door. "Dinner now, Mrs. Lister."

I gaped at her. "Grace!" I gasped. "Grace, far out!" For it was Grace Bettes, my old dance mate.

"What a world of surprises!" Grace said. And she retreated to the kitchen.

Every head was turned toward me. I felt flushed and hot with confusion. Clearly an explanation was required.

"We were in the Marine Corps together," I said, struggling to my feet.

I propelled myself into the kitchen. "Grace!" I said, close to tears. "You got your catering thing together!"

"I sure did," Grace said. "And you've still got your Boy Scout. This is my brother-in-law, Percy. Graham's in the living room with the hors d'oeuvres."

Grace was putting frilly pantaloons on the crown roast. She looked wonderful. She had perfectly manicured nails and beautiful eyelashes and, even in her taffeta uniform, she looked very glamorous. She told me that she and Graham had a house in Brooklyn and that they had four people working for them. In six months she was going to ease up because she had just discovered that she was going to have a baby.

"This pays ten times more than that cheap bastard Vernon ever paid me," she said, "and it's mine."

"It was fun," I said.

"Not for me. It was my way out. It got me out of the projects. I sweated my tail off. Now we plow all our profits back into the business and someday Ruby will beg me to cater for her. We're going to be b-i-g."

I asked her if she ever heard from anyone from the old days.

"Huh," she said. "I'm glad those days are over. Ivy got married and she has a little baby girl. Remember Harold Hicks, the drummer? He teaches music in a high school in Arizona. Hey, I gotta work—here's my card. Give a call."

Betty's guests were far too polite to ask me any questions, or perhaps they weren't interested in how Johnny's girlfriend knew Betty's cook.

Dinner was delicious but I was too distressed to eat. I sat in a fog. I heard Johnny explaining who Ruby Shakely was and how shy I was about my brilliant career. As I picked at my spinach soufflé, I remembered Grace and Ivy on stage in their dance dresses, throwing love beads and rose petals.

When we got home, I felt rather low. The feeling that everyone had organized lives except me caused me to collapse on the couch without speaking.

Johnny put his arms around me.

"I guess it was hard seeing Grace," he said.

I said it had been.

"I guess it demonstrated something to you," he said.

I told him it had, but on further reflection it was hard to pin down just exactly what.

PART TWO

Race Music

18

My darling Johnny was not too keen on Mary Abbott, my oldest and dearest friend. Perhaps this was plain jealousy; she had come before him in my affections and had known me longer. Or perhaps he intuited that I deferred to Mary. The fact is, she was my moral beacon.

Mary had dark hair, worn straight to her shoulders, and little round glasses. We wore the same clothes interchangeably and after a few years we did not have my clothes or your clothes, but ours. We spent our time drinking tea, listening to records and talking. I told Mary everything. From long habit as the eldest, she told me what she felt I needed to know. Thus, if she did not want to discuss what looked to me very much like a love affair she was conducting with one of her professors, we did not discuss it. I did not mind this a bit. It was part of what Johnny called Mary's quite unnecessary mysteriousness.

She was the oldest of four daughters in a liberal Catholic family that was constantly scrambling to reconcile the teachings of their church with the social problems of their times. They lived in a ramshackle Victorian house in a Connecticut suburb. Mr. Abbott was a chemist, and Mrs. Abbott was a reading teacher. They had a big Irish setter and a number of cats. The front porch was littered with bird and chipmunk guts. The dog, who was extremely stupid, was frequently lost and large search parties were constantly organized on his behalf. While my parents and I lived in slightly reduced grandeur and sat down every night to a formally set table, the Abbotts lived in a charmingly out-of-control messiness. In order to have dinner, any number of child or adult projects had to be pushed out of the way—this would have been quite unheard of in my parents' house.

I knew the smell of the Abbott house as well as I knew the house I grew up in. I knew Mary's likes and dislikes as well as my own. I thought everything about her was original and wonderful, from her taste in music (plainchant, which I found thrillingly exotic, and Tarheel Slim and Little Ann singing "It's Too Late") to the fact that she liked to combine hot and cold cereal for breakfast. Before she put her glasses on she was blind as a mole. She had an oldest sibling's sense of constant responsibility. Nevertheless, she had no fixed opinions, no vested interests, and she was perfectly free to see clearly who was a jerk and who was not. She was awesomely judgmental, but since her judgments matched mine, by and large, this was not much of a problem except when Mary turned her gaze on me.

She said that my good qualities were my bad qualities—this I have come to realize is true of everyone. On the one hand, I was game, eager and perfectly ready to see what was in front of me. On the other hand, I had no sense of direction or destiny.

When I decided to go on tour with Ruby, which I felt was the most focused decision I had ever made, Mary rightly pointed out that this was a stopgap, a charm on the bracelet of experience but not the bracelet itself.

"What will you do after?" she wanted to know.

And what would she do after? Mary's life was like a ribbon. She would get her degree. She would teach. She would marry some nice liberal Catholic and have a flock of children who resembled her sisters. She knew what she was: daughter, sister, Catholic, intellectual. And I was a terrible daughter, a lousy graduate student who was unable to cope with the hard stuff such as criticism or critical biographies. A proper graduate student did not lie around eating potato chips and reading Victorian novels for fun. When assigned some crucial critical work, the serious graduate student did not fling it across the room shouting "Oh, who *cares?*"

Mary said, "The fact is, you're a singer but you don't want to do all the work that singers do. You don't want to be ambitious."

This was true. I wanted experience to wash over me like a gentle wave. This was not the sort of thing that led to a really good job in later life. When the time came, she felt strongly that I should marry Johnny.

"For someone like you, he's the ideal mate," she said, making me feel like a lone, lame gorilla who had found her other. "The compromises he knows how to make would be good ones for you to be next to."

"I hate compromises," I said.

"I know you do," said Mary. "But the trouble with you is you hate them in a vacuum. What you have going for you is a nature that hates compromises, but you don't have anything you *do* with that nature except not compromise, so you ought to learn how it's done."

"What you're saying is I'm worthless."

"Don't be a jerk," said Mary. "What I'm saying is that temperament has to be attached to action. You did your thing when you went off with Ruby. If it's going to take you a million years to find out what you ought to be doing next, you ought to marry Johnny because he'll help you."

"And then I'll be a sellout like all those nice pals of his."

"If you think his pals are sellouts, don't marry him," Mary said. "Or do you just mean they know what they want and how to get it?"

"I guess I mean that. I mean, I hate to go to these parties where everybody is something except me. I used to be something. It's like once having been an alchemist or a dairymaid. My era has passed."

"You poor thing. So young and so washed up."

This conversation took place at what was increasingly Mary's apartment. My tiny room was so seldom used that Mary sorted her clothes in it. Each month, however, I gave her half the rent. I did not want to be stranded. I did not want to be forced to get married. I wanted a place of my own even if I never stayed in it.

Mary's room was positively austere, mine was underused, and the living room functioned as Mary's study. Unlike me, she knew what she was doing. She was writing her dissertation on the civil rights movement. Then she would get her Ph.D. and teach at a university. Her books and typewriter took up a large table, while her papers were generally spread out over our secondhand couch.

This was not a setting Johnny liked very much. Although his apartment was in what both our mothers thought of as a dicey part of town, it had a kind of raffish bachelor charm. The cast-offs of his parents' house—they had sold it to a nice young couple and moved into the city—were all good, solid and attractive. The building he lived in was on a street lined with trees and inhabited by old Ukrainians who sat outside their buildings on lawn chairs.

More than a year slipped by me. I watched the snow drift down in big, lazy flakes, stalling the traffic, quieting the street and forming white pelts on the fire escapes. I watched the little buds come out on the trees in the park. I watched children cooling themselves in fire hydrants in the summer. Then the leaves turned yellow and fell off the branches. Then it was winter and another year was gone.

Inside Johnny's apartment we were snug as a pair of mice. We were finally learning to cook. Thursday nights we practiced, and each Friday night we had a dinner party. On Saturdays we slunk around the neighborhood buying Russian jam, Hungarian sausage, Egyptian beans in cans, Latvian bread and Black Forest cake, which we snacked on over the weekend. On Saturday and Sunday we went to the movies or we kicked around with Johnny's childhood friend Ben Sennett. On Tuesday nights Johnny and Ben played squash, and I stayed at my old apartment with Mary.

Once a month we had dinner with my parents, and once a month with Johnny's. In the summer we motored up to Johnny's parents' house in Wickham, where I tried my best to be a sporting and energetic future daughter-in-law, but all I really felt was overwhelming exhaustion.

Johnny's mother, Dolly, was small and trim and full of energy. She was on the Wickham Library Committee, and she had formed a committee of weekenders (as opposed to year-round residents) to help the town council. People said over and over that there was no animosity in Wickham between weekenders and year-rounders because of people like Dolly.

Her society in Wickham was extensive. She knew the old residents, the founding families, the artists who had settled there in the thirties, the young couples loaded with money who had bought charming old farmhouses. Her annual cocktail party was as regular an event as the bake sale, the Memorial Day parade or the Volunteer Fire Department chicken fry.

Yes, there was a trick to it. You inherited your life, or you invented it. You figured out what you wanted life to be and then somehow or other you made it that way. Then, miracle of miracles, you liked it! I sat in Dolly's efficient, neat house, the material representation of her very being, in fact, and saw what would be laid out for me if I married Johnny. All I had to do was slip quietly into place.

I would help Dolly every year with her party. Johnny and I would eventually buy a sweet little old farmhouse nearby. Soon Dolly and I and my numerous children would do the annual party together. As time went by, I would take over and Dolly would supervise. My children would eventually take it over from me. We would all live together in a pattern as sure and unchanging as the seasons, if I would only knuckle under and get married.

19

"What's your rush?" I said.

"Listen, sweetheart. We're not getting any younger."

"Well, we're not getting any older."

"Arrested development is *not* the secret of eternal youth," said Johnny. "This is getting silly."

"In other words, you want to get married because it looks better," I said.

"I want to get married so I can begin my life."

This brought me up short. It was the beginning of his life, he felt, and the end of mine, I felt. At the moment I was nothing in particular, which was at least something. Being somebody's wife did not strike me as a role, an occupation or an identity.

"Listen," said Johnny. "We love each other. We're a good team. We even learned how to make pot roast together. We've confessed to each other that we admire Archie Bell and the Drells. Let's get on with it."

The corner I was being backed into got smaller and smaller. I hadn't any legitimate excuse. It was a question of how I felt, which had never been considered a valid reason for anything in my family.

"You said we would get married when you got a job you liked," Johnny said. "You've been at the foundation for over a year. You've catalogued every single female singer and now you're into blind guys. How much longer to we have to wait? Blind Lemon Jefferson, Willie McTell—what's next?"

"Blind guys with one leg," I said.

"Get serious," said Johnny.

"Okay," I said. "I will get serious. Here's the deal. I will marry you but we have to go to City Hall. Please, Johnny. I just can't take the white dress. I don't want my father to give me away. If we're gonna do it, let's just do it. Our parents can give us a party after, but I simply cannot go through one of those demeaning traditional weddings."

"Can I have the judge play 'Chapel of Love' before the ceremony? It only takes two minutes and fifty-two seconds."

"The ceremony?"

"No, the song."

"He can play 'It's Been a Drag' by James Wray, for all I care. I just want it over with."

At this Johnny looked sincerely hurt.

"I don't think you love me," he said.

"I do love you," I said. "It's all that other stuff I don't love. This is between the two of us. I hate all that dress and veil and cake shit. People should get married in seclusion."

"It's a public act," said my civic-minded husband-to-be. "It's in the public record. You can look it up."

"It seems like the most private thing in the world," I said.

So it was decided. Mary was my best man, so to speak, and Ben would stand up for Johnny. Both were sworn to secrecy.

I bought a genteel-looking dress and wore Johnny's pearls. Mary lent me a handkerchief and I wore an old blue garter from one of my dance routines. It was also suggested that I wear one of my fringed dance dresses. Johnny showed up with Ben, both wearing banker's suits, and we stood before the magistrate. When the time came, Johnny slipped a ring box out of his pocket and placed a plain gold band on my finger before I could say the words. To my amazement, I found the actual marriage part very thrilling. I could barely bring myself to look at Johnny when we were pronounced man and wife because I did not want him to see, after my years of protesting, that I had tears in my eyes. We did not get to play "Chapel of Love" but Johnny and Mary sang it all the way down the stairs in City Hall. Then the four of us went out for a tea lunch at a *dim sum* parlor in Chinatown, and that is how I became Mrs. John Franklin Miller.

After lunch, I allowed my shoulders to be scattered with a few grains of rice. Doubtless now that I was married, I would have a baby any minute. It occurred to me why newly married couples cling to one another—because the enormity of the change in their life makes them dizzy. I felt rather unsteady.

Johnny and I had both called in sick. As soon as the news was out, Johnny's partners would give us a big party and Dr. Willhall would mark the occasion by giving me a copy of one of his tracts, "The Sacred Home."

It was a cloudy, windy day in early fall. As we walked through Little Italy on the way back to what was now *our* apartment, it seemed to me that, if I looked back, I would see my unmarried past behind me, gray as a floating cloud. Before me stood the dreaded future: I was now an honest woman.

20

It made absolutely no difference whatsoever. My life changed not one whit, except that Johnny and I now had conversations about moving. His bachelor apartment was too small.

"It fit us before we were married," I said.

"Come on. It's a one-bedroom."

I began to get the picture. It was big enough, but only for us, not for the squadron of little Millers Johnny was contemplating. It wasn't that I didn't like children. I just didn't feel ready to have any.

Johnny tried a different tack.

"This is my bachelor apartment," he said. "We're married. We should have a new place to start out in."

"We've already started," I said. "If it's the bachelor vibes you're concerned about, we can always fumigate."

Of course, Johnny was not quite ready to become a doting father and he knew it. So we stayed put—my favorite mode of life—and nothing changed.

I got on the subway in the morning and stood packed with my fellow sardines as I made my way to the Race Music Foundation. A couple of afternoons a week I found myself sprawled on the couch at my old apartment, drinking tea and reading music magazines and watching Mary sitting at her desk doing useful work.

She had acquired a new roommate, a person called William L. Hammerklever who needed a place to sleep one or two nights a week and was willing to pay a month's rent to do so. Mary, who liked to control information, was not forthcoming about him, so it was hard to get this fellow's story straight. He was either married or had two teaching jobs, one in the city and one in the suburbs, where he maintained his principal residence. After a while, I began to suspect that William L. Hammerklever was Mary's lover.

"He's not around much," she said. Or, "I don't see him all that often." She did not say the things she might have said such as, "He's a perfect roommate—invisible." Or, "I just need the money but I wish he weren't here."

Mary's relationships with men had always been shrouded in mystery and indirection. I freely told her about my usually pointless love affairs conducted with feckless, unavailable or otherwise out-to-lunch boys. To all this Mary listened and then said, "The problem with you is that you don't want a real relationship. Because your mother never left you alone, you're afraid that, if someone really loves you, they'll consume you. Besides, you don't want to be loved for your real self because your mother doesn't love you for your real self and you feel your real self isn't worth it, right?" As usual, I had just sighed.

The first year in college Mary had conducted some sort of a relationship with a bespectacled, innocuous-looking guy named James Morton whose code name, necessary because he had a long-term girlfriend, was Chim. Chim's girl, a tiny blonde named Jenny, was also a friend of Mary's. For complicated reasons I can no longer remember, this was perfectly all right and I never found out whether Mary and Chim ever got around to going to bed together. She was very careful about what she told, a useful practice for the oldest of four girls. The unwritten rule was: she was my best friend and therefore I told her everything. I was her best friend and that meant I loved her best and would wait until she was ready to tell me anything.

When I finally met William Hammerklever, he was sitting at her table eating dinner as if he habitually ate dinner with Mary. It turned out, he did. He had curly salt-and-pepper hair and a blunt nose, and he wore old, soft, beautiful clothes. He was an older man who taught a Tuesday evening and a Wednesday morning class in statistics. The rest of the time he lived in Westchester and ran a computer company. It was not immediately clear if he was married, although later on I began to hear about a person called Madeline, who might or might not have been

William's wife. By this time he was an established fact of Mary's life and thus of mine.

Anyway, it was not a good idea to ask direct questions. Mary was like a turtle and only pulled her head into her shell. It was going to be a long time—if ever—before I found out what was going on between them.

I said, "I'd like to creep into my room, I mean his room, and steal all his cashmere sweaters."

"First grab is mine," Mary said. "After all, I feed him."

That, of course, was news to me, but then it all made sense. The day I saw her wearing William's sweater, I thought I knew what she had never told me.

21

Around my darling spouse I found that I had begun to walk gently, conversationally speaking—as if on eggs. I did not want the subject of babies to emerge as a topic of conversation. Our apartment was too small for a baby, and if we moved, my doom would be sealed. Therefore I never complained when the boiler broke down during a cold snap, since I did not want my sweetie to say, "It's too cold for you here. Let's move." Nor did I tell him when I was almost mugged on the street, even though my would-be mugger was chased away by three elderly Ukrainian men.

Besides, I loved my neighborhood. You never knew what you would see out on the street: strange-looking men with pet boa constrictors wrapped around their waists, old black men playing blues guitar in the park, girls in extremely long or extremely short skirts walking their cats on leashes or strolling with parrots on their shoulders. At night in the summer the fire escapes were padded with mattresses and the air rang with shouts and squeals in Spanish and English. I liked walking from the kosher delicatessen to the pork butcher to the place that sold empanadas, and around the corner to the six Indian restaurants. You could buy black toothpaste from India in the alternative drugstore, and a walk down the block offered many opportunities to buy poor-quality reefer. It was homey and strange at the same time, just the sort of neighborhood for me.

I also did not tell Johnny how isolated I felt at the Race Music

Foundation, or that during the workday my most significant conversations were conducted with two potheads called Ronnie and Luis who worked at Fred's Out-of-Print Records, housed in a dingy storefront a few blocks from the foundation.

The owner of this place, Fred Wood, was a morose-looking white dude who wore his pants hitched up high and favored the evil-looking, pointy little boots most people had thrown out years ago. He had a flat-top, little eyes and a long, cheerless face. I never saw him without a cigarette. It was rumored that he had made a lot of money on Wall Street but dropped out when his record fixation got out of hand. It was also rumored that he had been a speed freak, but he seemed so laid back that I often wondered if he had a pulse. He did have an encyclopedic memory for rock and roll, and every now and again I would need something I couldn't remember. These needs were as intense as any real addict's craving for drugs.

Fred did not seem surprised to see a white girl in this neighborhood, but then, he barely registered any emotion at all. He was more like a lizard than anyone I had ever seen.

"Hi. I need this record. I can't remember who did it or what it's called."

Fred Wood looked at me impassively and said nothing.

"It's from about a million years ago. Two black guys. I just remember it's something about love that you feel deep down inside."

"Yeah," said Fred Wood. "Luis, give her 'Deep Down Inside' by Bob and Earl. That's real obscure. They only played it a coupla times. Where'd you hear it?"

"I guess the coupla times it was played."

"Solid," said Fred Wood. He yawned. It was the only time his expression changed, but the cigarette never moved from his mouth. It was lodged in the corner.

"You useta be the white Shakette," he said, in his monotone.

"I did."

"Yeah. Ruby's going down the tubes. Violins and shit."

"Uh-huh."

"You still singing? You sang real good when Ruby let you."

"I work at the Race Music Foundation."

"Yeah? Good old Fred Willhall. *I do not play no rock and roll.*"

"He hired me for my research abilities."

Fred Wood looked me up and down. He was not a savory or healthy-looking person, but he had a kind of eerie charm which was strangely benign. When he looked at me I felt an undeniable thrill, the sort a married woman ought not feel for the creepy proprietor of a second-hand record store.

"Your research abilities," he said tonelessly. "Which are undeniably ample, I have no doubt."

"Don't you doubt it for a minute," I said.

Suddenly Luis returned with "Deep Down Inside" by Bob and Earl. Fred Wood put it lovingly on the turntable. He had long, boneless-looking fingers. His acoustical system was amazing. No matter how loud he turned up the sound, there was never a speck of distortion. The rig had been custom-made by an electronics genius and speed freak who got very strung out and split to California. This system was his greatest creation.

"It's his monument, man," Luis said.

Bob and Earl were of the gospel-inspired school of rock and roll. As the first notes rolled over us, we froze. We might have been hostages listening to the national anthem, and maybe we were. The opening had heavy gospel riffs on piano and shadow guitar. I felt my hair stand on end.

When it was over, a tear slid down Fred Wood's cheek. He took the record off the turntable with great tenderness and slipped it into its little paper jacket. Luis and Ronnie quietly went back to work with the air of people who had been chastened.

"It's really beautiful," I said.

"Oh, yes," said Fred Wood. He removed the dead cigarette from the corner of his mouth. He gave me the record in a used bag. "It is awesome."

22

For a long spell I was as happy as I could be. I was doing something I loved and I was marginal at the same time. My love for marginal people was a kind of lunatic variant on the fact that I had spent a good part of my childhood in secret pursuits. Who would ever know these people except me? The day I saw Fred Wood cry upon hearing Bob and Earl's "Deep Down Inside," my heart opened to him and I realized that I would always love him. I adored Ronnie and Luis.

My best and in fact my only friend at the Race Music Foundation was the overexcited acoustical engineer, James Hill, who referred to himself as "the Bopper." His mother, who came in once in a while to do the foundation's books, was known as "the Bopper's mother."

Every day he came bounding into my cramped little research space, slapped something on my turntable and said, "Hey, baby. Listen to *this* giant side."

The Bopper did not like blues or gospel, and he felt that Dixieland was to black music what early infancy is to people. He hated it. He liked very extreme jazz and he had convinced the Reverend Willhall that these strange, noncommercial wailings would disappear off the face of the earth if left uncatalogued by him. He was pressing the foundation to turn the conference room, in which no conferences were ever held, into a sound stage so that he could record the unrecorded musicians he found in jazz clubs. They often came to visit, some in what looked like the last stages of drug addiction, and some looking as fit as marathon runners, or wearing business suits and carrying electronic keyboards under their arms.

"Someday," he said, "the Bopper's gonna get together an interesting amount of money and open a club. Just for extreme jazz. Call it the Cutting Edge."

This sounded to me like a good way to lose an interesting amount of money, and besides, I told the Bopper, the Cutting Edge sounded like a beauty parlor.

I had a hard time with extreme jazz. It was like reading a book in a foreign language you haven't really studied. "I hear it, but I don't get it," I said.

"You rock and roll people are simple tools," said the Bopper. "You probably like 'Right on the Tip of My Tongue' by Brenda and the Tabulations."

I adored Brenda and the Tabulations.

I was also happy because I was secretly married. I had begged Johnny to let us have a couple of months before we announced it. He did not immediately understand the reason for this. I said I wanted the reality to sink in.

"In other words, set, as in concrete," he said.

Well, that was certainly the gist of it. Since I believed marriage to be private, and Johnny felt it was public, we made a deal. We would have the joy of a secret marriage for two months and then we were going to tell our parents *and* proclaim it to the world at large. An announcement in *The New York Times*. Parties. Then I agreed that we would move so we could have a housewarming.

These were, as any fool knew, the steps people take to emerge from the cocoon of their childhoods, sprout wings and become adult butterflies. I had never seen my true love so content. He liked *being* things: lawyer, husband. He was dying to tell everyone he knew. For a person who craved the marginal, I had married someone who loved being right out in the center.

Of course, he noted, everyone would assume that I was pregnant. I curled my eyebrow at him. And why, I wondered, would everyone think that?

"Well, secret marriage and all," Johnny said.

"Tell them I look like hell in white," I said. "Tell them we're so extremely assimilated that no rabbi would marry us, and since we're Jewish, no one else would either. Say we couldn't get married by a judge because I have a prison record."

"People get married in prison all the time," Johnny said.

"Oh, what's the big deal!" I said. "Tell them that's how we wanted to get married. You wanted to get hitched at the old Hud's Rock and Roll Hut but it closed."

"Hud's," said my husband dreamily. "It was probably like that place you go to. Fred's. A sort of dusty place that smells of vinyl and marijuana smoke. Every record ever made. I wanted to walk down the aisle to Garnet Mimms singing 'I'll Take Good Care of You.'"

"How I love Garnet Mimms," I said. "My mother is going to be awfully angry when we tell her."

"Not to worry," said my husband. "I'll take care of her. I'll tell her the truth: it was the only way I could convince you to do it at all."

"That won't go over too well either. She'll just complain about how abnormal I am."

"And I will say that's why I married you."

I looked at my husband with true love. Oh, the bliss of being married to a litigator who knew his way around difficult people, especially one who loved Garnet Mimms. It was almost too good to be true.

23

Our announcement did not go over very well with either set of parents. My mother was predictably aghast. She fixed me with a look I had known well in childhood: rage, and disappointment. My mother felt that defiance was the criminal activity of childhood.

"You must be pregnant," she said.

"I'm not," I said.

This made everything much worse. If I was not pregnant, then it was clear that I had only one reason: to defy her. To deny her a wedding. To throw it in her face.

"Listen, Gert," said my extremely agreeable husband, who knew how to twist a mother or two around his little finger. "It was the only way I could get the girl to have me. She really and truly doesn't approve of white dresses and flower girls and stuff. I'm not mad for it myself. You can give us a great big party and introduce us to all your friends and not have to go through the hell of planning a wedding."

My mother sat in a wing chair and took a lace handkerchief out of her sleeve. She was not so much crying as sniffing, which I had found very confusing as a child.

"To think of all the pleasure you've deprived them of," she sniffed. "Our friends were so looking forward to making a fuss. You two are very foolish. Just on a practical level—people do not send wedding presents under these circumstances."

I was about to say "We'll do without," when I saw Johnny's warning look. He had obviously found some way to play this and he didn't want it disrupted.

"Look, Gert," he said. "Think of it this way. The worst is over. We're married! A nice, hassle-free fact of life. No horrible wedding plans, no hysteria. Nice and easy. But we would love a party." At this he paused and looked at me. His look said, Shut up. We'd love a party. "You can tell your friends it was a quiet, family wedding, the nice, civilized kind, and now you can go crazy interviewing caterers, okay?" To my amazement, it *was* okay.

Johnny's parents were slightly less irate, but they were clearly puzzled.

"Are you two going to have a baby?" Dolly said.

"No, Ma," said Johnny. "We just wanted to be together quietly for a little bit, that's all."

"I'm afraid I don't understand you young people," she said. "In my day it was all different. These sorts of things weren't done."

"Oh, come on, Ma," said Johnny. "People have always done this. Wartime, and stuff like that."

"*Stuff like that* usually meant strong parental objection," said Dolly. "You two would have had our blessing."

It was Johnny's father's job to lighten things up. He was Dolly's perfect counterpoint: casual, easygoing and cheerful.

"Oh, come on, Dolly," he said. "I'd have been a lot happier running off with you than stuck in that horrible tuxedo, dancing in those awful patent leather shoes. What a wedding! You did the right thing, you two. I just wish you'd do it again so we could watch. I've never been to City Hall in all these years."

"Now, Herbert," Dolly complained. "We had a lovely wedding."

"I still have a bunion from those damned shoes, and your Aunt Lucy stepped on my feet when I took her for a spin. You've saved yourself years of wear and tear, footwise, Johnno."

I felt almost faint with gratitude. I was not used to parents who helped you out in this way.

As for Johnny's mother, I could not imagine why she was so happy that her darling boy had married a young woman who had spent her brief professional life jiving with black people, yet I knew that they had had few anxious moments about their precious angel. Perhaps they thought that with his own musical obsessions, he might find himself *married* to a jiving black person. Maybe they were happy that their boy had found the girl of his dreams. Johnny said that if he hadn't found me he would never have been happy. He might have married the dread Carol Adams, the bosomy blonde who had been on the *Law Review* with him. But as he pointed out, she couldn't dance, and her idea of rock and roll was what Johnny called "bubble gum music," the rather sickly kind made by underage white boys for underage white girls.

I knew, however, that in the back of Dolly's mind someone like Carol Adams might have made *her* a little happier. Someone she could really talk to. Someone who knew what a daughter-in-law should know: the right posture, the right way to sink comfortably into a family. I was not that person and, to tell the truth, adults, especially in the form of parents, had always made me extremely uneasy.

24

Johnny began to make more and more determined noises about moving, and finally I gave in. It was a drag not to have heat in the winter, and it was depressing to have a cockroach run out to say Hi! every time I got up at night and turned on the light in the kitchen to get a drink of water. It was even more depressing when a whole chorus line of roaches appeared in broad daylight. I was also bored listening to Johnny talking about how nice it would be to have a study, that he was a partner now and it was time to live like a real grown-up, and so forth.

Like a fool, I began to read the real estate section of the paper. My well-connected husband pointed out to me that this was not the way to go. "Don't worry," he said. "I'll ask around." Within a month we had signed a lease on a floor-through apartment in a formerly grand neighborhood. Johnny was in heaven, and I had to agree that it was a very compelling space. It had a large front room overlooking the tree-lined street, with a fireplace, a dining room, a kitchen, two small rooms—a study and nursery, no doubt—and a large bedroom on a street inhabited by artists, ministers, young couples and old people.

Mary Abbott put her finger right on it. "It's so well organized," she said as we wandered around the streets looking at the brownstones and peering into people's windows. "It's like a nice little village in which everyone is represented. Young couples with children, older couples with older children, grown-up couples with grown-up children, and then the grandchildren with their children."

"Do I fit in?" I said.

"Oh, give it a year or so," Mary said. "There's no reason in the world not to have a baby. You ought to. It would be good for you."

"And why would it be good for me?"

"Curative," Mary said. "Get some of those mother demons out of your hair."

We walked in silence. It was a magnificent day. Low, silver-colored clouds floated across the sky, and when they parted, golden light poured down. The maples had turned red, the ginkgoes brilliant yellow. Little children triked up and down the street and the leaves drifted slowly down like big flakes. In the air was a smell of wood smoke. In front of the third house a woman was sweeping leaves off the pavement and scooping them into plastic trash bags. A handsome black woman took a wooden basket of apples out of the back of her station wagon. My heart contracted and expanded. I longed to slip into a proper place alongside these normal-looking people—or at least I longed to long to. And on the other hand, I feared it. A pleated plaid skirt. A cashmere sweater. A baby in a pram. A broom to sweep the leaves off the sidewalk and a basket of apples. A station wagon! What, I wondered, would be left of me? I said as much to Mary.

"Your essential self," she said.

"Oh, don't be silly," I said. "I haven't had an 'essential self' since I quit Ruby."

"Nonsense," Mary said. "I would know you anywhere. Even a nice plaid skirt and a string of pearls won't hide you. Not even being married to Johnny."

Ah, Johnny! The golden mean. He managed to do good and make money at the same time. Doing good, he often said, was good for one's career, a beautiful dovetailing of civic-mindedness and self-interest. His secretary said of him, "Unlike some lawyers who would run over their dying grandmothers to get what they wanted, Johnny would move *his* dying grandmother to some nice, safe place and *then* go get what he wanted." That, in a nutshell, I felt, was the man I loved.

I was constantly amazed at his ability to get things done, to get people to do what he wanted, to make sure the people he needed to like and the people he liked were one and the same. And they *were* the same! He did not even have to manufacture his feelings. In some ways, he was the best-adapted person in the world. Being married to someone like me gave his life an edge—I was his safe road to rock and roll, to the rebellious boy he had been in high school.

And so I settled into life on our street, and greeted my neighbors and swept the leaves in front of the house, but it was at the Race Music Foundation that I felt most like myself.

Once in a while I caught Ruby on television. She was now a solo act, in an elaborate wig and a dress entirely made of bugle beads. When she did some of her old songs I said to myself, "My God, I used to do that!" It seemed to me an eon ago, in some vanished era, in a time warp, in Never-Never Land, in some place that I had invented.

"All right," I said to Johnny. "Let's have a baby."

25

It seemed to me that about three or four minutes later I was in the office of my gynecologist, who, I learned, I was now to refer to as "my obstetrician."

I told Johnny that Little LaVonda, or her brother, Little Milton, was definitely on the way. He was, needless to say, jubilant.

"Oh, how wonderful!" cried Johnny. "I'm so happy!" He grabbed me around the waist and hoisted me up in the air.

"Put me down," I said. "I feel sick."

"Lie down," he said. "I'll get you a pillow for your feet. Aren't you supposed to put your feet up?"

"I think that's supposed to help conception, or something," I said. "It's too late for that now."

"Well, I'll get you some tea. Or are you not supposed to have caffeine?"

I said I had no idea.

"No idea!" squealed my husband. "No idea! The harbinger of new life, and you have no idea!"

"Somehow I don't think harbinger is the right word," I said. "But look. I got this big bottle of pregnancy vitamins." I shook it at him. "They have lots of things I've never heard of before, like folic acid."

"Girl," said my husband. "Get your thing together. We have to get educated. Let's go buy some books."

"You go buy some books," I yawned. "I'm sleepy. The fetus is a parasite and this one is making me very tired. Wake me when you come back."

My sweetie came back with a shopping bag full of tomes. Advice for pregnant fathers. Nutrition and pregnancy. How the fetus develops. What you should and should not do while pregnant.

"Gee," I said. "It makes me tired just looking at them."

"And this one," Johnny was saying—he had not even bothered to take his coat off—"this one is in living color. Jesus, I wonder how they did this. You can see the fetus develop week by week. Yours—I mean ours—is this tiny little speck. Imagine that."

"Imagine that," I said, sinking into my pillow.

"Our parents will be thrilled," he said.

"How about not telling them for a while?" I said. "Let's get the first three months over with, okay?"

"Why?" demanded my spouse. There was a truculent note in his voice.

"High rate of miscarriage for first pregnancies in the first trimester,"

"Oh, no, not my baby," said Johnny.

"Aren't you arrogant," I said.

"Not my baby," Johnny said. "This baby's here to stay."

"Because of your fine, fine, extra-fine sperm, doubtless."

"Doubtless. Hey, let's tell 'em, for God's sake."

I turned over on my side.

"Boy," Johnny said, "you hate a public demonstration, don't you."

I was mute. All I really wanted to do was go to sleep, preferably for nine months, and wake up when it was all over.

"Okay," Johnny said. "It's a deal. After all, you're the mother."

These words chilled me to the bone. *You're the mother.* Mother of what? Something that looked like a speck or blob, and yet this little speck would soon develop fingers and toes, vital organs, a personality. And to think that I was the harbinger of all this! I found these thoughts quite daunting. They made me hungry. I demanded that my husband take me to an expensive delicatessen for an enormous pastrami sandwich.

He actually brought along the book about nutrition in pregnancy and read to me, out loud, about nitrates and nitrites while I wolfed down my sandwich, demolished the pickles and drank a large glass of celery tonic.

" '. . . the effects of which are unknown,' " Johnny read.

I looked down at my empty plate. I felt I easily could have polished off another entire sandwich but I contented myself by filching what was left of Johnny's.

26

It took about a month before anyone at the Race Music Foundation noticed any change in me. I did not look pregnant, but I began to look slightly less defined.

"Hey, you look terrible," said the Bopper "What're you, off your feed?"

I did feel rather off my feed. I felt I had shed whatever luster I had once possessed. Since the episode of the pastrami sandwich, I had lost my appetite, and although I was not sick, I could not have said that I felt precisely well. I found myself yawning a good deal. And curiously, I had a fierce desire to announce my condition to everyone, with the exception of my parents and in-laws.

Naturally I told Mary Abbott.

"It's all over," I said.

"Pregnant, huh?" said Mary, slumping onto her bed.

"Uh-huh," I said. "July, right in the middle."

"But you haven't told Gertrude, right?"

"Right."

"How thrilled she'll be," Mary said.

"Just for about five minutes, and then she'll discover that I'm not being pregnant the right way or not gaining enough weight or gaining too much weight or not wearing the right clothes. She always advised against summer babies. She thinks people should deliver before the middle of June to avoid the heat."

"Poor old Gertrude," Mary said. "She's always so anxious for everything to be right."

"Poor old me," I said. "I'm the thing that's never right."

"Oh, you'll do," Mary said. "William says the first three months are usually lousy."

"Oh, how interesting," I said. "And how does William know this?"

"He has three. He and Madeline live in adjoining houses since they have joint custody."

"I don't get it," I said. "Why don't they just live together?"

"They don't live together well and they can't divorce," Mary said. "It's a moral issue—they're Catholic."

"Oh, I see," I said.

Actually, I never did quite see. I never really understood the way in which Mary was Catholic. At college she had gone off to Mass and once in a while she had dragged me along with her. Although I never told her, I stopped going because I could not bear it when she got in line to take communion. At that moment it was glaringly clear to me how different we were. Not only was this experience closed to me, but I could not believe that Mary believed in it. If she did believe in it, a huge and important part of her was totally mysterious to me. I felt I bore this stoically: I could not bring myself to discuss it with her, but it pained me.

If I said to her, "Do you really believe all that stuff?" she would peer at me over her glasses and say with a quizzical voice, "Just because it's difficult to believe it is no reason not to."

On the subject of my impending baby, Mary said, "It will give your life some structure."

"Structure? I get up every morning. I go to the foundation. I do my work, do my shopping, come home, make dinner, visit Johnny's parents, go to his friends' dinner parties, see my parents. How much more structure do I need, for Christ's sake?"

"Internal structure," Mary said. "It's different."

I looked around her stark apartment, once partially mine. Evidence of internal structure was everywhere, from the neat little bed she slept in, to the desk she worked at, to her books about the civil rights movement piled neatly on the floor. Chapters of her dissertation were stacked on various tables and shelves.

Part of William Hammerklever's role in her life was to help her with her statistical research. Many an afternoon I had appeared to find them bent over the calculator.

As I was lying on the couch, figuring out how to break the news of my pregnancy to my mother, I heard a key in the lock and William Hammerklever walked in. He was one of those small men with a handsome, leonine head, a head that seemed meant for a larger man. He had a full mouth, green eyes and curly hair. His hands were strong, large-veined.

"Oh, hello, you two," he said, as if we were little girls. He put his coat in his room and came back and stood behind Mary at her desk.

Mary was illuminated by her gooseneck desk lamp. From where I lay, she and William looked like figures in a painting by Joseph Wright of Derby. When she looked up at him I saw an expression on her face I had never seen before. Oh, the things I would never know about her!

She was in thrall to him. He looked down at her and put his hand on her shoulder.

"I think you've finally got that data right," he said to her. It was clear that I was totally superfluous and it was time to go home.

27

The thing that is never emphasized enough in books on pregnancy is that it takes forty weeks, not nine months. On the other hand, it takes three trimesters of three months each, which equals nine months but does not equal forty weeks. The whole thing was explained to me by my husband, who shoved a hefty book at me and told me to read about the lunar calendar. I was emerging from my first trimester into my second, the harbinger of the miracle of life, as I liked to refer to myself.

Often when I could not get to sleep I made myself even more anxious by reflecting on the awesome notion that I would soon be responsible for forming another person's character. What if my darling child grew up and ran off to tour with some rock and roll act? A baby is one thing. A teenager is quite another. The whole prospect seemed too daunting for an exhausted person.

What was I going to do with a child?

I would teach it how to dance, and all the words to "Tutti Frutti." We would take it to concerts and oldies shows. We would take it to see *The Nutcracker* at Christmas and to the circus in the spring. And in between times, we would worry about enormous issues such as how to find an appropriate school for a young child, how to manage a temper tantrum, how to deal with colic, how to get a child to sleep through the night. The road you walked with a baby was a long, hard one, it seemed, what with teething pain, controversy about whooping cough inoculations and the prospect of chicken pox. You had to teach a child to be fair and considerate to its peers, to have nice manners, not to draw on the walls or furniture. All this, and breast-feeding too! To say nothing of labor and delivery, which, no matter how you sliced it, sounded like being drawn and quartered. I took a deep breath and realized that some of my anxiety came from the fact that I had not yet told my mother or father, or my in-laws, this thrilling news.

We decided to do it by telephone.

"Preferably from a crouched position," I said.

"Hello, Gertrude," Johnny said. "We have wonderful news. You are about to be a grandmother. I mean, in the summer. Here's your daughter."

"When did you find this out?" said my mother.

"Oh, just a little while ago," I said.

"It must have been a good bit of a little while, since it's almost the new year. You were pregnant at Christmas and didn't tell us?"

"Well, you know," I said.

"No, I don't," said my mother. "Perhaps you'd like to explain it to me."

"Well, there's a chance of miscarriage in the first trimester with a first pregnancy and I just wanted to get through it before I told anyone."

"*Anyone*," said my mother. "Your parents are *anyone?*"

"Well, I just wanted to make sure all was well."

"And you thought that your parents shouldn't go through this with you if all was not well?"

The answer to this was a resounding *yes*. My mother would have driven me insane on various points such as my choice of doctor, hospital and method of delivery. But after she finished venting, she and my father were genuinely delighted, and Johnny's parents were thrilled. They looked forward to a future lawyer or doctor.

As I grew larger I saw them giving my belly musing looks, as if to say "I wonder who she's got in there." At night I felt there was a lump under my heart—this was not the baby, I was assured by my doctor. It was some other heart in the shape of a valentine full of anxiety and uncertainty.

"They should make you take a test before you get pregnant," I said to Johnny. "To see if you're mentally and emotionally equipped."

"There'd be about four people on the planet who'd pass, Sweetheart," said Johnny. "Get real. Even morons have perfectly nice children."

"Really?" I said. "How do you know that? Do we know any morons?"

"You know what I mean," said Johnny.

"Well, what about Steve and Ginger's children," I said. Steve was a colleague of Johnny's, and Ginger, his repellent wife, was a city planner. Their two children, Jason and Samantha, were horribly ill behaved. They threw food, whined and had the posture of two almost empty sacks. They were the sort of children I liked least: scrawny and undercooked-looking, with what seemed to be some chronic nasal blockage that caused their mouths to hang open, giving them the aura of those very morons Johnny claimed to know something about. These gruesome children, who their parents claimed had the IQ's of geniuses, gave me new cause for insomnia. Supposing I produced a child like one of Steve and Ginger's?

"It isn't genetically possible," said Johnny, when I shared this new fear with him. "We're very good-looking and, frankly, Steve and Ginger are not."

"That doesn't guarantee anything. What about all the dope we smoked in our youth?"

"It's been metabolized out. Go to sleep."

"If I had a child that looked like Steve and Ginger's, I don't know what I'd do."

"Look, we'd give it to Steve and Ginger and start all over again. Now go to sleep."

28

One cold night Johnny and I went to hear the blues singer Bunny Estavez at a club called Smokey Minnie's.

"I wonder about the lung function of the developing fetus," said Johnny, surveying what looked like a roomful of smog.

"Maybe we can rent an oxygen tank for the evening," I said.

We sat at a tiny table—I was aware of how small it was in relation to how large I was. I now had the belly of a pregnant woman. I found myself patting it, and I noticed other pregnant women patting their stomachs, too.

Bunny Estavez was very old. His wife and son-in-law had to help him onto the stage. He looked like melted candle wax. He could barely sing and the sounds he emitted were more like croaking hums, vaguely on key. His guitar style had once been florid, but he was so old now, he had stripped it down to something that sounded sort of Japanese. When the set was over we stomped and clapped, and then it was time to go home. As I leaned over to get my coat, I felt a strange sensation, as if something were darting across my stomach *inside*. It was not precisely *in* my stomach but only in the vicinity, and it was not any flutter I recognized.

"Oh, my God," I said, sitting down. "It's the baby."

Johnny turned green. He had been reading quite a lot about premature labor.

"I'll call an ambulance," he said.

"Sit down, don't panic," I said. "I *felt* it. I actually *felt* it. It's totally amazing. It's like having a little fish inside. Oh, God! There it is again!"

We staggered through the crowd into the night. It was very, very cold and I was wrapped up in my warmest coat. I felt quite toasty. In fact, I felt cocooned. *I* was a cocoon, and inside me some little boy or girl was swimming around in all that nice warm amniotic fluid, which Johnny pointed out in wonderment was mostly baby pee. "They float around in *baby pee*," he kept saying.

"It's sterile," I said. "It makes a cushion against shocks."

"Baby pee," he said, shaking his head.

Now my baby was moving around in its little sac of baby pee and I was wrapped up in my big warm coat. I was the big warm container for this tiny little critter, just as the coat was a container for me. Suddenly I felt as placid and serene as a cow. It was a transporting experience.

At home I lay in bed in a dreamy state, hogging all the pillows.

"I should get the Nobel Prize because I'm pregnant," I said. "Women are so wonderful. Aren't you jealous?"

"I've never seen you like this," Johnny said. "It's probably hormonal."

"You could look it up," I said helpfully.

As the weeks went by, my little fish fluttered more and more often. "It's his or her way of saying 'Hi, Mom!' " said my doctor. As I got bigger and bigger, and winter turned into spring, these flutters became more like flutter kicks and then plain old kicks. One afternoon I felt myself the victim of a woodpecker drilling for bugs in my pelvic bones. I reached for one of Johnny's birth books, which I consulted to see what my developing fetus looked like. It now looked like an actual baby, only small. A drilling sensation, it said, is usually the fetus having hiccoughs." I dialed Johnny right away.

"Mr. Miller's office," said the smooth, cool receptionist.

"Oh, hello, Olivia. This is Geraldine. Is Johnny there?"

"I'm afraid he's not," said Olivia, as if she had never heard of me and had no idea what I wanted. Olivia was small-boned and taut and wore her hair in a chignon, never had a hair out of place, a stain on her sweater or a sagging hem. She was perfect and distant and at office parties I found it was necessary to repress the desire to kick her.

"May I take a message?" she said.

"Yes," I said. "Tell him his baby has the hiccoughs in utero. I thought he'd like to know."

"Thank you," said Olivia, and hung up.

29

As I got bigger and bigger, I found that I was a magnet for advice.

Mrs. Willhall took one look at me and said, "Coconut oil."

I asked her if I was supposed to drink it or cook with it or what.

"You rub it on yourself," she said. "It keeps the skin pliant. And you'll never get any stretch marks at all. I know this because, aside from Desdemona, the Reverend and I have seven others."

Although she did not look sylphlike, neither did she look like the mother of eight, so like a good girl I went around the corner to the botanica to get some oil.

I had passed this shop hundreds of times. In the window were holy candles, tiny plastic replicas of the Virgin Mary surrounded by what looked like the Seven Dwarfs, tin jars with labels that read "Power in Love" and "High Conquering Incense," and large bottles of some kind of cologne with shells, herbs and charms floating at the bottom.

The man behind the counter was a squat, white-haired person with spectacles.

"Do you have coconut oil?" I said.

He produced a large brown bottle. "For ju," he said. "Ju need candles? Or lotion? We also have these for praying. Ju have bad foot, ju take this." He pulled out a little foot made out of shiny, silvery metal, which Mary later told me was called an ex-voto. "Or for a good baby, here." He put into my hand a flat silver baby wearing an adult-looking smile.

"I'll take it," I said. "Thank you very much."

"Ju are going to have a gwomang," the man said.

"Really?" I said. "A woman! I wondered who was inside there."

Back at the foundation I showed my silver baby to the Bopper.

"Oh, you went to the voodoo store, yeah?"

"I did."

"They sell some weird shit in there," the Bopper said. "I had a Puerto Rican girlfriend once. She wanted me to marry her. She went and got this stuff called Agua Conunga. I woke up one morning smelling like a French whorehouse. She put it all over me while I was asleep."

"Did it work?"

"Well, almost," said the Bopper. "Then she painted it on this other guy and *he* married her. I got some for my sister. I told her, 'This stuff is Get-him-to-marry-me lotion.' It worked on her boyfriend."

"The guy in the botanica told me I was going to have a gwomang."

"You're not," said the Bopper. "I've got a great record on this. You're having a man, take my word."

As I sat in my local coffee shop one morning putting Tabasco on my scrambled eggs, the woman next to me said, "Never eat pepper when pregnant. It makes the children excitable."

I was told not to travel on the subway (because of squashing) or the bus (because of jolts) or by car (potential crashes). I was told to drink large quantities of milk (for bone development) or no milk at all (because it makes babies mucousy) and to eat lots of meat (for protein) or no meat (possible parasites).

As for my mother and mother-in-law, between the two of them I felt more squashed than in any subway. Finally they had me where they wanted me. I was something they recognized. The daughter who had run off with a rock and roll act and who refused to dress nicely, the daughter-in-law who worked up in God-knows-where for God-knows-who, had turned into a classifiable object: a pregnant woman. With Gertrude on one arm and Dolly on the other, I felt about to be led off to jail. They took me to a nice ladies' luncheon place and fed me chicken salad sandwiches.

"I'll have coffee," I said.

"No, darling," said Dolly. "Coffee's bad for the baby."

"All right. Tea."

"Tea has the same amount of caffeine and is more corrosive," said my mother. "Now, after lunch, we thought we'd take you over to Saks to see about a layette."

"I don't want a layette," I said. "It's not even April Fools' Day. This kid isn't due till the Fourth of July. It's bad luck."

"You ought to be prepared," said Dolly. "My mother saw to it that I was totally outfitted long before Johnny came along."

"Besides, first babies often come early," said Gertrude. "Like that poor Feldman girl. Her baby looked like a mouse."

"A mouse," I mused. "How interesting. Then it would have been way too small to fit into any regular stuff in a layette, right?"

The real purpose of this lunch was to get me to quit my job.

"We're very worried," said Dolly.

"There are too many variables," said Gertrude.

"It isn't a safe part of town," said Dolly. "Johnny's really frantic."

"After all, it's *our* grandchild you're carrying," said Gertrude.

"We'd be happy to go up with you and explain everything to that nice minister you work for."

I closed my eyes and tried to envision the Reverend Willhall, surrounded by his wife Queenie and Desdemona, being confronted by two white matrons in mink coats.

I said, "I'm not quitting. I get fed a terrific lunch every day and I love my job."

"I think you ought to have a better sense of priorities," said my mother. "You may be endangering your child."

"I don't think working in Harlem endangers my child. After all, there are tons of children in Harlem."

"Yes, darling, but not *our* children."

"Ma," I said. "That really sounds like a first-class racist remark."

"That's very unfair," my mother said. "You know how many colored members of the Artists League there are. I have many black colleagues.

30

For a while it seemed to me that my condition would make social life easier. After all, a pregnant woman is a conversation starter. Didn't strangers on buses ask me when my due date was or where I was going to deliver? I figured Johnny's colleagues—at least the women colleagues—might ask me a question or two and I could give a normal answer. But it was not to be. Nobody, it seemed, wanted to talk about having babies. They had either had them a long time ago, like Betty Lister, or had decided not to have any for a while, or had had them a few years ago and now were more interested in things like social adjustment and reading scores.

However, I could not be denied. Johnny and I went to another of the Listers' dinner parties—they loved a dinner party as hogs love mud, and Betty must have felt that it was rude to let me sit there like some excrescence without giving me so much as a flicker of acknowledgment. Besides, I was quite a sight. A brief tour of the shops that sold maternity clothes had convinced me that I would rather be fried in boiling oil than wear what was considered proper for a pregnant woman. It was strange enough to be pregnant without having to redo my style totally. So instead I found a skimpy, yet shapeless black garment which I wore with black suede boots. I found myself drawn to eye makeup and would have worn my old false eyelashes from my dancing days had I not been stopped by my husband.

We sat having drinks in the Listers' living room, or rather everyone

Eva Toussaint is on the board with me, a lovely woman. It isn't about black people. It's about the neighborhood you work in."

"Which is full of black people," I said.

"Now, Geraldine, you are hardly being fair to your mother," said Dolly. "We both have a perfectly legitimate cause for concern."

"In my pregnancy book it says that harassment of the pregnant mother by mothers and mothers-in-law is bad for the developing fetus," I said.

Dolly and my mother sighed and drank their glasses of white wine. We finished our lunch, but the subject was far from closed. For the rest of our time together we discussed such fascinating subjects as why breast-feeding was old-fashioned (neither of them had done it), why I should have a baby nurse (since I obviously didn't know what I was doing, and *they* had had baby nurses) and how good it was that I was having a summer baby but not a *late* summer baby so it could ripen up and gain weight for the cold weather. Apparently it was the only thing I had done right, so I didn't have the heart to tell them it was a matter of pure luck.

had a glass of wine and I had ginger ale, since alcohol was damaging to the developing fetus. Betty's foundation gave money to a group that did prenatal outreach to poor women and encouraged them not to drink or smoke and to have frequent checkups.

"If no one was permitted to drink, there would be no babies born in France," said Adrien McWirter, who was also drinking ginger ale. He had gone on the wagon and was now allowed back at the Listers' hearth. I had longed to meet him. Hadn't he slipped a cornichon down the dress of the wife of the dean of the law school? Hadn't he once tried to sit on the lap of the Chief Justice of London?

"Now, Adrien," said Betty. "You know that isn't true."

"Don't be silly," said Adrien. "My three children are perfectly civilized and intelligent, and Helen drank whatever she pleased through each pregnancy. And it didn't do them a scrap of harm."

"But we know better now," said Betty. "Besides, think how many of their brain cells might have been killed off. They might have been geniuses."

"They *are* geniuses," said Adrien. "Maybe Helen was just *pretending* to drink. Maybe it was white grape juice all along and the old girl was having one over on me."

"Oh, Adrien, do shut up," said Betty fondly.

"I will shut up, if you let me sit next to that nice young mother-to-be at dinner."

"Now, Geraldine," Betty said, sitting down next to me. "Here are the most important two words of advice I can give you—I'm an old, old hand at babies. *Stein Agency.*"

"Are they in the music business?" I said, confused.

She laughed. "No, dear. They're the best baby-sitting agency in the city. They'll find you baby nurses and nannies and night sitters. They are perfectly wonderful, and totally reliable. We used them for years and years. Our baby nurse came from the Stein Agency and so did both our nannies, and when our regular baby-sitters—we had a nice squad of teenage girls in the neighborhood—when they couldn't make it, we'd simply dial up Stein and they'd send some really wonderful person over."

"You mean, you left a baby with someone the baby had never seen before?"

Betty Lister gave me a kind of consoling look. She said, "It isn't the way it sounds at all. Children take terribly well to someone whose only apparent interest is *them*. You'll see. The most important thing is your relationship with Johnny. So many women of my generation let that go all to hell. Baby this! Baby that! Walking around with baby spit-up on their shoulders, looking a fright! Never going out! Totally fixated on their babies. That's not good for anyone."

Here at last, I thought, was the second opinion.

"I went straight back to work," Betty said. "I was just starting out at the foundation. Let me tell you, between you and me, babies are just a tiny bit boring."

Naturally this conversation depressed me. It seemed so likely that I might be the sort of person who fixated on my baby and had baby spit-up all over my shoulders. Besides, I had hated baby-sitters as a child and I thought the idea of leaving a baby with someone it had never seen before was sort of sociopathological.

I perked up considerably at dinner. Adrien McWirter sat next to me.

"Please don't put a cornichon down my back," I said.

"Aha!" he said. "My beautiful reputation precedes me. Now listen. You and I know . . ." He leaned over and whispered into my ear. " . . . that Betty is really full of shit. Her children are now the most awful fascist slime. Don't listen to her. Babies are delicious. When mine were little I was working at home and I sniffed 'em and bathed 'em and changed their little diapers. I personally adore baby spit-up, and you will too."

"Gee, I hope so," I said. "I hear there's quite a lot of it. Everyone's talking about it."

"Ah, birth. Amazing. Sitting next to a pregnant woman makes me feel all tingly. I adore what you're wearing, by the way. Most women wear the most terrible things when they're in pig—to cover up the essential fact."

"Essential fact?"

"Sex, heat, eros," he said. "That's what it's all about, yes? I get on the subway and see all these pretty young women big as houses. Christ, they're *apartments,* with little babies rattling around inside, and you can't but look at them and speculate about the way they got there."

"Mostly it's the usual way," I said, mashing my spoon delicately into my chocolate mousse. "Although sometimes it's more high-tech."

"You know what I mean," he said. "You imagine them *at it.*"

For the first time in my adult life, I felt myself blush.

"You wouldn't have lunch with me, would you?" he whispered.

"I don't think that would be too cool," I said.

"What are you two conspiring about down there?" Betty said. "Come on, join the conversation. We're talking about Latin America."

"I'm trying to get this young woman to have an assignation with me," said Adrien McWirter.

"Now, Adrien, try to be good, you silly man," said Betty.

"You seemed to have a lot more fun tonight," Johnny said. "Being pregs is a big asset. Was McWirter really trying to pick you up?"

"No," I said. "He was just being silly."

"That's what we thought," said Johnny.

"How lucky," I yawned, "of you to be right." And I fell asleep on the spot.

31

Finally the spring burst forth. The leaves shot out on the trees and the buds exploded into flower, causing hay fever sufferers to suffer. The Reverend Willhall, solemn and funereal on the best of days, now seemed to be a man in constant tears. He was allergic to almost anything that grew and he was a mess. He walked around the foundation, his eyes streaming, blowing his nose into an enormous handkerchief the size of a pillowcase.

I myself felt wonderful, but I could barely overcome my constant urge to nap. At my desk I yawned constantly. Tears from yawning spilled down my cheeks and onto my papers. My unborn baby, now known as "Little," had become a positive acrobat. When I sat down or curled up to take a nap, he or she began a strenuous aerobics routine.

My mother was not pleased that, although I had had the test for genetic abnormalities also revealed gender, Johnny and I had decided against asking what we were having.

"It's just nonsense," my mother said. "Your doctor knows. Why shouldn't you know?"

"My doctor also knows what my cervix looks like, Ma," I said.

"It's hardly the same thing," said my mother. "Think of all the planning we could do if you knew."

It was her opinion that only girls kicked so ardently. I had kept her awake night after night after night. Now I was kept awake. My baby knocked around inside me all night long, and then spent the morning knocking the coffee cup off my lap. It was only when I walked that he or she took a nice little snooze, and all I really wanted was a little snooze, too.

Eventually it occurred to me that I must quit my job. In truth I had run out of things to do. Johnny wanted to go to his parents' summer house for a week, and I was tired of dragging myself up to the foundation. As much as I hated to do it, I knew I had to. On a hot day in June, I did it.

"Reverend Willhall," I said. "I think I have to quit." As I said it I burst into tears.

The Reverend blew his nose. Tears were streaming down his cheeks. He began to sneeze violently.

"You have done fine work," he said. A series of extremely loud sneezes followed. "But your future work is more important. The care of a newborn soul. Please have this pamphlet," he said. He slipped into my hand a little bound tract entitled "New Life from Heaven," which began: "The newborn child is an angel from God."

"You will not be replaced," said the Reverend Willhall. "We are phasing out this part of our research and our next move is the development of the Race Music Foundation Gospel and Blues College in Natchez, Mississippi, under the direction of my brother, Reverend Archie Willhall, and my brother-in-law, Antoine Fontenez."

"I see," I said.

"We will put you on the mailing list," said the Reverend Willhall, blowing his nose.

"Thank you," I said. "Well, goodbye."

"God bless you," he said, and he shook my hand. The last I saw of him he was standing at his desk, in front of the poster that read I DO NOT PLAY NO ROCK AND ROLL, and sneezing.

I said goodbye to Queenie, to Desdemona and to the Bopper's mother. Finally, I said goodbye to the Bopper.

"Hey, c'mere," he said. "Before you leave, I want you to listen to something. But make sure the door is closed."

With the door properly closed, the room was totally soundproof.

"Okay, sit down," the Bopper said. "This is gonna put a cut in your strut and a glide in your slide."

I sat down. The Bopper threaded a piece of tape into his machine. At once the room was flooded with sound: a clear, beautiful voice singing the first lines of "You Don't Love Me Like You Used to Do." It didn't sound like Ruby or anyone else. Perhaps it was some discovery of the Bopper's

"So?" said the Bopper.

"It's beautiful," I said. "Who is it?"

"Baby, it's you," he said.

"Don't be ridiculous," I said.

"Hey, I spliced it right off a piece of documentary footage. The Bopper has his sources. Now listen," he said. "Let's make a million dollars. Let's record you singing some of those groovy old blues songs you catalogued. I provide the backup with some of my degenerate out-of-work jazz buddies. I make the demo and sell it. It'll be our big break."

"I'm sorry, Bopper," I said. "I'm really sorry."

"I don't get you," the Bopper said. "You run with spades, you go on tour, you work up here. What's your story?"

"I'm like the Reverend Willhall," I said. "A purist."

"So what's impure about singing some folk songs, for crying out loud. This is the music you grew up with."

"I'm not a blues singer," I said. "Going on tour was a kind of lucky fluke. I went for the music, not to have a career. I'm not a singer. I'm —I don't know what I am, except a mother-to-be. Eventually I'll have to find my next thing."

"Hey, I'm *offering* you your next thing."

"I'm very flattered, Bopper, really I am," I said. "I just can't do it. I love this music with all my heart but I don't honestly believe it's mine to sing."

"You and Willhall," the Bopper said. "Boy, was he ever right to hire you. Who would have thought that a white chick would have the interests of Afro-Americans so close to her heart?"

"Don't be mad, Bopper," I said. "I loved working here, and I loved working with you."

He sighed. "Maybe you'll change your mind. I'm told changing diapers over and over can drive a person nuts."

I kissed him on the top of his head.

"Let me know when you have your man," he said.

Unlike workers at normal offices, I did not have a big bag of personal possessions from my office to take home. All I had to do was close my desk drawer. My days as a researcher at the Race Music Foundation were over.

I paid a last visit to Fred's Out-of-Print Records. Luis and Ronnie were at lunch, and only Fred Wood was in, slumped over his counter, smoking a cigarette and looking morose. I hadn't been there in some time.

"Knocked up, I see," he said.

"Almost ready to roll."

"Still up at Willhall's?"

"I just quit. Too tired."

"Pregnant women are very groovy," said Fred Wood.

"Really, do you think?" I said.

"Oh, yeah," said Fred Wood. "Extremely. I just don't get many in here. You might be the only one."

"Gosh," I said.

"Yeah," he drawled, exhaling smoke. "They always look very . . . ripe."

I felt if I looked at Fred Wood the wrong way, he was going to take me into the stacks and do things to me.

"Well, goodbye," I said.

"Yeah, take care of yourself," he said, running his piggy little eyes up and down my body.

There was obviously a breed of men definitely into pregnant women. Of course, it *was* about heat and sex and eros, but by the time you were very pregnant it was mostly about family, stability, crib toys and concepts of early learning.

"When the kid cries," Fred Wood continued, "sing it 'Come On Baby Let the Good Times Roll.' That'll generally put it to sleep. If you get bored in the next month or so, come and see me and I'll deal with it."

"What a good idea," I said.

I got on the subway and when I got out I found myself meandering into a toy store. There I bought a mobile of fish and frogs chasing each other, which you were supposed to assemble yourself. It had been made in Japan. At home, in a spate of heat and sex and eros, I attempted to put this thing together. Two hours later it was still unassembled, and I was awash in tears for what I had just given up and for what was ahead of me.

32

Now that I was unemployed, I found myself constantly rearranging the furniture. On nights that Johnny played squash with his friend Ben Sennett, I lay around the house with Mary Abbott, figuring out where to put what and listening to the B sides of obscure records.

The nursery was ready. In it stood a plain wooden crib that had been sitting in the attic of the Listers' country house, and an old pine bureau from Johnny's mother, plus two of my mother's best watercolors—one of me wearing a straw hat, and one of a baby curled up in a rosebud —were nicely hung on the wall in gold frames. The Listers had sent us a humidifier, with a long note from Betty about the delicacy of newborn skin and a copy of a hospital report attached. From the Race Music Foundation came a wicker basket lined with patchwork, for carrying the baby around. The secretaries at Johnny's office sent striped receiving blankets and his partners presented us with a fancy pram that turned into a stroller. We were all set.

"I feel like a time bomb," I said to Mary. "Everything's ready and waiting for me to go off."

"You *are* a time bomb," said Mary. "Stop fussing about where to put the rocker. Put it in the baby's room and shut up."

"I barely see you anymore," I said. "I'll have this baby and I'll never see you. If I had any religion, you could be the baby's godmother."

"Well, get some and I'll be," said Mary.

"It's too late to get some," I said. "Will you be its unofficial godmother?"

"Can't," Mary said. "In Catholicism it's a real thing. I can't be a pretend godmother, but I'll be its courtesy aunt."

"Do you promise?"

"I do," Mary said.

"You'll marry William," I said. "You'll move somewhere. Then I'll never see you."

"I'm not going to marry William," Mary said.

"Then what are you doing with him?"

"I'm having a friendship," Mary said, settling in on the couch. "It's a kind of friendship of struggle, and when I get through the struggle I'll know something important."

"Like what?"

"If I knew I wouldn't have to struggle."

"I see," I said, but I never saw. What was a friendship of struggle? Did that mean she wanted to sleep with him but wouldn't, or vice versa? The equation of our friendship was that I told her everything and she told me what she wanted to tell me. My role was to understand this—Mary liked to incubate an idea, and when she was ready she would present it to me. The fact was, she was very secretive about her dealings with men.

It was now truly summer. We sat in the air-conditioning, drinking iced mint tea. I lay on the couch feeling my baby go thump, thump, thump inside me.

"I think it's going to happen soon," I said. "I feel odd all the time. Imminent."

"It will be revealed to us in the fullness of time," said Mary. She had brought a batch of brownies and we were polishing them off. Outside it was steamy and dark, probably as steamy and dark as where little LaVonda or Milton was working out.

The weeks dragged by and suddenly I was almost two weeks past my due date.

"Your baby has gotten itself into a weird position," said my doctor. "It's called the 'transverse lie.' It's in there crossways. Here's its little head, over here on the left, and here's its little feet, over here on the right, kind of like a person on a couch. I hoped it would wriggle itself around, but it hasn't. I think we ought to section this baby very soon. Why don't I book you in? You go home and get your things and your husband, and I will meet you at the hospital."

"You mean today?" I said.

"Certainly."

"But I'm not ready," I said.

"Are you packed?"

"Yes."

"Is the baby's room ready?"

"Yes."

"Then what?"

"What?" I said. "I mean, I'm supposed to be someone's mother by this time tomorrow?"

"Why not?" said my doctor cheerfully.

"Why not? Well, you're not somebody's mother." I found this so overwhelming that I had to take deep breaths.

"You'll be a wonderful mother," said the doctor. "You've been a wonderful patient. Now, go call your husband and let's get this baby out into the world."

From that point on I felt that I was on a train hurtling out of control. I went home. Johnny met me. We drove to the hospital. I was put on a gurney and a large Algerian threaded a catheter into my spine which made the lower half of my body numb. I was wheeled down a hallway, with Johnny, all in green, running next to me. My heart was flopping like a caught fish.

They painted my stomach with Betadine. "Don't look," said the doctor to Johnny. I, of course, couldn't look, since there was a screen in front of my face. I felt something tugging at my stomach.

"You can look now," said the doctor. "It's a big beautiful boy."

"Oh, boy!" said Johnny.

Suddenly a little wet thing was put on my chest, a thing with dark wet hair and covered with something that looked like cold cream. He had entered the world with a loud shriek but seemed to have regained some equilibrium. He opened his little slate-colored eyes. I looked down at him, and I felt that he looked up at me. A wave of the most intense feeling came over me. So this, I thought, is a transcendental experience.

With my tiny slimy boy in my arms, I felt suddenly and irrevocably that I had found my true purpose—or at least a part of it—for the first time in my life.

PART THREE

Little Franklin

33

Our son, Franklin Ross Miller, named in honor of Johnny's paternal grandfather, the federal court judge from Savannah, was a winsome little creature from the moment he bounced into life, shrieking like a demented chicken. His chickenlike hair stood straight up. Johnny called him Frankie, but he would always be Little Franklin to me.

I was totally swept away by this minute person whose hot, velvety head nestled so perfectly against my shoulder as he spit up mother's milk all down the back of my shirt. There was much less spit-up than I had anticipated after all that talk.

How smart he was! Just a few days old and he could yawn, make a fist, blink and stretch. It was love at first sight, just like in the songs.

My adorable Little Franklin! Asleep in my arms, he was unaware that the person holding him was out of a job, had no profession and had in fact outlived an era. Little Franklin of course didn't care, and I didn't much care either. I had a purpose in life: to sit in a rocking chair mindlessly musing on my baby while I nursed him and burped him and rocked him. I sang him "Come On Baby Let the Good Times Roll" and "Hi-Heel Sneakers," and when he was fretful I threw on "Everybody Is a Star" by Sly and the Family Stone and danced him slowly across the floor.

The first question people asked me when I brought him home was "Where are you going to send him to school?" The second was "When are you going back to work?"

Since I had no work to go back to, I concentrated on the school issue. "Johnny and I feel he should not go to school until he is at least seven weeks old," was my standard response.

We answered this question again and again, for as soon as Little Franklin was home and in his tiny Moses basket, it seemed that everyone Johnny or I had ever known showed up for a viewing.

"Our child is just like the pope," I said. "He has audiences."

Mary felt he looked rather like Queen Victoria, but I thought he resembled the poet Wallace Stevens.

"Basically," I said to Mary, "he looks like a little veal roast."

"It's amazing," she said. "There are bags of kitty litter that weigh more than he does."

"Why don't you let me baby-sit, and you and Johnny go out?" asked my mother or Johnny's mother.

"Because Franklin is on a two-hour schedule at the moment."

"We raised children, too, you know," they said.

"As you know, I'm nursing him."

"Well, we certainly hope you're not going to get carried away with *that*. All babies like bottles. Besides, he *should* have a bottle so you can have some freedom."

"I don't actually feel like having any of what you call freedom. I'm very happy." I said.

"Well, breast-feeding is all the rage among you young women," my mother said. "I can never quite get used to it. The other day I saw a woman doing it in a *restaurant.*"

"Oh," I said gaily, "I do it in restaurants all the time."

"Well, it's awfully hard on people of my generation," Johnny's mother said. "We simply didn't do things like that. Immigrant women did it, but not people *we* knew. How long are you intending to continue?"

"I thought I'd wean him right before he goes to high school."

"Now, seriously," said my mother. "I'm told three months is best."

"We'll see how Franklin feels," I said.

Johnny's mother said, "How *Franklin* feels. Geraldine! Little babies don't have feelings about things like that!"

And then there was Betty Lister. Once Franklin was born, every time I turned around she was standing at my door. Perhaps she felt I was some project her foundation might do a rehab job on. She usually came armed with data.

"I'm just stopping by on my way to the Barradas-Elitzer Center. It's right in your neighborhood. Do you know them? They're one of our oldest outreaches. They do vocational and legal counseling. So I just wanted to bring you something that came in the mail. It's quite fascinating. Early visual stimulation of newborns can lead to much better test scores in the later years. Now, are you two getting out at night?"

"We're not even sleeping at night," I said.

"Well, dearie. It's all in Dr. Spock. You just encourage that little baby of yours *not* to want to eat every two hours. Take him outside, get him in the car!"

"At four o'clock in the morning?"

"Use your imagination. All this breast-feeding. I know it's supposed to be better for them, but all the reports say that formula is *denser* and they sleep better."

"I don't care if he sleeps better," I said. "I like getting up at night."

"Well, you look very tired, if you don't mind my saying so. I'm telling you, one call to the Stein Agency and all your troubles would fly away."

"I don't see this as trouble," I said.

"Oh, but you will!" said Betty. "You will as soon as you want to get anything worthwhile done."

As soon as I was alone with my baby, I sat with him in the rocking chair and sang "I Sold My Heart to the Junkman," which began, *"I gave my heart to you, the one that I trusted. You gave it back to me all broken and busted."*

Little Franklin seemed to like this song, and he liked the songs I made up for him. One, based on Big Joe Turner's immortal classic, "Feel My Leg," began: *"I want to bite your nose, I want to bite your toes."*

When Johnny came home the first thing he said was, "Where's my beauty?" This, I knew, meant Little Franklin. It did not bother me in the slightest. He was my beauty too.

"Hey, John. How 'bout keeping our mothers off me, huh? And Betty Lister too."

"Oh," said Johnny, holding his beloved in his arms. "Bum day with the old girls?"

"They think only peasants breast-feed," I said.

"Did you tell 'em about all those groovy immunities?"

"I forgot."

"Don't answer the door," said Johnny. "Gosh, this critter grows in the space of a couple of hours."

"Also, how about telling Betty that she's bringing harmful contaminants into the house. Look at this! We're supposed to get big black shapes and put them near his crib so he'll have better test scores in later years. What are the Listers' children like, anyway?"

"To tell the truth, Bill Jr.'s a wimp and Penny's a jerk."

"We don't have to do any of this stuff, do we?" I said.

"Naa," said Johnny. "Our baby will have naturally high test scores without all this junk."

34

Often, as I was hanging around the neighborhood with my beloved boy, I would think of the old days when, instead of a baby sling
or pram, I tore around in a chartreuse dance dress with Day-Glo fringe
on it. Those days were gone forever. There were no acts like that
anymore, except for groups like Jean and the Bee-Bops, but they were
retro and only did oldies shows. When I was with Ruby, we were *new.*
Like an exile, I knew that I could never return to the home of my
childhood. It had vanished—but not, however, without a trace.

When Little Franklin was six months old, a documentary came out
called *It Will Never Die,* which included footage of Ruby and the Shakettes during the time that I was a Shakette. My own husband bought a
print of it at great personal expense.

"Franklin will want to see this when he grows up," Johnny said.
"Isn't it great! You actually sing solo on 'Baby Come Home.' "

"I sing one line," I pointed out.

"Yes, but what a line," he said.

The night it aired I watched it solemnly. Johnny was in a wonderful
mood: he thought this sort of thing was historic. He loved old family
photos, too, even those that made him look like a little creep.

"I wish Franklin was awake to see this," he said.

"It probably wouldn't mean much to a baby his age," I said.

The documentary attempted to explain the origins of rock and roll.
It showed gospel singers, old bluesmen (including the late Bunny

Estavez), rhythm and blues men, girl groups, a cappella quartets and finally, after Chuck Berry and Bo Diddley and Fats Domino and James Brown and the Famous Flames, a short section on Ruby.

Ruby, according to this documentary, began in the old tradition and then entered the twenty-first century. The first shot was of her new show: a big set, a huge orchestra and Ruby, in a spotlight, wearing a short sequined dress festooned with fringe made out of tiny glass beads. That dress probably cost as much as she once made in a year.

It mentioned that she and Vernon were the first to break the color line by hiring a white Shakette. There was an interview with Vernon, who seemed, after all these years, entirely unchanged. He said, "It didn't never make no never mind to us. We treated them all the same."

And then there was some footage from my time: Ivy, Grace and my own self, on a plain, nasty-looking stage. I squinted and saw that the curtain on the stage read "Toledo Auditorium." And there I was.

We were backing Ruby on "Get Your Own Boy, Girl," which had a fast backbeat to which we did one of our more complicated routines, including a lot of shimmying. There I was, frozen in a moment that existed only in history. It was the saddest thing I had ever seen. Then we did "Baby Come Home" and I sang my solo line.

"God, you guys were great," said Johnny. He sounded positively awestruck. "Come on, admit it. You were hot stuff."

I sat on the couch and did not say a thing.

"Say out loud, black and proud," said Johnny, eating a handful of popcorn.

"Oh, shut up," I said. I looked around me. Our living room had high ceilings with ornamental moldings in each corner, a fireplace, a coffee table and two sofas that faced it. In a nook was Little Franklin's Moses basket for when I was sitting around and wanted him near. What am I doing here? I wondered. What happened to the person on the stage?

"I'm so jealous," Johnny said. "You really have a past to be proud of. I mean it."

"It's just like watching Little Franklin," I said finally. "Each day I say to myself, 'This is the last day he will be exactly this age.' Soon he will learn how to crawl and talk and he will never again be the way he is right now. His babyhood is melting away in front of my eyes."

"That's why the motion picture camera was invented, Honey," Johnny said. "Now everyone can be a historian, and if you get it with the audio attachment, you can be an oral historian, too. I was just browsing the other day in front of that discount camera store and now I think I'm going to take the plunge. I mean, his newborn state has been fully photo-documented. Now let's get some action."

I leaned my head on my husband's shoulder. What a comforting person he was. Yes, melancholy could easily be banished. Confused about memory or history? Buy a camera! Easy as pie! And the amazing thing, I realized, was that he was right.

In a few years maybe Little Franklin would want to see this film of his mother. Maybe he would say, "That's pretty cool, Mom, but it doesn't really look like you." Or maybe he would say, "That's pretty retarded-looking, Mom." Or maybe Johnny and I had produced some incipient straight-bag, an uptight white boy on his way to the Harvard Business School who would look at me sternly and say, "Mother, can't you be appropriate, ever?"

35

"*You* know," said Johnny one morning over breakfast when Little Franklin had become a real baby, with a few teeth and a beautiful grin. "People are getting very interested in rock and roll again. I mean, the good stuff."

"Is that so?" I said. "Franklin, spit that out!" My darling son was sitting in his high chair stuffing a large piece of toast into his mouth. He obligingly spat a wet lump of partially chewed bread into my hand.

"I mean," said Johnny, "I mean you ought to write something about it. After all, you had firsthand experience."

"Johnno," I said. "I am raising your son. I am not a writer. I don't want to write about rock and roll. I am very happy. When the time comes for me to find self-fulfilling employment, I will go and look for it. I still have money socked away from Ruby. And for the moment I am perfectly happy to be Little Franklin's mother."

"Ginger says that after a while being just a mother is bad for a person."

I wheeled around at my husband. "Bad for a person! It's bad for her with those two horrible-looking little weasel children. If I had had children like that, I'd have gone back to work *the next day*. I am the harbinger of new life, and don't you forget it. I'm sick of everyone expecting me to be something or other. The only person who likes me for myself is Little Franklin."

Little Franklin watched this performance with wide eyes, and then he began to cry. I took him out of his high chair and held him in my arms.

"Listen," I said. "I had this baby and the first thing everyone wanted to know was when I was going to send him to prep school so I could do some useful work. Then they wanted to know when I was going to have a second one. You people are insane. Your child is being raised by his parents, not by a bunch of nannies. I *like* being his mother. I don't want to be anything else for a while. He's a *baby*. When he gets a little older, you can send him to law school. Maybe you're ashamed of me because all the other boys in your firm have wives with babies and big jobs, too. Maybe you're embarrassed because I'm just nobody."

"You aren't just nobody," Johnny said.

"No," I said. "I am Little Franklin's mother."

But really none of this bothered me very much. Having withdrawn from the foreign country of the Race Music Foundation, I crossed the border and entered another exotic place: the world of babies.

I took Little Franklin to the park, where local mothers met to discuss diaper rash, the acquisition of teeth, nursing, sleep schedules and where to get the many appliances necessary to upscale baby life: baby swings and contraptions that helped them to jump up and down, and portable high chairs. As our babies began to look more like children, we discussed nursery schools, finger food and toilet training.

But while other mothers perused catalogues of baby items as their little angels took their naps on blankets under the trees, I read *Billboard* and *Cashbox*. I read these on the sly—I did not want my husband getting any funny ideas. While other mothers read articles about toys that would raise the IQ's of their toddlers, I followed the career of Vernon and Ruby and the scores of other acts we used to travel with.

It turned out that Veronica LeBlanc of Veronica and the Vee-teens had returned to Charleston and opened a knitting shop called "Vonknitique." Gladys Williams had died in some drug-related incident. King Carter had filed for personal bankruptcy. His sidemen, the Bell Brothers, were doing well in their private security company and performing their old hits such as "Bad Girl," "Gumdrop" and "Honey Mine" at oldies shows in the San Diego area. As for Ruby, Ruby was golden, a million-dollar act.

Donald "Doo-Wah" Banks, Ruby's former saxophonist, was writing the score for a feature film about a black detective by a hot black writer named Will Bartholomew. As I pushed Little Franklin gently on the baby swing, my crush on Doo-Wah came back to me full force.

I could see him now in his work garb, which consisted of a thick white sweatshirt with the sleeves cut off, old black trousers and beat-up cowboy boots. With shades, he looked somewhat sinister. With his shades off, he was the kind of man children run to when they need a splinter removed. I myself, when overcome with despair on tour, would creep into his room. Although he constantly refused to sleep with me—it was unprofessional, he said—he always made me a sherry flip after a recipe of his grandmother's. Wah traveled with a quart of milk, a six-pack of eggs and a pint of sherry. This always picked me right up, and once in a while, if I was particularly downcast, he would permit himself to kiss me. This was also bracing.

As I stood there, consumed with longing for Wah, I said to myself: You ought to get your thing together. Here you are, a wife and mother, daydreaming about a saxophone player when you ought to be thinking about your child's developmental stages.

One summery day I found a letter waiting for me from a person I had never heard of, forwarded to me from Flame Records. Every once in a while I got a fan letter from someone who wondered what had happened to me. Often these letters were forwarded by the nice woman in Cleveland who was the president of the Ruby Shakely Fan Club. (One letter had read: "Where are you, my white Shakette? You drove me crazy in the old days." I did not answer this letter, although I could have said: "Yes, and I drove myself crazy in the old days, too.")

This letter was written on glossy stock. At the top, in heavy engraved red letters, was the name Spider Joe Washburn. On the bottom it said: "A friend of Rock and Roll." Spider Joe, as he signed himself, was writing a book about girl groups, with photos, and he claimed he was desperate to interview me. As I stared at the letter, Little Franklin began to shriek and I realized that he was still strapped in his buggy.

That night, after Little Franklin was asleep, I wrote a note to Spider Joe telling him that I would consent to be interviewed at our mutual convenience. "I am married and have a baby son," I wrote. "Although I no longer sing or dance, I keep up with current trends in popular music."

This letter contained a number of lies. I did not keep up with trends in popular music. I played the same old music over and over again, only occasionally straying into a Latin music parlor to buy a few Ricardo Rey discs. Furthermore, although I was certainly married, it could no longer be said that my son was a baby.

36

Spider Joe was a sort of depraved-looking person, the type that used to hang around the rock and roll scene wearing extremely expensive clothes. I thought these people had disappeared off the face of the earth. He had on ostrich-skin cowboy boots, tailored blue jeans and a workshirt that looked as if it had been made by English shirtmakers. With these Spider Joe wore a string tie, an Australian hat and a Navaho silver bracelet on his wrist. He wore little round glasses with tinted lenses and his moustache was in the style of Fu Manchu. He came at nap time, as I had suggested.

"Oh, you mean you'll be asleep?" he had asked.

"No, my child."

"Yo, child," he had said. "What a gas."

It took him quite a while to set up his recording gear, what with making and taking telephone calls. "I gave your number, babe," he said. It was impossible to hear anything of these calls since his voice dropped to a deep, inaudible murmur.

"Yo," he finally said. "Let's get on it. Testing. Testing. You read? Dig." He played this back to himself. "This is an interview with Geraldine Coleshares, the white Shakette. Yo, Geraldine. Those were the glory days, right?"

"Wrong."

"I mean, we had a lot of fun, right?"

I peered at Spider Joe. Suddenly he looked very familiar to me.

"Did you used to be an act?" I asked.

Spider Joe turned off his machine. "Yeah," he said demurely. "Just for like a minute. I was with Brute Force and the Invaders."

"That's not where I know you from," I said. "I never saw Brute."

"I used to manage this act called Homard Roti out of New Orleans, with Huey Moscogne," said Spider Joe.

I considered this. I remembered Homard Roti, but not Spider Joe.

"Oh," I said, slapping my forehead. "How could I be so dumb! Spider Joe's Rock and Roll Web! Gosh, I was a teenager then. Is that you?"

"Yeah," he said. "But I don't, like, dwell on it. That was, like, television for teens."

"Well, bless my soul," I said. "You must be a hundred years old."

"Spider Joe is a cat, babe. A cat has many lives. But let's roll. We made great music. When you look back, what do you see?"

"Well, I'm one who believes with the Reverend Arthur Willhall, at the Race Music Foundation, that rock and roll co-opted black music. I mean, it *was* great music. In the beginning it gave everybody in it a taste. But then it turned into a kind of corporation of its own. Remember Penny Bones? Her big hits were 'River of Love' and 'Middle of the Night.' I read the other day that she used to listen to herself on the oldies stations while she was working as a cleaning lady."

"That's life, babe," said Spider Joe.

"It isn't the business I went into," I said.

"Yeah, well, let's talk about then, okay? You used to sing real good, right? Weren't you on that Shakette single?"

"You mean 'I'm Not Yours'? That was three studio singers and Ruby got the money."

"Yeah, but *you* sang. I saw you."

"I sang solo on 'Baby Come Home,' 'You Don't Love Me Like You Used to Do' and 'Nobody's Out There.' "

These were considered my finest moments. The fact was, I loved to sing, but it was my heart's desire to be a backup, not a singer. I said this to Spider Joe.

"You lie, babe. Everybody wanted to be a star."

"Actually, everybody did *not* want to be a star."

"But let's talk about those wonderful days. All of us together. Ruby broke the color line."

"Doubtless you mean our color-coordinated dresses," I said.

"I mean integration, babe."

"Oh, come on," I said. "I was a novelty, like those singing chipmunks, or the dogs that bark 'Jingle Bells.' If it hadn't meant bucks, believe me, there wouldn't have been a white Shakette."

"Yeah, but Ruby made the statement."

"Yes, and as soon as she hit the big time, I was out."

"You bitter about those days?"

"I am not," I said. "I just don't want to be nostalgic about a time I *didn't* have. By the time we hit the trail, there was no color bar. We all stayed in the same hotels. I loved being a Shakette, but that doesn't mean that we made a lot of money or got treated very well. Ruby and Vernon turned into *business people*."

Spider Joe switched off his tape. "This is a drag," he said. "I can't use this. I want some color, action, some groovy memories about how it was. I don't mean to sound like hostile, but this is a disappointment."

"Well, go interview someone else," I said. "Go see if you can find that girl Pixie Lehar who danced as Venus Cupid, if she's not dead from being a hairoyne addict."

"I know her," said Spider Joe. "She lives around here someplace. Her name is Paulette 'Pixie' Goldberg. But she got fired before the tour, so I can't use her. Do you mind if I use your phone on my way out?"

This interview left me with a sense of gloom which was dispelled by my cheerful son, who woke up from his nap full of unfocused smiles. He and I had a standing afternoon date with his little friend Amos Potts, and Amos's mother, Ann.

Amos and Little Franklin had met when they were three months old. On my first trips to our local park, the lawn was full of well-turned-out young matrons with their immaculate children in perfect prams and buggies. At the far end of the park I spied a private-looking person sitting alone, wearing leopard-print stretch pants and espadrilles. She was reading a fashion magazine and smoking a cigarette. Her baby lay sleeping on a woven blanket, shielded from the sun by an oversized, battered alligator handbag. "That's a mother for me," I thought, and I was right. Ann and I were the same age, and so were our boys. We were now fixtures in each other's lives.

Ann was a poet who lived with her husband, Winston, in what had once been a chic white loft.

"Now it's a chic white loft with handprints," she said.

We spent our afternoon gazing upon our boys with disbelief. From babies wriggling on sheepskin rugs they had grown into rosy-cheeked toddlers who could cruise around the kitchen pulling dangerous implements down.

"Isn't it amazing," I said to Ann. "So accomplished, and all from two cells. There must be a God."

"Maybe there are just two amazing little cells," Ann said.

"Don't these things dog your heels? God, religion and all that?"

Ann blew a smoke ring. "We thought about having Amos baptized until we read the Book of Common Prayer and Winnie said, 'I am not having someone renounce Satan and all that crap.' I myself think all religion is bad."

"So does Johnny," I said. "He says it leads to war. I told him I felt we should join a synagogue, and he said if it meant that much to me I should go and find one."

Ann said, "Well, there certainly are a bunch of them around."

I sighed. The greatest minds in history had grappled with this God issue, but it was not a big deal to Johnny. This was his greatness and his flaw.

Amos and Franklin sat on the living room floor engaging in what early childhood experts call "parallel play." Franklin was placing his extensive collection of plastic elephants in a circle, and Amos was building a flat structure out of blocks.

"A guy came to interview me today," I said.

"Do tell," said Ann, who was sitting on the floor drinking coffee.

"About my former life as a backup singer," I said. "It seemed so odd to be thinking about all that with Little Franklin asleep in his crib. They seem a universe apart. Is Amos interested in sleeping in a bed?"

"Don't change the subject," said Ann. "What did you say?"

"I didn't get the feeling that what I said was very interesting to him. This guy has his big idea of what it was like and I think he's looking for people who agree with him."

"What *was* it like?" Ann said. "Singing and all that."

"It was perfect heaven," I said, yawning. "It was sort of like life is now—being very tired and singing a lot. Also being on your feet all the time. That's what I should have told him: it's exactly like having a small child."

37

Although I had nowhere to go and nothing much to do, one afternoon a week a very nice girl from the local design college—a redhead who wore yellow and purple in combination—came to baby-sit Little Franklin, who also wore yellow and purple in combination. Her name was Mirandy Rubenstein, and when I came back from my outing my dining room table was covered with newspaper, and the newspaper was covered with clay, paint, crayons and glue.

When Johnny asked me what I did on my day out, I said I did errands or went shopping, which was often true, but more often than not I found myself browsing at Huey's O.P. Records, TCB Enterprises, Inc. (TCB stood for Take Care of Business.) It was too far to Fred Wood's, and Huey's was just like Fred Wood's. In fact, every out-of-print record store I had ever been in was like every other. They smelled of cigarettes and cardboard, and the faint, plastic smell of vinyl. The proprietors were either laconic and depressed, or depressed and hyped up.

You never knew what you might find in these places. If you were patient, you might stumble on an old Howlin' Wolf cut, or some old sides by Bobby Blue Bland.

One balmy afternoon I pushed my way over to the always crowded rhythm and blues section. I felt awfully low. That morning I had taken Little Franklin to his play group—a bunch of one- and two-year-olds in a pretty room in a church, where I was the lone biological caregiver in a sea of baby-sitters. All the other mothers had gotten their thing together and gone back to being lawyers or graphic designers. At lunchtime Franklin said, "I have no baby-sitter."

"You have Mirandy," I said.

"She isn't," Little Franklin said.

"But she comes and baby-sits for you," I said.

He looked at me intently. "She isn't brown," he said. "She has red hair."

As I browsed through the records, reflecting on the fact that I had deprived my child of early independence from me by not having a full-time Jamaican baby-sitter, I felt an arm press against me. I looked up and there was Donald "Doo-Wah" Banks."

"Wah!" I said. "How amazing!"

"Well, well, well, well," said Wah. "What brings you into this neighborhood?"

"Huey's," I said.

"Pee-Wee over at WIS says you have a baby."

"I have a big, huge boy," I said.

Doo-Wah looked remarkably fine. He was wearing a white sweatshirt and cowboy boots. His hair was short and he had done away with his sinister shades.

"You look great, Wah," I said.

"I'm an ugly critter," he said. "You have always been blinded by love."

He *was* a sort of ugly critter, blunt and big, but imposing, like a tugboat or a brick wall.

"Let me take you for a drink," he said. "What's your boy's name?"

"Franklin Ross Miller," I said. "I call him Little Franklin."

"Great name," said Wah. "Has he cut any sides yet?"

"He made up a song he says is called 'Kitty Roll Over,' but he won't sing it for me."

I was so used to having Franklin with me that being without him made me feel light and anxious. To be loose around town without a cookie, a box of raisins, a copy of *Curious George Rides a Bike,* an extra T-shirt, a supply of juice and two tiny molded-plastic elephants, made me uneasy. I kept checking my pockets, until Wah asked me why I was wriggling so much.

We walked a few blocks to an old saloon that had a barbecue in the back. It was two in the afternoon and there was almost no one around, except a guy at the bar and another guy fooling around with the jukebox. As we sat down, the entire place was suddenly drenched with the sound of Fats Domino singing "When My Dreamboat Comes Home."

How I loved that low, growly, mellow bass. At the sound of it, I put my head on Doo-Wah's warm muscular arm.

We were sitting in a dark corner. Wah drank a beer, and I drank a Coke. He would have fed me mine with a spoon if I had asked him.

"Now, tell old Wah what's up your mind," he said.

"I guess sometimes it makes me sad that I'll never be a Shakette again," I said, overcome.

"Oh, come *on*," said Wah. "Don't be sentimental. Aren't you glad? You're a mama! And you don't have to bust your butt or get on that nasty bus again."

"I'm not my old self anymore."

"History," said Wah, sipping his beer. "We are constantly living the history of our own lives, you dig? You used to be your old self, now you're a new self, and someday you'll be some other self and what's now will be your old self. Honey, my kids are almost in *college*. When I started with Ruby, I was paying off *my* college loans. Look at your own kid—what's he, almost two? Where'd the baby go? Vanished! History! Don't sweat it."

There was no question but that I was in the state of mind that allows people either to lecture or to hector you. This was the same rap I got from Johnny: even Wah came on like a guidance counselor in high school. I told Wah about the Race Music Foundation and how I had run into Grace.

"She's doing great," Wah said. "Catering a lot of music gigs these days. Got nine people working for her. *She* doesn't look back."

This pep talk did not cheer me up. I wanted Wah to say to me, "Girl, my crib is around the corner from here. You come with me and we'll finish some unfinished business, and Wah'll make you feel real good."

But it was not to be, since I was now a respectable wife and mother.

•   •   •

That night Johnny noticed that something was up. He knew what it was and he gave me a variant form of the Doo-Wah lecture.

"Oh, leave me alone," I said. "I have enough trouble trying to pass for normal with all those other mothers in the park."

"I thought you *liked* those women."

I was silent.

"You like Ann Potts," Johnny said.

"Well, look at Ann Potts," I said. "She wears leopard-skin clothes, and remember when she put that green streak in her hair? That's the kind of mother I like."

"I don't know what to do with you," said Johnny. "First you just want to be Little Franklin's mother, then you see Doo-Wah and get all upset because you can't be a Shakette. You say you blew it with Spider Joe Washburn. What do you want?"

" 'We don't understand it better by and by,' " I said, quoting a hymn from my album of Bahamian spirituals.

Johnny looked disturbed. "Are you unhappy being married to me?"

I told him that he was the only person I could have stood being married to, even if he was like a Boy Scout. When he sat transfixed listening to John Lee Hooker and singing along in a strange voice, I knew I had married the right person. Besides, he had known me when I was a Shakette.

"Look," he said. "You know what I found? Look at this."

He took the wrapping off an oversized book entitled *The Golden Years: A Rock and Roll History.*

"Look in the index," Johnny said.

I did, and there I was on page 413.

"It's finished," I said.

"But it's never over," said my husband.

38

In what seemed like half a second, Little Franklin turned two, and that fall he entered a program for two-year-olds at the Malcolm Sprague School, an old, venerable progressive school in our neighborhood. Three mornings a week, along with his close personal friend, Amos Potts, Little Franklin and eight children played with clay, blocks, little squares of cloth and water, or they painted with one color on a flat surface so as not to have to cope with drips. These materials, I came to learn, were called "open ended" since they had no fixed purpose and could be used in any number of ways at the child's discretion. I often stood in the doorway wishing that I could go to the Malcolm Sprague School, too.

The second month there, as I was waiting to pick up Little Franklin, I noticed a woman giving me what used to be called "the hairy eyeball." She stared and stared. Finally she came over.

She had a quantity of fuzzy yellow hair, freckles and a diamond ring on her finger that probably made it hard for her to lift a fork or spoon.

"You don't know me," she said.

"I don't," I said.

"But I know you."

"You do?"

"I used to be Pixie Lehar," she said. "I'm Paulette Goldberg."

"Oh, right!" I said. "Spider Joe Washburn told me you lived in this neighborhood."

"That sleaze," she said.

"I thought you were probably dead from being a hairoyne addict," I said.

"Vernon," she said. "What an old lady. I only snorted a few brown flakes once or twice, but you know what that does to a girl's eyes. Vernon thought he could spot a junkie a mile away. What a nance! But you were a good girl. That was the buzz. What are *you* doing here?"

"My little boy just started the twos program," I said.

"My daughter, Cilla, is in the nines, and my son, Otis, is in the sevens." She took a lipstick out of her bag and painted her lips bright red. "I'm on the parents' committee," she said.

"Do you keep up with anyone from old times?" I said.

"Keep up!" she said. "Are you kidding? It's bad enough to be hit on by a jive-hummer like Washburn. It was a phase, you know. Sort of fun at the time, but I'm glad it's over. I mean, look what washed up on the shore! All those dumb girls in their little dresses drugging their brains out and thinking that they had a million years till adulthood set in. I mean."

I sighed. Probably I was just like one of those girls, except I hadn't drugged my brains out.

"How did you get," I asked, "from there to here?"

"Hmm," she said. "Well, let's see. I was a very bad girl at college. I mean, a girls' school, can you believe it? I dropped out and, you know. One thing. Another, then another. I used to dance at the old Bombsite, remember? Then I backed up this group called Big Thing and Little Ed. Remember them? They were sort of nowhere but I was with Little Ed at the time so it seemed like a good idea, and then we opened for Ruby one night, God knows why. We were pretty terrible, but loud. I still think I have partial hearing loss in my right ear from jumping around in front of those speakers. Then Vernon fired me. It was your very friend Spider Joe Washburn that I used to get smacked up with. He hung around the scene, that scunge. What a jerk! Then I worked for that guy Lenny Decatur, he repped all these acts. You probably don't remember him. Another sleaze in the music business. Like my father used to say, a real American Indian: a Schmohawk. Just when I thought the light at the end of the tunnel had just about gone out, I met Bob Goldberg, who had nothing to do with the music business really, except that he happened to be Lenny Decatur's cousin and when they were in college they had collaborated on that song 'You Make Me Go on Fire.' Remember? '*Ooh woo, smoke! Smoke!*' It was kind of a novelty song and made a million dollars. So we got married and eventually I had Cilla and Otis and now I work at *Kids* Magazine. And yourself?"

I said I had quit the tour and worked at the Race Music Foundation, got married and had Little Frankln. It sounded totally reasonable, a straight line. "I don't know what next," I said.

"Next," said Paulette, "I have to go pick Cilla up for her dentist appointment. Catch you later."

I looked at my watch. It was time to pick my baby up.

Oh, Little Franklin! The look of happiness on his face when he saw me waiting made my heart open and close like a sea anemone. I had never imagined I could love anyone so much, and when people asked, as they did incessantly, when was I going to have another, I was always struck dumb. I had one husband, one mother and one father. Why was I supposed to have two children? The idea of sharing myself with some other child and Little Franklin seemed to me totally out of the question.

At night I tossed and turned and wished that in the welter of books about child development there was one about stages in parent development. What about separation anxiety among parents? What about stages of independence from your child? At night I held my darling Franklin in my arms and realized that I would never know him as an old man. Johnny said, "In a couple of years you won't know anything about his bowel movements. Think of that!"

I did think of that. I thought and thought about that. Franklin on a bus by himself. Franklin and his buddies going off to play hockey. In my imaginings I myself grew smaller and smaller, like a person seen through the wrong end of a telescope. Pretty soon the whole idea of having a mother would be a joke, from Franklin's point of view. "Aw, Ma," he would doubtless say. "Lemme alone. Don't kiss me goodbye in front of school, okay? It looks queer. Nobody else's mother kisses them." And sooner than later I would hear, "Aw, Ma. I can get home by myself. It's no big deal. Stop treating me like a baby." *Stop treating me like a baby*—the same words I and millions of other developing children had uttered time after time, and soon my little baby boy would utter them to me. Out on the street I felt lost wandering around without my child. I felt I ought to wear a pin that said: *I have a child who is at school at the moment.*

When I smiled at mothers with their children in the supermarket, they stared at me as if I were insane, and perhaps I was. There was no book to tell me what I was supposed to feel, but one thing was perfectly clear: eventually, I was going to have to get a job.

39

How lucky, I thought, were people who had known from earliest childhood what they wanted to do. All the children in my grammar school, who said they wanted to be doctors, had grown up to become doctors. This was also the case apparently with firemen, veterinarians, songwriters, and race car drivers.

I had opted for a kind of pure experience, which, as Doo Wah had pointed out, is not usually something you get paid for. I did not want to write a book about it. I did not want to write so much as an article. I wanted to be left alone with my experience and go on to the next thing, whatever that was. I had once been something. Now it was time to become something else. Being someone's mother was not enough.

Ann Potts (whom Mary referred to as "the Smoking Poet") and I discussed these issues endlessly as we sat at "Carole and Peter" Café, a little joint in our neighborhood that sold sandwiches, cookies, coffee and groceries. We had taken Franklin and Amos there as babies and as toddlers, and now we brought them in after school for ice cream. In the mornings we sat by ourselves drinking coffee, reading the paper and conversing in a meandering sort of way. I found these mornings lazy and beautiful.

"I think I have to look for a job," I said.

"Here," said Ann, handing me the paper. "You can have the want ads."

"Very funny," I said. "At least you know what you want to do."

"Don't be ridiculous," Ann said. "You don't think I'm sitting at home writing sonnets in my five minutes of spare time, do you? Eventually I'll have to see if I can get my job back at the Poetry Society, if they haven't given it to some beautiful young thing. Of course, *I* used to be the beautiful young thing. What a tragedy! I keep thinking I'll call them but I keep doing the laundry instead. It's kind of a tic."

"Laundry," I said, yawning. "I never really understood about laundry before. It's a kind of Möbius strip—no end and no beginning."

"Men never understand about laundry," Ann said. "I mean, Winnie doesn't. I guess he doesn't get much call for clean laundry at Squirrel Productions." This was the name of Winnie's design company.

"I'm sure at Johnny's firm they do the laundry for them," I said. "They seem to do everything else."

Ann spun the magazine racks. Among the fashion and news magazines were those for women, the very magazines that said we must be totally available but make our children independent.

As the mother of a young child, I was supposed to be totally related to my child but not so much as to cripple his emerging sense of self. By being completely available, I would also be able to know when to let go. All this, and laundry too!

" 'Fun dads,' " Ann read. " 'More fun, more time.' These fun dads give me hives. Carole, do you mind if we buzz through *Vogue* if we promise not to get any smudge marks on it?"

" 'Care-giver for small child,' " I read from the want ads. " 'Academic family.' Hey! Here's my job!"

"I'll give you a reference," Ann said. "Amos thinks you're a very nice mother."

"I'm a lovely little mother," I said. "Turn that page around, will you? We have to go out this weekend and I have no clothes."

"Endless laundry and nothing to wear," Ann said. "Isn't it a bite? How 'bout one of your little fringe dresses, or is it a formal affair?"

"Even my formal clothes have child smearings on them," I said. "Of course, that's only a manner of speaking. I have no formal clothes."

We sat in the yellow sunlight, drinking our coffee. The café smelled enticingly of coffee and salami.

"We're going out, too," Ann said. "So I guess we can't baby-sit for each other."

"I hate going out," I said.

"I love it," said Ann. "The bliss of going to the ladies' room without having someone under three feet in there with you." She yawned and stretched her arms. "Last time we went out, I found that I had packed a box of raisins in my handbag."

I said: "I hate leaving my nice warm house right when I'm most exhausted and then going out somewhere with awful food and where everyone has a swell, high-powered job, plans to take their six children under four skiing in Tibet, and full-time child care. It makes me tired."

"It's all guilt. You feel guilty because you stay home and they feel guilty because they don't."

"I guess part-time work is the answer," I said.

"Then you feel guilty because you're not giving either thing your full attention. Gosh, I'm sleepy. Amos won't go to bed anymore. He stays up until eleven without a nap and then he falls into a kind of coma on his bed and turns the color of a white cabbage."

"Really? A white cabbage?" I said. "I'm sort of a white cabbage myself. I've been up since quarter to six."

"Gosh," said Ann, turning a page of her magazine. "Get this! Velvet and suede. How gorgeous! Only one year's tuition at Malcolm Sprague and I could have it. Maybe I should read more role-appropriate trash, like *Kids* Magazine. Speaking of which, what's the name of that attack dog who works for it?"

"Pixie Goldberg. She's really very nice," I said. "She's just a little aggressive. She was one of Ruby's backups, you know."

"No," said Ann. "You're kidding. *Her?*"

"Oh, yes," I said. "And furthermore, Vernon fired her because he thought she was a hairoyne addict."

"Otis and Cilla's *mother?*"

"Yup," I said. "She wasn't, but there you are. Accused of being a hairoyne addict and now she has a rich husband, a mink coat, live-in help and a full-time job."

"Gee," said Ann. "I don't know, but she makes being a drug addict look good. I smoked a lot of dope and I don't have any of those things."

"You're a *poet,*" I said. "She sits in her office and writes headlines about fun dads."

"I have nothing," said Ann. "My cigarettes are my friends. Gosh, look at the time! We have to go get our boys any minute, and I bet neither of us has our dinner menu planned."

We ambled off to the greengrocer's and then we picked our darlings up at school and went back to the café for a snack. I took Little Franklin home, settled him down for a nap or an attempted nap, did the laundry, picked up the toys, put away the dishes, folded the laundry, got the mail, and then relaxed for two or three minutes before rest time was over.

Then off to the park, or to the supermarket, or to buy new shoes or a raincoat, or to Amos's house, or to the bakery for a snack if Ann and Amos were coming to visit us.

Then it was time to make dinner, to serve Franklin dinner, to scrape some of the dropped dinner off the floor. Then bath, time for Daddy's homecoming, story reading, good-night kisses, drinks of water, adjustment of the night light. When Franklin was asleep Johnny and I had dinner, during which I propped my head on my hand to keep it from falling into my plate.

And so another day slipped by, at the end of which I was totally exhausted and had done absolutely nothing whatsoever about my future.

40

I did not wear my dance dress to Simon and Alice's dinner party. I did not get drunk, throw up or try to seduce Simon, a small, intense person whom Ann Potts would doubtlessly have labeled "verbally aggressive." Their two horrible-looking children were on show for half an hour before the haggard French au pair girl put them to bed. Alice and Simon did not approve of a second language for young children, but, "in context," it was different, and it was so nice to have Geneviève around.

"I didn't know you guys spoke French," I said.

"Oh, I had it in college. I can make myself understood," Alice said. "It's important for the children."

"We're thinking of getting a Chinese au pair," I said. "It's definitely the language of the future, and it would be so helpful later on in Chinese restaurants." Johnny gave me a terrible look.

"What a great idea!" Alice said. "You know, there's a program—I can't remember where—that offers Chinese to young kids. I mean, it would be such fun for them to learn how to write it!"

"I think Franklin should learn to write his own language first," I said.

"You mean they don't help them with it in pre-school?" asked Alice, her eyes wide.

"They don't officially teach reading at Franklin's school until they're seven," I said. "You know, in some Scandinavian countries it's illegal to teach reading before six."

"Well, of course that's the way things would be in a perfect world," Alice said. "But life is so *competitive*. Amanda could write when she was three, and David really knows how to read already and he won't be four for seven months!"

By the end of the evening I had been told how wonderful it was for the children to have two parents who worked because it made them independent. How they had never cried at school or had any problems separating from their parents. ("We simply popped them in and left!") How children, whose mothers stayed home, were less well adjusted later on.

"How interesting!" I said. "I sat around in Franklin's class for a month or so and a lot of the kids had a hard time for a while."

"It entirely depends on the school and the child, of course," said Alice, who had also remarked of breast-feeding, "I just didn't see what was in it for *me*."

"Let's never, never, never see them again, okay?" I said.

"They *are* kind of nauseating in combination," said Johnny. "I guess it's because at work Simon and I talk about cases. He's really incredibly smart. When he gets around Alice he turns into a kind of deformed jackass, as you would say."

"You mean you boys never talk about your kids? You mean you never heard him say, 'Of course, we really don't approve of the sort of school that makes the children wear uniforms, but Amanda looks so adorable in hers'?"

"I guess I haven't."

"Ann Potts is needlepointing a pillow," I said.

"Yes," Johnny said, uncomprehendingly.

"It will have a quote from Dorothy Parker."

"Yes?" said Johnny.

"It will say *I hate men. They irritate me.* She picked out some extremely pretty colors for it at that yarn shop near the park. Teal, scarlet and yellow."

Johnny said, "So kill me because I don't talk about children with Simon. Would you want me to?"

"No," I said. "But I don't see any reason to see them again, ever ever ever, and I'm not going to. Besides, I don't think Franklin will ever like that nasty little David. He hasn't forgotten the time they came here and David hit him with a truck."

"That's just kids playing," Johnny said.

"Oh, yeah? What would you know? That is *not* kids playing. That is *angry* kids playing. I hope that little creep grows up to off his parents."

On that note I took off my dress, which, I could tell, Alice Crain had found only marginally tasteful, and I got into bed. I reflected that if you were going to ask people for dinner, you ought to do a little better than overcooked round roast—that staple of retrograde dinner parties —undercooked rice and nothing for salad. I was not a great cook by a long shot, but at least I could put together something people could chew.

Before I fell into a not too refreshing sleep, I reflected on the whole subject of parents. How suspicious of them I was. My own, Johnny's, the parents of my friends from high school, the Listers, Alice and Simon. As I lay there thinking, listening to my husband showering in the bathroom, I realized it was probably grownups I feared in general, and parents in specific, since they were grownups who felt justified. And here I was, a grownup and a parent. Would Little Franklin, the light of my life, learn to hate me? Would some subtle change overcome me as I grew older? Would I begin to criticize his friends, tell him who he could and could not play with, and foist on him the nauseating offspring of my friends? Often I wondered if he truly liked Amos Potts or simply was forced to put up with him because I was a friend of Amos' mother. What an amazing welter of things there was to feel terrible about!

"Your problem," Mary often said, "is that on the one hand you feel better than other people because you have never sold out or knuckled under, and on the other hand you feel worse than everyone else because you perceive them to be doing better or behaving better than you. You don't want to take a chance either way, and to stay marginal —the way you like to be—is nice and safe."

There it was in a nutshell. Little Franklin's marginal mom! What good are pure ideals in a vacuum? I would have been better off if I had wanted to be a star and devoted myself to my career, or if I had been born in a time when women were *supposed* to be mothers—when motherhood was considered something to do.

"What are you muttering about?" Johnny said, slipping in beside me.

He wore an old T-shirt that said on one side I'D RATHER EAT WORMS THAN
RIDE A HONDA and HARLEY DAVIDSON MOTORCYCLES on the back, and a pair
of striped pajama bottoms. His hair was wet. He sat up in bed with his
shoulders slightly hunched, reminding me of Franklin, who often
looked like his little clone. In my observations of children I had for-
mulated the maxim that all babies walk like their mothers, but the
exception was my boy, who had his daddy's springy, energetic, well-
balanced walk.

I loved Johnny best when he appeared to be a little cracked. I liked
him to do his imitation of John Lee Hooker or to go around the house
singing "Lonely Teardrops" in falsetto. This was our common language. I loved to dance with him, not that anyone had dance parties
anymore. He was my ideal dance partner, and sometimes at night,
when I was not too exhausted and Little Franklin was in bed, we threw
some sides on the stereo and danced as in olden times.

On my best days, I felt that his struggle was my struggle: the work of
trying to stay true to your school and fit into an orderly society at the
same time. I hated him most when he came home at night in his lawyer
clothes, mooing lawyer noises and sounding like the dread Bill Lister,
a man who actually used the word "heretofore" in normal conversation. I wanted my Johnny to retain his jagged edge. I wanted him never
to stop being my Boy Scout from Mars, my weirdo from Normalsville,
who knew how to maneuver in the world. I seemed totally unable to
do it. Doubtless this was a burden for my adorable husband, who was
now bent over a small stack of papers.

"Hey, man," I said. "Why not trash those papers and let's have a little
fun."

"I have to be in court tomorrow, girl."

"Oh, come on, baby. Let the good times roll," I said.

"Okay," said my well-organized husband. "Give me two minutes and
we'll roll all night long."

41

Every so often I felt it wise to go out on my own at night. Once in a while I went to a movie. More often, I found myself lying on the couch at Mary's, doing nothing in particular except enjoying a break from being someone's wife or mother.

It was easy as pie to slip back into my old self. I lay on the couch, reading through a stack of magazines or meandering through some choice Victorian novel, while Mary sat at her desk and worked. How many thousands of hours like this had we put in? Half an hour of reading, half an hour of music, a break for tea. We had established this rhythm our first week at college and it seemed to me that in Mary's apartment I had drifted back in time to some other self, some person who found the idea of a quest a challenge rather than a burden.

Sometimes for a treat we repaired to a club to watch a beloved performer from our past. My enduring image of Mary was of her sitting next to me in a smoky place, wearing her round-collared blouse and her little round glasses, with her hair parted like Alice in Wonderland's. She had never changed her style in all these years.

One dreary night I lounged on her couch, watching the rain slip down her not terribly clean windows.

"Today Little Franklin asked me what heaven was," I said.

"How interesting," Mary said. "How did he know to ask?"

"His baby-sitter, Mirandy, said her dog went there," I said. "I told him it was a place some people think people go when they die, and then he told me that he and Johnny have this spot on River Road, up by Johnny's parents, called 'the squashed frog place' because they once spent a lot of time looking at a squashed frog. He asked if the squashed frog went to heaven. I always feel like such a jerk about these things. How lucky you are to have religious structure in your life."

"What did you say?"

"I said yes. It seemed like a good idea at the time."

"Heaven's always a good idea," Mary said. "By the way, would you and Johnny like to buy my car?"

"Oh, are you selling it?" I asked stupidly.

"Well, obviously," she said. "It's in really good condition. William found it out on the Island. It doesn't have too many miles on it and it's only five years old."

"I'll ask Johnny," I said. "Are you getting a new one, or are you just tired of having a car?"

"Listen, Geraldine," Mary said, "I have something to tell you. I've been thinking about telling you for months."

I held my breath. "You're marrying William."

"I'm going to be a nun," Mary said. "Sometime within the year. It's a monastic order. I'm going in as a postulant. Then I'll be a novice, then a junior. If I make it, I'll be professed in five years and then I take life vows."

I sat bolt upright on the couch and gaped at her. I felt as if I had been struck.

"They're Benedictines," she continued. "You might like to borrow this copy of *The Rule of St. Benedict*. It's a very good description of the way they live. You take vows of stability to your chosen house and then you stay there for life."

"You stay there for life," I repeated.

"Don't look so sick, Gerry. I'm really very happy. I've been thinking about this for years."

"Do you mind telling me," I said, "why you never bothered to mention this in all these years?"

"I guess I wasn't sure myself," she said. "I guess I didn't want you to tell me not to."

"Not to!" I cried. "Haven't I been your best friend and supporter all these years? Haven't I hauled your furniture around and run your errands and listened to every single thing you've ever said to me?

Didn't I love you enough? Wasn't I a good enough friend? Or did you think I was too spiritually undeveloped to understand?" I burst into tears. "It's the place upstate, isn't it?"

"It is," she said.

"I hate you," I said. "I can't believe you've hidden this from me. Oh, fuck it. I'm jealous. I feel I have to invent every single thing in my life. The whole structure is there waiting for you. All you have to do is take your place in it. Now I'll have to invent some way of being myself without having you around."

"Don't be silly," Mary said. "You have Johnny and Franklin. How's that for structure? You have your friend the Smoking Poet. Don't you think I'm a little jealous? I didn't go through nursing and teething and measles shots and infant fevers with you. She did."

"You're my history," I said.

"I still am," Mary said. "You can come and see me. And we can write to each other."

"Oh, swell," I said, looking desolately around the only other place in the world that felt like home to me. "Most people are such sellouts and jerks," I said.

"Most people do the best they can," Mary said.

"I don't want 'the best I can,'" I said. "Neither do you."

"I know you don't," Mary said. "That's one of the reasons why I love you."

"You're the only person in the world who understands why I don't have any interest in a singing career," I said. "Every time I turn around someone wants me to perform."

"You are a pilgrim," Mary said.

"And what is that supposed to mean?"

"Someone on a quest. You can't imagine how much I admired it when you went on tour, even if it was a kind of dodge. I was amazed that you did it and amazed that you stuck."

"It wasn't about singing and dancing," I said. "It was about *being.*"

"I know," Mary said. "It's not unlike being a nun."

"I hate people who compromise," I said.

"Oh, really? Does that mean you hate Johnny?"

"I love him," I said. "He's very adaptable. It scares me. What happens when he comes home and announces that he's taken on a case I find morally bankrupt and reprehensible? That worm Simon Crain is defending a gas company against a bunch of workers who were injured in an explosion."

"Maybe he won't," Mary said. "He's married to *you*, after all."

"Oh, me," I said. "It's all very lovely to have purity of heart and a right mind when you don't really live in the real world. Johnny thinks rock and roll keeps him clean. He thinks it strikes into that unpolluted core of his and that if he can still boogie he'll keep a cool tool."

"He's a useful person," Mary said. "If everyone were like us, the world would probably collapse. Let's have some tea."

We went into her dark little kitchen, sat at the table and drank tea as we had a thousand times before. We were like sisters without the rivalry. We had worn each other's clothes and finished each other's sentences and told the same jokes and read each other's moods. We had known each other at the end of our childhoods and the beginning of our adult lives. I would never in my life make such a friend again.

When it was time to go, I put on my slicker and stood by the door. I had signed on to find Mary black cotton tights, a bolt of black wool cloth and a gray blanket.

"Thank you, Gerry," Mary said. "Thank you for not making this hard. Almost every nice thing I have was a present from you. You're the only person who remembers all those small things, like what a person likes to eat and how a person likes to smell. The hardest thing about going into a monastery is how much I'll miss you."

"I'll talk to you this week," I said, and closed the door. I could not bring myself to say goodbye, but as I left, I truly felt as one of Ruby's songs had said, that I had cut my heart in half and left one part behind.

42

It took a few days before it really struck that I was going to spend the rest of my life without Mary in it. Then I felt as if I had been flattened by a tornado. I could hardly bear to speak to her, although I found her the black cotton tights she needed and went looking for black lisle socks of exactly the length specified by the monastery. In an antiques store in my neighborhood I bought a plain tin box and filled it with the required shoe polish, brushes and polishing cloth. All the while, Mary was struggling to finish her dissertation and get her life in order, while my life appeared to be unraveling before me.

"You're behaving as if she were about to die," Johnny said.

"It's worse," I said. "If she was dead I'd simply never see her again, but she's not going to be dead. She's going to be alive in some other reality, and she'll never be my friend again."

At this my husband gave me a baleful look.

"I don't get you two," he said. "Never mind, I'm just a guy. I couldn't possibly understand this sacred bond."

"It's just that your idea of a best friend is someone you play squash with year after year," I said.

"That's a perfectly sound basis for friendship," Johnny said. "Ben and I have known each other all our lives and I feel we understand each other perfectly, except that you ladies talk all the time and we play squash."

I felt as if I were about to grind my teeth.

"Now take Winnie Potts," he continued. "You accuse me, as a member of the male race, of never making friends with other fathers. Remember you said, and these are your exact words: 'It's the difference between men and women.' Well, Winnie and I have put in quite a lot of time together. While you and Ann have your days off discussing the higher things of life, Winnie and I are crawling around in various parks together with our kids."

"And you have never had a personal conversation," I said.

"Who needs it?" Johnny said. "We're task-oriented."

I sighed. My life was a cloud of gnats. One of the most important and ongoing conversations of my life would soon end. For Johnny, as opposed to me and Mary, the great issues of life were easily resolvable. For instance, I found myself obsessed with the fact that I had almost no Jewish upbringing, and neither had Johnny. I felt some nascent spiritual longings as well as some desire for a historical context. This was the sort of thing Mary and I could easily have spent a couple of years on.

On this issue Johnny was clear as a bell. "Go find a synagogue and stop agitating," he said. "They have classes. You could go and talk to someone. Just go find it."

There it was, easy as pie.

Meanwhile, the days meandered by and I meandered with them. Time was running out for me. The days of Little Franklin's babyhood seemed haloed in fuzzy golden light. Never again would I carry him next to me in a sling, or Chinese style on my back. He was becoming a completely separate entity, a little boy who swung his arms when he walked and would hold my hand only to cross the street.

It seemed to me that I was spending my life sitting around the C&P Café with my son and his best friend and his best friend's mother.

"We are whiling away our golden youth," Ann said.

"Maybe you are," I said. "My golden youth burned out a long time ago." I looked across the table at her. The green streak in her hair had almost grown out, leaving a shiny, iridescent stripe. I felt as if I had known her all my life. In some way I had. Just as Mary would begin her life in religion when she entered her monastery, so I had started my life as a mother when Little Franklin was born—millions and millions of hours ago, many of which I had spent with Ann.

"What's your little book?" Ann said. "You've been carrying it around for weeks. Oh! *The Rule of St. Benedict!* How cute."

"My friend Mary is about to become a nun."

"Oh, right!" said Ann. "I forgot. How retro."

"There's a lot of retro going on," I said. "That little worm Alice Crain said to me, 'Oh, that funny old music you used to sing.' She'd probably die if she heard the funny music they sing in monasteries."

"I wonder what it's like," Ann said, stirring her coffee.

"It sounds very orderly," I said. "They have a farm and a pottery and a weaving room, and they study and they never have to wonder what to wear or what they ought to make for dinner, and their day is planned, and they don't have to worry about their careers."

"How restful," Ann said. "But, of course, they wouldn't want lots of little cars and blocks lying around, so they won't take us."

"Mary says they have a very nice guest house."

"Yes, but do they let you come *encumbered?*"

"Ladies only," I said.

"Heaven," said Ann. "But hardly possible. My, wouldn't it creep Winnie out if I told him I was going to visit a monastery. I do find the idea of a habit very relaxing."

"Yes, and the laundry gets done for you," I said. "I find that a most compelling feature."

We finished our coffee and ambled over to the supermarket.

"Hey," said our regular checker, a sort of dumb boy. "You guys are in here every day, almost. Don't you have anything to do?"

"No," said Ann. "We have nothing to do. We are totally useless and have no sense of occupation. We are mothers, you stupid little shithead."

"Hey, geez," said the checker. "I just mean I see you in here all the time."

"In fact," Ann said, "we're looking for work. Perhaps we'll take *your* job."

Out on the street Ann patted my shoulder. "Don't despair," she said. "My oldest friend lives in Hawaii on a tiny little island and we're still close."

"It's not the same thing," I said. "Or, maybe it is."

"We both need work," Ann said. "Just remember our pact. When they hit three, off we go."

It sounded so possible but also very far away.

43

Franklin turned three. He changed from a round little baby into a tall little boy. I could never watch him and his pal Amos walking down the street together without a pang of amazement. What had happened to those babies who had taken naps in the same crib, who had spent hours creeping around on the floor? Now they spent their afternoons pretending to be *Mike Mulligan and His Steam Shovel.*

I felt the rug being pulled from under my feet from any number of directions. Ann Potts revealed to me that she was going back to work part-time at the Poetry Society, and that three days a week a girl engineering student from China would pick Amos up from school. Wiped away in an instant were those days of sitting at C&P's, of strolling around together with the boys. Everyone seemed to be doing something. In desperation I called the Reverend Arthur Willhall, who said I should come and see him.

I had not been up to Harlem since before Little Franklin was born and I brought photos of my boy along on the remote chance anyone should want to see him. Although some things looked a lot worse—the subway station exit, for one—a lot of things looked better. The Race Music Foundation looked positively rich.

A beautifully dressed receptionist, I had never seen before, sat in front of a complicated Japanese telephone system and showed me into what had once been an office and was now a freshly painted reception room. Along the back window was a sleek new conference table.

No one was left. The Bopper had quit to work for a record company, and Desdemona was now a full-time fund-raiser who traveled constantly. According to the glossy brochure I found waiting on a table next to my chair, the foundation had branched out. It now incorporated several smaller foundations: the Fund for Black Studies, the Afro-American Textbook Alliance and the Afro-History Foundation. On the last page was a picture of the Gospel and Blues College in Natchez and, underneath, a long list of sponsors of the foundation, including Ruby and Vernon Shakely. I wondered if the Reverend Willhall still had his I DO NOT PLAY NO ROCK AND ROLL poster.

He did not, although his office was unchanged in any other way, and the Reverend himself looked as somber as ever.

"Gee, it looks a lot different up here," I said.

"We have expanded the focus of our work," said the Reverend.

I said, "Reverend Willhall, my baby has turned into a three-year-old boy and I need a part-time job."

"We no longer research," the Reverend Willhall said. The thing about the Reverend Willhall was that talking to him was like talking to a foundation. "The Race Music Foundation archive has been taken on by the Archive for American Music, I am happy to say. This has left us free in many ways."

"Do you know anyone who might need a researcher?" I said.

The Reverend Willhall pressed his two long hands together, and closed his eyes as if in prayer. He uttered a humming sound. This I knew meant that he was thinking.

"I have considered," he said finally, and taking one of his pens, the kind you see in old-fashioned banks, he scribbled something on a sheet of paper and handed it to me. It read "The Hansonia Society."

"What is it?" I said. "Does it have anything to do with Hansophie Records?"

"They are one and the same," said the Reverend Willhall. He explained that they were run by the Regenstein family, the late Hans and Sonia Regenstein, who had come here in the 1920s. These pious Europeans of Jewish heritage fell in love with race music, and it is because of their efforts that much of it was preserved on Hansophie Records. I believe Sophie was the name of both their mothers."

The Hansonia Society was run these days by Bernard Regenstein (the nephew of Hans's much older brother) and his wife, who were the executors of Hansophie Records, and also the executors of many small estates. They also handled the works of Hans and Sonia Regenstein, whose *Delta Blues Singers of the 1930's* was an essential text. They were family-run and they often needed someone to work in their office. He said I could use his name.

"Thank you, Dr. Willhall," I said. "And please tell Mrs. Willhall and Desdemona that I send them my best wishes."

"Mrs. Willhall has gone to her eternal reward," said the Reverend Willhall.

I assumed this meant dead.

"In heaven," said the Reverend Willhall. "She passed on to her eternal glory last year."

If a person has passed on to her eternal glory, was it right to say "I'm sorry," or were you supposed to say "How nice"?

I said, "That must be quite a loss for you."

"The Lord is my shepherd," said the Reverend Willhall. "I shall not want."

We sat in silence for a few moments, as seemed appropriate.

"I'll never forget that wonderful vegetable soup," I said.

"I will call my friend, Bernard Regenstein, and tell him you will contact him."

His intercom, something he had not possessed in the old days, buzzed. The Reverend Willhall put the receiver down and shook my hand.

"Thank you," I said.

"The Lord be with you," he said. With that, I was dismissed.

By the time twelve thirty rolled around—at the Malcolm Sprague School, three-year-olds stayed for lunch—I had had enough solitude and was ravenous to see my boy. I was used to having him with me for lunch. Now he was gone into the bosom of his little companions and I was under the Tyranny of the Lunchbox: every day Little Franklin set out with a proper, interesting and varied lunch dreamed up and prepared by me. He told me that there were two tables at school: a round one and a square one. The round one was the silly table and the square one was the serious table.

"And which do *you* sit at?" I said.

"The silly," he said. And there it was. Little Franklin now had a private life, a day at school about which I knew nothing since I wasn't there. He was off without me, building structures out of wooden blocks and practicing his social skills. I supposed I was happy to have the telephone number of the Hansonia Society in my pocket.

That night my mother had at me. To keep our parents in line, Johnny suggested monthly dinners and it was my parents' turn. I mentioned that I had a job possibility as I served the second course.

"It's about time," my mother said. "It isn't healthy just being at home."

"I see," I said.

"It's good for young women to get out," she said. "Besides, I've always thought that part of the reason you were so stuck on staying at home was that you couldn't seem to find a career for yourself."

"Oh," I said. "You mean you feel my decision to be Franklin's primary care-giver during his first two years was simply a dodge. In other words, my being with him is essentially neurotic and selfish, is that right?"

"I didn't mean that," my mother said.

"You did!" I shrieked. "I'm sorry I have no art gene so I can't be a painter. I'm sorry I didn't get a doctorate in some worthy subject. I apologize for being my unidentified self."

"Geraldine, calm down," said my mother.

"I have a better idea," I said. "You guys have dinner together and talk about *your* careers. So long!"

I flung on my coat and slammed the door behind me. Johnny flew out in pursuit.

"I hate her," I said. "I hate everyone."

"Here's twenty bucks. There's a great double bill at the Showbox. The second feature starts in fifteen minutes. They'll be gone by the time you come home. Call Ann and see if she wants to go."

"What will you do?"

"I'm going to tell them that you are an award-winning mother, and then I'm going to terrify Gertrude into good behavior."

"She's not wrong," I said. "Don't say I went to the movies, okay?"

"I'll tell them you vanished into the night mist."

"I don't hate *you*," I said.

"Gertrude adores and fears you. She worries about you," Johnny said. "Give her a break."

"She can go to hell," I said. I threw the twenty on the floor. "So long, sucker."

44

I had absolutely nowhere to go, a humiliating thought. Here I was, the mother of a child, and I had nothing. What would I do with myself? I did not want to go and see Mary. I was not fit company for anyone. Perhaps I would do what I generally did when depressed: buy an expensive fashion magazine and drink a cappuccino.

I ambled over to the magazine store. It had begun to drizzle a fine, late-spring rain. I had stormed out of the house with only a light coat and I was cold.

There, browsing over a glossy Italian magazine was none other than Ann Potts, wearing a man's hat and a trench coat.

"Oh, hi there!" she said. "What are you doing here? I thought your parents were coming for dinner."

"I'm running away from home," I said.

"What a great idea!" said Ann. "It's too bad we have nowhere to go, because I am too. Winnie and Amos have formed this primitive tribe that finds women useless. I thought little boys were supposed to be in love with their mothers in this stage."

"Franklin finds me moderately amusing, but fun dad is where the action is," I said. "Let's go get drunk."

Ann yawned. "I told Winnie I was going out for cigarettes but he'll never miss me. If I came home at six in the morning he would say, 'Oh, I bet you ran into Geraldine and had a little chat.'"

We meandered into a glossy bar. Our neighborhood was slowly

being upgraded. The seedy saloon that seemed to have only one customer, and smelled of cat pee, had been replaced by a sleek bistro with a long marble and brass bar in the front and a restaurant in the back.

"Are we dressed?" I said. I was wearing blue jeans and a turtleneck, and I realized I had no wallet. Ann and I rifled through our pockets and created a pile of rumpled dollar bills and quarters in the middle of the little round table.

An extremely handsome waiter appeared. His hair shone in the soft light, and he appeared to be quite put out to have to wait on us.

"Can I get you ladies something?" he said, looking at us as if we were a mess on the floor.

"I'll have a beer," Ann said.

"We have Palm Ale, Fisher from India, Watney's Red Barrel on tap, Silas Mountain Beer from Idaho, Cliff Davies Natural Lager from England, Anchor Steam, Meridia Ale, Palace, Guinness, Brown Ale, Foster's and Cabinet Home Brew."

Ann considered this. "Don't you have any of that tasteless American beer?"

"I'm so sorry, we don't," he said.

Ann narrowed her eyes. "Well, can you repeat what you just said?"

The waiter clamped his jaw. "I suggest Foster's. And you?" he said, turning to me.

"Do you have more than one kind of coffee?" I said.

"We have ten kinds of coffee," he said.

"Do you have more than one kind of decaffeinated coffee?"

"Brown roast, French roast and Swiss process Vienna roast," said the waiter.

"I'll have that," I said. "Do you have more than one kind of hot milk?"

"Plain or steamed."

"Steamed," I said. "No, plain."

"Steamed," said the waiter. "Thank you."

The beer came in a frosted glass, the coffee in an oversized cup. "Gee, I hope we don't have to call the boys to send a runner over with some money," Ann said. "Let's see. We have nine dollars and fifty-seven cents."

"That ought to cover it," I said. "If we don't leave a tip."

"If we don't leave a tip, that guy will come out and spank us."

We stretched our legs and watched a group of well-dressed people walk past us on the way to their tables.

"I guess they all have baby-sitters," Ann said, staring at them. "How did we come to this? I mean, motherhood."

"Oh, in the usual way," I said, filching one of her cigarettes. "Unless you and Winnie did something weird."

"It's like a costume party," Ann said. "You put on some silly dress and you get married. Then you put on an even sillier dress when you're pregnant. You find yourself wearing the same thing day after day and you're a mother."

"I often wonder about my own mother," I said. "I remember her closet. Blue tissue paper. Ostrich shoes. Little shoe trees made of some kind of stuffed fabric. Those things you hang on hangers that make your closet smell good. Lingerie bags."

"Life was different then," Ann said. "We missed out on the silver tea services and the frilly aprons. I remember my mother sitting with us when we played with clay and she was wearing a *dress.*"

"My mother cooked with a white pinafore over her suit," I said. "I guess we don't make it as real adults. For instance, do you remember your mother coming back from the hairdresser?"

Ann blew a smoke ring. "I haven't been to the hairdresser since I had that green streak put in."

"How I loved your green streak," I said. "I've been so hoping you'd put in another."

At the exact moment our glass and cup were empty, the waiter reappeared.

"Is there anything else I could possibly get you?" he said.

"You could get us a different waiter, but we'd be happy to have the check," Ann said.

Out on the street she said, "Well, we'll never be welcome in there again."

"Oh, to hell with them," I said. "They're open for lunch. We'll take the boys. That'll show 'em."

We ambled around the neighborhood. Our usual haunts were closed. The park lay quiet and still. In the dark the jungle gym looked like the bones of a prehistoric creature. The C&P Café was closed and the gates were locked over the windows. The evening dog walkers were out, wandering down the street with the abstracted look that seems to go with dog walking. The air was misty and still and there were haloes on the streetlights.

"It's so mournful here at night," I said. "I guess it's time to go home, or perhaps you'd like to invite me in for a sleep-over."

"Swell," Ann said. "I'll send Winnie over to Johnny. Gosh, look at us. Renegade matrons on the loose."

We walked around the corner. The street spread before us, house after house full of yellow light. Carefully parked cars. Carefully planted front gardens. Fuzzy buds on the trees.

"I used to live in a loft in Chinatown," Ann said, yawning. "Can you imagine?"

"And I spent my youth in a tour bus," I said. "And now look."

Johnny was waiting for me outside on the stoop.

"I gave your mother a lecture," he said. "She apologizes. I told her she should be proud to have such an upstanding daughter with such intact values. I told her you find compromise intolerable and because of that Little Franklin will grow up to be another Abraham Lincoln."

"My hero," I said.

"It's easy for me," he said. "She's not *my* mother."

As we went up the stairs I felt a warm surge of optimism. I would call the Hansonia Society. They would hire me because of my intact values. Little Franklin would grow up to be another Abraham Lincoln. I would find my place in life. It seemed, for the moment, a total snap.

PART FOUR

*Goodbye
Without Leaving*

"Well enough for *what?*" he said.

"Well enough for a graduate student, I guess I mean."

"Are you a graduate student?"

"I'm a mother," I said.

"Really? The mother of what?"

"I mean, I'm not a graduate student at the moment. I used to be one. I have a little boy who's three."

"Do you also have any office skills?"

I had never asked myself this question and now I found I had to think about the answer.

"I was a researcher," I said. "At the Race Music Foundation. The Reverend Willhall sent me to you."

The man looked totally blank.

"Are you Bernard Regenstein?" I said.

"I am Bernard Regenstein, Junior."

"Oh, I see," I said. "Well, then I must have spoken to your father."

"My father is in London."

"But didn't I speak to him on the telephone?"

"You spoke to *me*. As far as I'm concerned, you've got the job."

I stared at Bernard Regenstein, Jr., who, I began to see, was gazing intently at the front of my sweater.

"This is very confusing," I said. "Aren't you supposed to tell me what this job is?" I had never had a job interview before but it seemed to me that this could not possibly be a normal one.

"We need someone to answer letters, answer the telephone and, in general, help out. This is a very small office. It's just me, my mother and my father."

A loud series of barking coughs could be heard from an inner office.

"That's Dr. Frechtvogel," Bernard junior said. "*He* doesn't really work here. He kind of sits here."

"I see," I said.

"What we really need is someone who doesn't have a lot of fixed ideas about how an office should be, because we get a lot of crazy types in here. My father also represents a lot of writers and illustrators. Mostly they're refugees and they sort of hang around. A lot of people would find that strange in an office."

I said it sounded fine to me and that I had no fixed ideas whatsoever

45

The office of the Hansonia Society was a series of small, connecting rooms. I had called up and a man's voice said that they were in fact looking for someone to do part-time work and told me to come for an interview. I set off on a fine morning, a week after Franklin's school started.

The door to the office was frosted glass. Painted in gold letters, backed in black, was a list of names:

> THE HANSONIA SOCIETY
>
> HANSOPHIE RECORDS
>
> BERNARD REGENSTEIN, AGENT AND EXECUTOR
>
> THE KINDERVATER TRUST
>
> VOGELWEIDE PUBLICATIONS

I opened the door. There, sitting at a calculator with a scowl on his face, was a person I took to be somewhat my senior. He was wearing an expensive cashmere sweater with a silk ascot, and he ran his fingers through disarranged, thinning hair.

"Yes?" he said without looking up.

"I came about the job," I said. "I'm Geraldine Coleshares."

"Uh-huh," he said, still fixated on his calculator. "Can you type?"

"Oh, well enough," I said airily.

The young man finally looked up.

about offices. At that moment a very old man, of medium height and a shuffling gait, appeared. He wore an aged blue suit, a sweater vest, white shirt and skinny black tie. Stuck in the corner of his mouth was a little cigar which shed ashes down his front. His skin was as translucent as parchment, with the same sheen, but his hair was brown, and his immense eyebrows shot up from his little eyes, giving him the look of an astonished beaver.

"Who is this voman?" he said. He pronounced his *w*'s as *v*'s.

"Ludo, this is Geraldine Coleshares, who is going to work here."

"How do you do?" he barked, extending his hand. His hand was pale and soft and had probably never done anything more strenuous than hold a pen or a cigar.

"This is Dr. Ludwig Frechtvogel," Bernard junior said.

"Are you a doctor?" I asked.

"In Vienna everyone is a doctor," said Dr. Frechtvogel. "I am a doctor of law. Are you capable of hard work?"

"I think I am," I said.

"Yes, but what can you do? Anyone can work hard," Dr. Frechtvogel said.

"I used to be a researcher," I said. "I researched female blues singers of the twenties and thirties. I did archive work."

Dr. Frechtvogel peered at me. A cloud of blue smoke hung between us. Never since my days on tour with Ruby had I seen anyone able to talk, yell and never once take the cigar out of his mouth. I had once stood in absolute wonderment when a blues belter named Bones O'Dell who opened for us did an entire set without removing his cheroot.

"And before?" demanded Dr. Frechtvogel. "These are the things Buddy has forgotten to ask you."

"Are you Buddy?" I said to Bernard, Junior, who was clearly embarrassed.

"It's my family nickname," he said.

"And before?" barked Dr. Frechtvogel. "What did you do before, or did you do nothing?"

"I was a backup singer for a rock and roll act called Ruby and Vernon Shakely," I said, looking Dr. Frechtvogel straight in the eye. "I was a backup singer and dancer. I was a Shakette."

"Very nice!" said Dr. Frechtvogel. "A Shakette. What is this?"

"It's not the sort of thing you might put on your résumé," I said, although I had no résumé.

"This is not an office," said Dr. Frechtvogel. "It is a lunatic asylum. You will see. Dancing experience may come in handy."

"He likes you," Buddy said. "You've got the job."

"What about money?" I said. "What about your parents?"

"Oh, money," said Buddy grandly. "Come over by the calculator and we'll work out what you want. As for my mother and father, they'll be happy to have someone here. Our last office person just quit."

"A catastrophe," said Dr. Frechtvogel. "A nice, steady young man."

The telephone rang. "Answer it," said Buddy. "Let's see how you do."

"What do I say?" I asked.

"You figure it out," said Buddy.

"Hansonia Society," I said. "Good morning."

A sweet, girlish voice asked for someone called Ludovic. I covered the receiver with my hand. "Is there someone called Ludovic?" I asked.

"This is myself!" said Dr. Frechtvogel, snatching the telephone from my hands.

"Hello!" he barked, and continued the conversation in what sounded like angry German. Then he shouted "Servus!" and slammed the telephone down.

"Mrs. Rosenstiel," Buddy said to me. "One of his girlfriends."

"What does 'servus' mean?"

"It's a sort of sign-off from old Vienna," Buddy said. He looked down at the papers on his desk. "Can you start tomorrow?"

I was unprepared for this, but why couldn't I start tomorrow? I would take Little Franklin to school, and then what? I could start my job. I could go up to the office at school and give Bernice, the secretary, an actual work number. What a statement! Then everyone could tell me how I was endangering the welfare of my child by working, just as they had once told me that he was being warped by my not working. Three days a week I would be wearing grown-up work clothes, as opposed to grubby child-care clothes. Sure, I said.

Out in the street, I did not call Johnny. I called Mary Abbott from a pay phone to tell her my interesting news and then I went off to pick up my boy.

46

"*I've* never heard of these people," said my mother. "Who did you say they were?"

"I said they were called Regenstein. And I can't imagine why you would have heard of them. They started out as collectors of delta blues singers."

"I suppose you'll have to get some sort of baby-sitter for Franklin," my mother said, stirring her coffee.

"I won't!" I said brightly. "Because I'm only working part time."

Oh, mothers! What did they mean to say? Did she mean it was a good thing or a bad thing that Franklin would not have a baby-sitter? Was I doing the right thing or the wrong thing by going to work?

A baby-sitter—if I had said there would be no baby-sitter—would have been a better choice in my mother's eyes, because my job would take up my energy and I would be tired and therefore unable to give Little Franklin the full attention he deserved when I came home from work. Had I said I had decided to get a baby-sitter, my mother would have doubtless told me how bad for Franklin this might be, since no baby-sitter can ever love and console a child as a mother can, and so on. This, of course, was the conflict of my mother's generation, lavishly handed down to mine. Why hadn't I seen it before? I remembered the baby-sitters I had had as a child—older women I and my little friends had tried to torture as my mother sat in her studio, torn between her desire to paint and her responsibilities as a parent. There was no end to these things—they were like laundry. You felt that you had gotten them clean and folded and put away and suddenly there they were—a tangled mess, everywhere you looked.

I said, "You know, Ma, you were lucky. You had work you loved to do and you could do it at home. The work I loved to do I had to go on tour to do. You can't do that sort of thing and have a child and a husband."

"That's all in the past, darling," said my mother. "Now you ought to find something you can be happy with. This new job sounds very minimal. What about going back to school?"

Or going to law school or writing a book or consulting on a documentary film about rock and roll? How about deciding on a singing career? What about finding someone like Doo-Wah and putting together an act? How about finding something that would put my heart at rest?

"It'll come along," I said. "Right now I'm going to work part-time and hang out with Little Franklin, since my days are numbered in that regard."

"Well," said my mother. "What are your other friends up to? I never hear you mention Mary anymore. Did you two have a falling out?"

"She's going to be a nun," I said.

"Oh, good gracious!" said my mother. "You girls! What next? Why ever is she doing that?"

"Well, Ma, she *is* a Catholic, you know."

"Darling, there are millions of Catholics. That's hardly a sufficient reason. Oh, her poor parents!"

"She feels she's being called," I said. "She's going to enter a monastery upstate. They keep a farm and spin their own wool."

My mother looked pained. "Farming and spinning," she said. "Why?"

"They live by the rule of St. Benedict. Work and pray, live self-sufficiently. I've done a lot of reading about it. It sounds very nice. I find it restful to think about."

"I'm sure they don't let Jewish women with children into monasteries," my mother said.

These days any planned thing looked good to me. What heaven to have your work cut out for you, to be part of the Big Picture—a picture you did not have to paint yourself.

"Perhaps this new job of yours will lead to something else," my mother said.

"Yes," I said. "Perhaps I'll get the Nobel Prize in physics."

"Now, Geraldine," my mother said.

"Now, Mom," I said. "My instinct tells me this is the right job for me."

"But you say that young man hired you the minute you walked in the door. He knows nothing about you."

"It's just as well," I said. "Maybe his instinct told him to hire me."

"Oh, you young people," said my mother. "Instincts. Monasteries. What does it all mean?"

From down the hall we suddenly heard Little Franklin. "Mama," he called. "Can I have some ice cream right this minute?"

"Our little prince is up," said my mother. "Darling," she called to him. "Your Nanny is here and she has hazelnut ice cream for you."

At these words Little Franklin came bounding down the hall. Hazelnut ice cream was my mother's ace in the hole. She led Franklin, who had not bothered to acknowledge me in any way, into the kitchen Several minutes later I found them deep in conversation.

"Is there any ice cream left for me?" I asked.

"Not too much," said Little Franklin putting his little hand over his dish.

47

My first meeting with Bernard Regenstein, Sr., was not auspicious. He had coughed in my direction and then disappeared into his office. For a long time, if he wanted me, he called to Gertje (who instructed me *not* to call her Mrs. Regenstein) to fetch me. I often felt he was unclear about my name, and for months after I had been hired I would find the occasional note to me addressed to the man I had succeeded.

Bernard was tall and cranelike, and he stooped like a crane. He had a beautifully formed, egg-shaped head, bald and polished. He wore old, tweed jackets with a long silk opera scarf around his neck. In winter he wore a beret and an enormous old raccoon coat. He was delicate in his lungs, Gertje said, although he smoked a pipe. The imported tobacco he preferred was kept in stock at the smoke shop in the lobby.

Gertje was a big, handsome woman who wore a cape. Her hair was cut rather like Franklin's, but longer and gray. She had a bobbed nose and hazel eyes. Her face was a mesh of fine, distinguished lines. It was clear she had been a great beauty in her youth.

On my first day she had held out her hand and said, "How lovely to meet you!" as if I had been a tea guest. "How clever of Buddy to hire you! Our dear Paul Robinson left us just like that!" She snapped her fingers. "He was studying science. And when his fellowship came through . . . pffft! Vanished!"

She had a sweet, girlish voice. Her accent had mellowed, but not much. After a month or so at the Regenstein office I began to think that it was a feature of all German women to have beautiful voices.

I answered the telephone, typed letters, made photocopies and filed letters. I also began the task of reading my way through the files. In the Regenstein office was a copy (or a photocopy) of everything Hans and Sonia Regenstein had ever written. An entire file drawer was devoted to contracts concerning another of their classic texts, *Music of All People*, a book every schoolchild in the Western Hemisphere had been brought up with.

Hans and Sonia Regenstein had plunged into the culture of their adopted country with a passion. They had written several books for young people, *What Our Colonists Wore* and *What the Pilgrims Ate*, as well as *Musical Instruments and Interests of Colonial People*. They had written monographs on corn-husk dolls, chain-gang songs and quilting styles.

What interested me most about them was why two cultivated Europeans from the Old World would come to this country and find themselves in a Studebaker with a lot of primitive recording equipment, listening to old blues men and women in the middle of the Deep South.

"I will tell you something," Gertje said. "Bernard's aunt and uncle came here and they fell in love. You Americans have no idea what this country looks like to a European. The old world was crumbling. They felt that terrible things were about to happen. They did not think Hitler would simply go away. Hans was in the first war—a Jewish war hero. His comrades believed that no one would harm a Jewish war hero— they all perished! Hans and Sonia came here and they saw a big, open country with lots of room and lots of food. Bananas! Pineapples! I myself was a grown woman before I ever tasted such things, and I was rich as a girl. A huge country where everyone speaks one language! The army does not try to overthrow the government! A constitution! No kings or royalty! Paradise." She took a sip of coffee from a blue and red cup.

No matter how long Gertje had lived in this country, no matter that she had raised an American son, she remained exotically and essentially European. She wore a kind of heavy stocking I had never seen before (sent to her from Germany by a cousin), and white shirts she bought on her yearly trip abroad, and heavy yet elegant shoes.

The things she kept in a cupboard in the inner office were a European's emergency larder: raspberry jam, imported biscuits, a flat, round tin of herrings rolled up with pickles, and four cartons of cigarettes.

"Someday I stop smoking," Gertje said. "But until that time . . . when I am down to even two or three packs, I begin to feel anxious. You know, in the war cigarettes were gold. They were diamonds! To have a cigarette meant that for a little time everything was all right. Of course, everything was not all right. You cannot imagine what it is like to come here and see cigarettes everywhere! I used to go by a tobacconist's near where I lived and I would stare at such abundance. Boxes and boxes of cigarettes! You cannot imagine, Geraldine, what an amazing sight a cigarette *machine* is, that spits out the cigarettes, so! But now I keep my little stockpile and it makes me feel calm."

She also kept a small tea cloth for the table, in case of guests, and a pack of fancy paper plates, but she could not abide plastic forks and so, in a little wicker basket, was a set of silverware. There were wineglasses, too, for special occasions. In a tiny office refrigerator, the size of a doll's house, were a few bottles of sparkling water, a tin of peach nectar and a bottle of champagne, lying on its side.

As the months went by, I felt more and more at home at the Regenstein office. Gertje was sincerely interested in Little Franklin, who came to visit once or twice on his way to the dentist. But Gertje, Bernard and Dr. Frechtvogel were as exotic to me as the Reverend Willhall. They were all from a world I had never known and to which I had only the most minimal access.

Bernard and Gertje were often out. They went to Europe, they had business lunches, they spent four-day weekends at their house in Vermont. Often I was left alone with Dr. Frechtvogel.

Dr. Frechtvogel's occupation was to sit in the back office dispensing advice to Bernard. Once he had opened the mail and finished his coffee, he waited for Bernard and Gertje to come in. Then the three of them sat smoking and arguing in German until I came in and threw the window open to let the smoke out.

Gertje told me that Dr. Frechtvogel had been a lawyer in Vienna and that he had made a pledge never to work again once he came to this country, although a good many elderly Europeans came to the office for consultations with him. He had dozens of lady friends who called the office all day long and he claimed, as a young man, to have lived with a trapeze artist who, because of a scar, had never taken off her face paint for the duration of their affair. My happiest moments came when Dr. Frechtvogel and I were alone and he would talk to me.

We had lunch every day in the back office, providing he was not out with one of his ladies. Each day I ordered him the same thing: roast beef on dry toast with black coffee. Each day he gnawed his sandwich and then made terrible noises about the terrible coffee, until I was moved to get up and make a fresh pot for him. I lit his cigars and brushed the ashes off his clothes. I found his glasses for him when he lost them, and remembered to have the mail stacked neatly at his place on the coffee table. I discovered that he adored those hard black Dutch toffees that come in a tin and bought them for him. When he was angry he called me a brainless American, but I noticed that it was crucial that I kiss him goodbye before I left each day. He was the grandfather I had never had.

"You were a singer," he said one day. "Why do you no longer sing?"

I explained that I hadn't really been a singer, I had been a backup. He had no idea what this was, so I explained it to him. I told him that my purpose was to punctuate the lead singer but that every once in a while I got to sing a very small solo.

"Sing something to me," Dr. Frechtvogel said.

"I'll sing you Brahms' Lullaby."

"Stupid girl!" he said. "I mean something you sang on your job."

"Okay," I said. I was sitting on the sofa and he sat in his big leather chair. I sang "You Don't Love Me Like You Used to Do." He sat quite still, allowing the ash on his cigar to grow. I sang, fixated on the cigar. When I finished, the ash was scattered all over his jacket.

"That is an extremely stupid song," he said. "Brush me off. Now, do you know this song called 'The Tennessee Waltz'?"

I said I did.

"And do you know how to waltz?" he barked.

I said I didn't.

"You must learn. I will teach you. You sing," he said. "I will keep time."

He stood up and held out his arms. I put my arm around his waist. He held me away from him. "Sing," he said.

I began to sing and he began to count: one two three. He lumbered and shambled like a bear, but he pushed me around the floor. "Sing it again," he said.

I took about ten steps to his one as I pivoted around him.

"They don't teach American girls to waltz," I said, slightly out of breath.

"Sing more," said Dr. Frechtvogel.

He spun me around and, when I opened my eyes, I saw a man standing in the door of the office watching me.

"There's someone here," I whispered. The person was tall and dark, with horn-rimmed glasses and a camel hair coat. The faintest smile played across his otherwise serious features.

"Hello, Ludwig," he said.

"*Ach!* Leo," said Dr. Frechtvogel, dropping my arm. "Geraldine, this is Leo Rhinehart. You are just in time for our dancing party. Leo, here is Mrs. Geraldine Miller who works in this office. She was at one time a singer and I am now teaching her to waltz, as American girls are deficient in this skill."

Leo shook my hand. He had dark brown eyes and seemed to be a few years older than I was. My heart seemed suddenly to flop around in my chest, but of course I had just been dancing.

"Take your coat off, Leo, and dance with this person," Dr. Frechtvogel said. "Leo is an excellent waltzer."

"Oh, no!" I said. "I've got to run. I'll be late to pick up my little boy at school. Goodbye, Ludwig." I turned to Leo and extended my hand. Europeans seemed to shake hands at every turn: hello, goodbye, nice to meet you, sit down. His hand was strong.

"I'm glad to have met you," I said. "Goodbye. Goodbye."

I took a deep breath and bolted from the office. The sight of Leo Rhinehart had unscrambled me. I felt hot and cold and shaky, and I hoped it would be a long time before I ever saw him again.

48

In the back office, in a special cabinet, was the original album of photos documenting Hans and Sonia Regenstein's first trip to the rural South.

In these photos, many of them sepia prints, Hans wears striped suspenders and a straw hat, and smokes the kind of enormous curved pipe you see in travel posters of Switzerland. Sonia, in her flowered print dress, garden hat and lorgnette, does not look like anything indigenous to these shores. In many photos they stand with one bluesman or other against the background of a field or shanty. They recorded field hands, chain gangs, sharecroppers, old women sitting on their porches.

For many years these recordings were pressed and issued by Hansophie Records, but after Hans and Sonia died, and record technology improved, Bernard sold the archive to the American Folklore Society, which kept it intact. Bernard and Gertje, through the Hansonia Society, were still executors.

In several of the photos, a tall, extremely handsome, dark young man stands off to the side. This, Gertje told me, was the great Felix Kindervater, often called "the Heinrich Heine of the twentieth century," and one of Hans Regenstein's closest friends. Kindervater was a poet, author of *The New Hebrew Melodies*. His account of his American trip, *An Austrian in Dixie,* had been a best-seller here and in Europe.

Hans and Sonia begged him to stay: as a Jew and a socialist, they felt him to be in danger.

He left anyway. His two most famous books, always published under their German titles, *Es Kommt Mir Vor* (*It Seems to Me*) and *Es Tut Mir Leid* (*It's Too Bad*), his forebodings on the European landscape just before the war, had been published secretly and eventually caused his imprisonment. *Es Tut Mir Leid* was smuggled out of Buchenwald, across the border and finally to England, and then to the office of Hansophie Records, where Hans Regenstein decided to publish it himself under the imprint Vogelweide Publications (after Walter von der Vogelweide, the medieval poet and author of "Unter den Linden"). The rights to this work had been sold by Bernard and Gertje in almost every language. One entire bookshelf was taken up by editions in every known, and several unknown, languages.

On quiet days, of which there were many, I sat in the front office reading. I read my way through the works of Hans and Sonia and through Felix Kindervater, just as I had worked my way through female blues singers of the thirties. I began to feel that someday I would put all this together and it would yield some sense. In the meantime, I was happy in the way of a fulfilled graduate student, and I was always pleased to be interrupted by one or another of the Regenstein regulars.

For example, Mr. Ratlitz, a tiny, stocky Pole who wore flashy socks and sandals. He had been in the underground in the Vilna ghetto and had written a novel about Auschwitz. He believed he had been swindled by an Off-Broadway producer who had an interest in an adaptation of the novel for the stage, and who had died. Ratlitz was suing the producer's son on some grounds I could not quite understand, but every other Monday morning he appeared with a large sheaf of documents to be copied on our primitive and often out-of-order copying machine. These he thrust at me and said, "Copy, please," and retreated to the back office to schnor a cup of coffee and one of Dr. Frechtvogel's cigars.

I never minded standing in front of our copier, feeding sheet after sheet of paper into its maw. Frequently the thing misfired and I would have to take it apart and pull a piece of slightly charred paper out from underneath the rollers. When this happened, I swore loudly, which called Ratlitz's attention to me. He stood watching with his mild, expressionless blue eyes as I sweated over this infernal machine.

I did not mind making up address labels for him, or typing letters for him to sign. I did not, in fact, mind anything. For the first time in my life, I felt totally useful. These people were Europeans and they had suffered. I was an American, as round, untouched and pure as a cotton puff. Nothing bad had ever happened to me—at least not in global terms. I had never seen a country blown up or my family loaded into a boxcar (as described in Ratlitz's autobiographical novel). Gertje was right. To be an American was to be blessed with a kind of idiotic but very useful innocence. I often felt like a nurse on a battlefield, capable, in my freshness, of dispensing cheer to wounded people. I did not flinch during a thunderstorm as Gertje did. To see her face—the face of an old child—was to understand everything. No matter how jolly, how eager, how life-embracing she was, the matter of cigarette anxiety, or thunderstorms, gave her away.

Every second Wednesday the Regensteins' accountant appeared, a well-groomed and elegantly dressed woman named Hannah Hausknecht. She had red hair, always freshly set, and pink cheeks. It was hard to tell how old she was. Her coat came from Saks Fifth Avenue. I saw the label when I hung it up for her, and I always brought her a cup of coffee and one of Gertje's biscuits, for which she was lavishly grateful. When I admired her clothes, she was voluble. Saks Fifth Avenue, it turned out, was one of her favorite subjects.

"You know, Geraldine, I will tell you something," she began, just as Gertje always began. "When I first came here I went to Saks and, you know, there are really such excellent lingerie fitters there. And then, such a surprise! I went one day to buy a brassière and a lady looked at me for a long time. This woman was the head of the lingerie department, and you cannot imagine! She was the aunt of my best friend! I did not even know she was still alive."

She took off her suit jacket and rolled up the sleeve of her striped shirt. I could see a series of blue numbers on her wrist; she was the first person I had ever seen with a concentration camp tattoo.

"This suit," she said. "Drastically reduced—isn't that how you say? But not drastic enough. Geraldine, I will tell you. Shopping is like hunting. The hunter must creep with great patience and must also take the risk that someone will get the beautiful red suit before she does. I watched this suit for weeks and finally I see that a button is missing and a tiny smudge is on the lining. So for the lost button and the smudge, the suit is mine very cheap!" She broke off because she saw me staring at her wrist.

I was mortified. "I'm sorry," I said.

"Oh, Geraldine. Please do not be silly," she said. "Why should a nice American girl not look? These things do not happen here, thank God."

"Where were you?"

"Auschwitz," Hannah said. "I will tell you something. I only remember the good times. I was in the children's section and it was near the end of the war. We made up songs about cakes—big chocolate cakes with thousands of sugar roses and whipped cream, and almond horns and petit fours with pink icing and little silver balls. Then we were liberated and went to Israel. My mother had survived, my father and brothers not. We looked everywhere for a baker. However, the Israelis are not such good bakers. But in New York! *Ach,* New York is the true promised land. A land of milk and honey and almond horns and beautiful Danishes such as I had as a child. Please don't look so upset! Here is my handkerchief."

She gave me a little flowered square and I wiped my eyes. There is nothing so morally tepid, I thought, than weeping over something horrible that happened to someone else and will never happen to you.

"But look!" she said. "I have grown up so plump and happy. The day we are made citizens, my husband and I and my friends, some who survived the war like us, all celebrated at the Little Vienna Pastry Shop, at a big table, and we ate all the things we dreamed about! Delicious coffee and hot milk! No, really, I am very content."

I asked her how she had stood it.

"You have no *idea* how much people can stand, she said, smiling."

I asked her if she understood why Hans and Sonia Regenstein had been so enamored of the kind of music many Americans had never even heard.

"I have read their books," said Hannah. "Obviously their subject is music, but they are also about the *idea* of this place. Myself, I have been unable to connect with this music—we have all the records, you know. But to listen to them is to think that you are having the *experience* of America. It is like nothing else. You know, Geraldine, last spring my husband and I were in Paris and I said, 'Even Africa must be like Europe. All those handsome Africans in business suits!' It is the Old World still. But here! Here it is always new!" She broke her biscuit in half.

"Some people come here to reinvent themselves," she said. "But, you know, exiles and refugees are forced away from the things that invented them. Coming here is like climbing into a nice clean bed after a terrible series of nightmares. Now I must get to work and not chatter all the morning away."

49

After a while I noticed that Buddy never seemed to be around until lunchtime, so I supposed that he either slept late or had some other business ventures to attend to.

I was still reading my way through the files when I came across a somewhat battered blue folder marked BUDDY: PERSONAL, in Bernard's handwriting. There was another file for Gertje, which held photocopies of her naturalization papers and various medical forms. Although I never thought of myself as a snoop, I could not help myself. There, on the top, was Buddy's birth certificate, and it said he was seventeen years old. I naturally assumed that this was a mistake, but a further look revealed report cards which seemed to corroborate this mystifying information.

I went to my desk, which faced Gertje's. I had originally assumed it was Buddy's desk.

"Gertje, why is Buddy never here in the morning?" I said.

Gertje's face fell. She lit a cigarette. "So," she said. "You have discovered the big secret."

"You mean it's true? I thought he was a grown-up."

"*Ach*, Geraldine," said Gertje. "He *is* a grown-up. When he was fourteen he started a little business on his own, a little newsletter and mail-order service to find various out-of-print books. He began this with our friend Leon Weiss, who has a bookshop near our house. Some people have music prodigies, and some people's children are over developed at math, but mine is a business genius, and I can tell you that before he is twenty-one years old, he will make a million dollars. It is hard to believe. Both my parents were painters. When I was little, we lived in a big house in the country and we thought that America was like a vast forest full of red Indians. Now I am a citizen and my child will be a tycoon! One never thinks that life will be so strange."

"I have the feeling he will never forgive me if he knows I know," I said.

"It will be our secret," said Gertje. "You know, when he was a little boy I kept myself from sleep at night worrying that since I was not an American mother I could not envision a proper American childhood for him. If I put jam on his pancakes I worried that I ought to use maple syrup. I made him little sandwiches of brown bread with egg yolk and brown sugar. At night the only songs I knew to sing him were the lullabies of my childhood, all in German. I said to myself, I know nothing of these baseball players or these footballers. I do not understand what American teenagers are like. These really were like Martians to me, Geraldine. In Europe when I was a girl, teenagers were big giggling children. But here! Such energy! Such confidence! Here little children talked back to their teachers and called grown ups by their first names! I found it so thrilling and liberating and bewildering."

I felt exactly the same way. Somewhere there were women who knew exactly what to do. They knew the correct way to talk to children. They knew how to take their places as mothers, with all the authority and command that goes with the role. I myself felt like Franklin's big, adoring friend. I wondered if he took me seriously at all.

And, of course, I was to my own mother what Buddy was to Gertje. Gertje, who did calligraphy and watercolors, who had grown up under the old order, did not expect to spawn a millionaire, and my mother in her proper, tailored suits, with her mahogany dining room table, her sense of order and propriety, did not expect to raise a daughter who would someday stand on a stage wearing a dress the size of a camisole, jumping up and down and singing with a bunch of Afro-Americans.

"I often wonder what Franklin will turn out to be," I said to Gertje.

"One can never predict anything," Gertje said. "This is what a war will teach one. None of us ever believed we would someday live in America, and yet you see how well we do. Look at Hannah Hausknecht.

She has come here and made the best of it. Go home and read *An Austrian in Dixie.* You know, Geraldine, if it had not been for the war, life would be very rigid. Things cannot be the old way forever. Even horrible things must happen to make changes. Felix Kindervater had been analyzed by a colleague of Freud. He believed that the events leading up to World War II were like the rebellion in an old-fashioned family in which the whole situation explodes. The Old World was very, very tight, and now it is blown to bits and here we are! My little boy is going to be a mogul. Someday he will buy this agency from his father. And your Little Franklin will step into a world made by people like Buddy. It is hard to think of it."

It *was* hard to think of it.

"Your Little Franklin is lucky," Gertje said. "Because you and he speak a common language. You are his American mommy and he is your American boy."

"No one seems to think that's enough," I said.

"Geraldine, I will tell you something," Gertje said. "Americans are very busy and ambitious. They do not rest. Sophie Regenstein describes Colonial mothers at home, always spinning, weaving, sewing. No one ever stopped to relax or think. That is what Americans are like. I look at my own Buddy and there he is, planning and plotting and scheming. He eats his supper and makes little notes on the napkin. He has his lunch on the telephone. Here no one ever thinks that it is enough merely to *be.*"

This seemed right on the money to me, but as I pointed out to Gertje, it probably made it easier to *be* something to begin with in order merely to be it.

"Spoken like an American girl!" said Gertje.

50

For several months the office was turned upside down by what Gertje called the affair of Manfred Kirschbaum, who claimed to be an old friend of Felix Kindervater's and said he had in his possession a hitherto undiscovered novel of Kindervater's which it was his intention to publish. His letters hinted, in the most elegant and polite way, that he intended to do this with or without the permission of the estate.

I had typed dozens of letters regarding this matter: to lawyers, to foreign publishers, to various heirs and editors. Then Manfred Kirschbaum appeared in person. He was accompanied by his mistress, Mrs. Lucia Bonfiglio. They were quite sensational to look at. Ruby, at her most dramatic, paled beside them.

Mrs. Bonfiglio was six feet tall. She wore a coat of dyed orange mink. Her brilliant orange hair was piled up on top of her head and affixed with an enormous green silk ribbon. On her hand she wore a diamond, the size of one of Little Franklin's plastic building blocks, set into an enormous hoop of yellow gold. She wore dark green stockings, alligator shoes and a great deal of green eye shadow.

Manfred Kirschbaum was similarly magnificent, although somewhat miniature: small, rosy-cheeked, with glossy white hair worn a little too long, and cold little blue eyes. His yellow cashmere scarf was long enough to wrap around his neck three or four times. His socks were lavender and his suspenders gray, embroidered with a design of alpine flowers. He wore a yellow and white striped shirt, a hacking jacket and tweed trousers. I greatly admired his shoes, which were a kind of orangy suede. He and Mrs. Bonfiglio smoked little black Sobranie cigarettes with gold tips. I found it hard to take my eyes off them.

Dr. Frechtvogel, who knew everyone in the world, had known Manfred's brother Wolfgang, who had once collaborated on the libretto for an operetta with one of Dr. Frechtvogel's friends.

He shook Kirschbaum's hand cordially. "Your brother is dead, yes?" he barked, spewing ashes.

"Indeed he is not!" said Kirschbaum, whose accent was a mixture of British, Middle European and German. "Very much alive, my dear fellow! And whom have I the pleasure of addressing? My memory is not so keen."

"I am Frechtvogel," said Dr. Frechtvogel.

"Ah," said Manfred Kirschbaum, signifying that the name meant nothing to him.

Gertje greeted them with overpowering formality. It was clear she felt nothing but contempt, yet she sat them down and insisted several times that they have coffee. She provided a number of large glass ashtrays. Her normally girlish voice was pitched ever so slightly lower.

Bernard greeted them with a look of rattled distraction. The KIRSCHBAUM/KINDERVATER file lay unopened before him. He did not think in personal terms; he thought about strategy and logic. Human emotions, so far as he could tell, played no interesting part in anything.

"Geraldine, come sit," Gertje said. "And please to take notes. This is important."

Take *notes?* Her expression said clearly "Write fast and fake it," and I realized that I was a useful office ornament: the secretary.

Soon the back office was thick with smoke and perfume. Mrs. Lucia Bonfiglio sat without moving a hair, while Kirschbaum reiterated what he had already written to Bernard in countless letters: he and his best friend, Kindervater, had been habitués of the Café des Modernes in Vienna. When Kindervater came back from his American trip, and things began to look bad, he vouchsafed his unpublished novel to Kirschbaum, who was about to flee. According to Kirschbaum, he had said: "Take this with you and do nothing with it until you feel the time is right."

Bernard cleared his throat. "And why was the time not right before now?"

"Ah," said Kirschbaum. "This is not a work that would have appealed to Hans and Sonia Regenstein. It is not about war or politics or culture. It is about love . . . eros. It is lighthearted, almost stupid."

"His early letters are not exactly lighthearted," said Bernard. "We must see the manuscript."

"I have brought with me a faithful reproduction by the most advanced methods."

Dr. Frechtvogel, like Mrs. Lucia Bonfiglio, had been posing as a wax dummy. Suddenly he sprang up, spraying cigar ashes right and left.

"We must see the original at once!" he shouted, and then sat down.

"My dear fellow," said Kirschbaum languidly. "This is totally impossible, as it resides in a safety deposit box in Paris, where Mrs. Bonfiglio and I have our flat. I am perfectly willing to endow the Kindervater Trust with it, should you permit me to advance its publication."

Gertje narrowed her eyes and a look of pure scorn crossed her otherwise mild features.

"And you intend to *sell* this manuscript," Gertje said.

"My dear lady, of course!" said Kirschbaum. "One must live, must one not? But the heirs, I believe, his sister Mrs. Jacobson, of Toronto, and her three children, will richly benefit. And now, I leave this manuscript and we must go. We are due for lunch."

Mrs. Bonfiglio spoke for the first time. Her voice was a low, bored drawl. "And with whom do we lunch, Manfredo?" she said.

"Paola and Hugo," said Kirschbaum.

"Oh, really," said Mrs. Bonfiglio, snuffing out her cigarette. "I really can't stick them." Her coat was held out for her. She slipped her arms into it, and then, in a cloud of Guerlain perfume and Sobranie smoke, they were gone.

After they left, Gertje threw the window open.

"They're so beautiful," I said. "Like figurines."

"Darling, Europe is littered with people like them. And he says life has been *kind* to him. He means the Bonfiglio has been kind to him. He lives off her. Ask Ludwig. He knows all about her." She closed the window. "Ludo! Come tell Geraldine about the Bonfiglio."

"A horrible person," said Dr. Frechtvogel. "First she is married to Hoffheimer, a manufacturer of drainpipes. Then she married Bonfiglio of an Italian pottery fortune, but he then died and now she lives with Kirschbaum off the Bonfiglio money. This man is a total fraud. You will see. He is a swindler and we will never see him again. Now please let us never open the window again. I do not like fresh air."

51

I had never seen anyone like Mrs. Lucia Bonfiglio or Manfred Kirschbaum before, and now I saw them everywhere. Tall women in mink
coats and heavy silk scarves, decorated with tassels or roses or horses
or eagles, rushed past me speaking French, Italian or German. Men,
wearing lavender socks and enormous silk mufflers, held them by the
arm, strolling in and out of very expensive shops. This was not the sort
of thing you saw around the Malcolm Sprague School or the Race
Music Foundation, or even on the tour, where it was not unknown for
a really big star to appear in an oversized Cadillac and a floor-length
chinchilla coat. But this was different: these were Europeans.

They made me feel like an American Indian with leather leggings
and a papoose on my back. These creatures fluttered and floated in
from Vienna, Paris, Chile via Poland, or Berlin. All of them had been
through the war. Mrs. Lucia Bonfiglio, according to Dr. Frechtvogel,
had lived in a drainpipe—the very same manufactured by Hoffheimer,
the man who would later become her husband—in the spring after
the war. She had it outfitted with a camp table and had rigged up a
clothesline as a closet. And yet here she was, hair ablaze, carrying an
ostrich handbag as if nothing more trying than a missed dressmaker
appointment had ever vexed her.

As for Kirschbaum, his story was unknown, although he dropped
hints, Gertje said, that he had been in the Underground. I asked her if
she thought he had been.

"Geraldine, I will tell you something," she said. "You can never, never tell. Europe was full of charlatans and heroes and fanatics in those days. People did all sorts of things to protect themselves, and the most unlikely people turned up doing the most unlikely things. My own grandmother, to whom servants were expected to *bow*, hid hundreds of Jews. Our land was up at the top of Germany, near Denmark. She ran an underground railroad, I think you call them, but by boat. And the boat that took people across! It was owned by a friend of my mother's who did nothing before the war but have massages and manicures and never cared for another thing. But this woman herself took these people across because her family were accomplished pleasure sailors. She rigged up her sail and pretended to go fishing and hid people under bunks and disguised them as her servants. Now she sits in a chair surrounded by real servants and when I go to see her she says, 'Look, Gertje dear. So many letters from Israel, where these people went!' And her little hands are always perfect: pink nail polish and a big diamond ring. So who is to know? Great patriots denounced their neighbors, and cleaning women were saints. It is hard to tell anything. Here it is easier. The bad guys are more identifiable. Americans have fewer hiding places, I always think."

"And," I said as casually as I could, "what about Leo Rhinehart?"

He had come to the office several times to see Dr. Frechtvogel, always in the morning when I was around. The sight of him seemed to turn me into a nervous wreck. I had learned that he was a nephew of one of the Mrs. Kleins—either Mrs. Charlotte Klein or Mrs. Gusta Klein, I could never remember.

When I looked at him I felt strangely warm and embarrassed, like a thirteen-year-old girl with her first crush. From the moment I first saw him, I had been unable to stop thinking about him. My quest was to ferret out information without seeming to be very interested. At the same time I felt deeply mortified by my interest, but it was easy enough to justify: I worked in an office of Europeans, and Leo, although he had been born in Europe and came from an Old World household, had grown up an American boy. This made him, for my present purposes, irresistible.

"*Ach*, Leo," said Gertje. "His father was not a Jew. After Leo was born, the father left the mother. He said if she did not divorce him, he would denounce her. So she left with that little baby and went to Shanghai.

Many Jews ended up there. Children could go to the Peter Pan Nursery, which was run by Australian ladies, or to the Kaiser Wilhelmschule. Imagine—in *China!* And then they came here, and Leo's father was killed in the war, and his mother, Lilly, is Mrs. Lotte Klein's sister."

Three weeks later, I found myself sitting across from Leo Rhinehart in a small, dark restaurant called The Coffee Bean attempting to eat a sandwich, unable to concentrate on anything.

He had come to see Dr. Frechtvogel, and after half an hour I was summoned to the back office.

"Take these papers," Dr. Frechtvogel barked, "and make copies in the machine."

"Ludwig, please don't," Leo said.

"Yes, yes, this is her job," said Dr. Frechtvogel. In his hand were three chapters of Leo's dissertation.

"I'm happy to do it," I said.

"It isn't right," said Leo.

"It is entirely right!" shouted Dr. Frechtvogel. "This is what an office girl must do."

"Ludwig, really . . ." Leo said.

"I *am* the office girl," I said sweetly. "Is this your thesis?"

"Well, yes," said Leo.

"I'm happy to do it," I said. "I used to be a graduate student."

I ran the copies happily but without any comprehension. There were a great many graphs and charts and equations. When I was finished, I handed the manuscript back to Leo, who suddenly became shy, as if he had come to pick me up on a first date.

I did not see him for a week. Then he appeared late one morning when Gertje, Bernard and Buddy were at a meeting and Dr. Frechtvogel had gone off to lunch with Mrs. Eva Muller.

"No one's here," I said.

"You're here," he said.

"I mean, no one you want to see."

"I want to see *you*," he said. "I'd like to take you out to lunch to thank you for all that work."

"Oh, that's okay," I said.

I found that I was having a hard time looking at him.

"I mean it," he said.

"Okay," I said. "I'll just put the answering machine on. But you'll have to have lunch near my son's school. Is that all right?"

"How nice that you have a child," Leo said.

We took a cab to the Coffee Bean. In the taxi, we did not say a word.

We did not say very much while we looked at the menu. Once our order was taken, I felt a little desperate.

"What did you do before you worked for the Regensteins?" Leo asked.

"I had a baby," I said.

"And before that?"

"Well, I worked for this foundation that preserved Afro-American music, and before that I used to be a rock and roll performer."

"Oh, really," said Leo.

"Yup," I said. "I used to sing with Ruby Shakely and the Shakettes. You probably never heard of them. You were probably off somewhere listening to the Brahms string quartets."

" 'Shake and Boogie,' " said Leo. " 'Love Me All Night Long.' I'm a man of my generation. Did you sing those?"

"Oh, sure," I said.

"How fascinating," Leo said.

"I have nothing to show for it," I said.

"Oh," Leo said. "Are you supposed to have something to show for things?"

"Well, of course," I said. "My God. You have the experience of going to college and you get a degree and then you use the degree to do something. You have the experience of being pregnant and you get a baby. I mean, I just have the memory of the experience."

"I heard you singing 'The Tennessee Waltz.' " said Leo. "You can still sing, after all."

"Those days are over. Nothing came of it," I said. "I mean, people who really *do* things have professions, and vocations. Maybe I'm one of those meandering types and being in the music business was a form of meandering."

"Meandering types are often very interesting to know," Leo said.

All at once I looked him in the eye. Did this mean he wanted to know me?

"Maybe some are," I said. I realized that it was costing me a great deal of effort not to grab his hands.

We drank our coffee. Then I said, "Did you go to the Peter Pan Nursery?"

He put his cup down and smiled. His eyes were a very dark brown but, when I looked at them closely, I could see varying shades in them, like the rings of trees.

"I went to the Kaiser Wilhelmschule," Leo said. "But every day I had tea with two old British ladies who taught me English. When I came to this country I wore an Eton suit and spoke with a British accent, and the other little boys beat me up."

I thought of Little Franklin. What sorrows would *my* little darling have to face?

"Now that I work at the Regensteins'," I said, "I feel totally amorphous. Gertje talks about what America is like to Europeans, but I don't quite identify with what she describes. In some ways, nothing ever *happens* in America. It's like a sponge. I feel as if I have no qualities whatsoever."

"Really?" Leo said, smiling. "No qualities whatsoever?"

"I'm a fabulous driver," I said.

A few weeks later, I lied to Johnny about where I was going. I went to Leo's apartment on the pretext of borrowing a book and shortly thereafter I went to bed with him.

52

It was snowing when I left my nice warm apartment, my nice warm husband, my sleeping child. I had made a meatloaf for supper. The dishes were washed, the laundry was done, folded and stacked on the dining room table. Little Franklin had been fed his supper, bathed, settled into bed in his striped pajamas, read to and kissed good-night. Johnny sat at his desk in a corner of the living room going through a pile of papers. I left the house without a pang.

I said I was going to the movies with Mary, a safe lie since she was on a retreat at her monastery. Without my boy, without a bag full of crackers and Mickey Mouse statuettes and little boxes of grape juice with straws attached, and extra mittens, to say nothing of the battered elephant I was required to carry with me when accompanied by my son, I felt totally unlike myself: light, unanchored, an unidentifiable person on the subway.

I had arranged with Leo that I would stop by on my way to visit my friend Mary Abbott, who lived in his neighborhood. I was going to borrow a book called *Kindervater's Vienna*, the English edition of which we did not have at the office. As far as I could tell, Leo thought I was a nice, ordinary, married person with a child.

I felt I was being compelled toward him. I felt I would die if he did not kiss me. It had nothing to do with Johnny or Franklin; it had to do with me. Just for a minute, I said to myself, I want to be in Leo's arms. Then I will somehow be fortified and can go on with the rest of my life. I was sort of a blank slate and Leo was a school. I needed the experience of him. He would kiss me and I would turn into Hannah Arendt. I would definitely be a better person for it.

I was the innocent American, making trouble right and left—a microcosm of imperialism, except that I only sought to colonize a tiny portion of Old Europe. A small, green elevator took me to the sixth floor. I rang his doorbell and in a minute we were face to face.

"Hi!" I said, in a bright, rattled way.

"Come in," said Leo. "Take your coat off. There's snow all over you."

I took my coat off and threw it over a chair in his hallway.

"I'm sorry to look so grubby," I said.

"You don't look grubby," Leo said. "Would you like a cup of tea?"

"Oh, yes!" I said, feeling that the voice of some jaunty, moronic member of the Junior League had entered my body.

His living room looked disorganized and rich, like a room in a domestic Victorian painting: an old couch covered with a paisley shawl, lamps with the kind of heavy paper shades that throw off yellow light. These things, he told me, were found by his flea-marketing mother and given to him. Two walls were covered in books.

I followed him into the kitchen, a small, functional space, and saw that he had one of those old enamel French coffeepots with a top that looks like a pagoda. In his kitchen he looked slightly over-lifesized. A person could have just thrown her arms around him from the back while he filled the kettle. I felt that if I opened the cupboards, which I longed to do, I would find a jumble of exotic things I had never seen before, but when Leo himself opened a door, all I saw was peanut butter, Rice Krispies and grape jelly.

On a tray he put two cups, a teapot and a plate of wafers he took from an ornamental tin. "They're Carlsbad *Oblaten*," Leo said. "My mother makes sure I always have some around."

I looked at him with longing.

"Food of my childhood," he said. "Come into my study."

At the end of another small hallway were two rooms separated by a bathroom. One was a bedroom—I could see the bed and a bureau. The other was his study, with a desk, a reading chair and an ottoman. The walls were covered with bookshelves and his desk was covered with papers. The reading lamp had a paper shade too, which made me feel that I was sitting in the middle of a pool of yellow light.

Leo poured the tea and I stared at his large, strong-looking hands.

"When I was a little boy," he was saying, "my mother used to take me to Kleine Café every Thursday afternoon after school. I guess I must have been about eight, because I had already turned into an American boy. I wore blue jeans and Keds and played baseball instead of soccer. I sort of looked forward to it and dreaded it, too. There would be all her friends, sitting and drinking their coffee and eating those little cakes with the decorations on them. I wanted to go home and eat Oreo cookies like my friends, but my mother had no idea what they were. I knew I was being a good boy since it meant so much to her to have this weekly outing, and I hated her for it, too."

"Oh," I said.

"You have a little boy," Leo said. "Ludwig mentioned what a wonderful child he is."

"Yes," I said. "He's the most wonderful person I have ever known."

"It's nice to be from the same place as your child," said Leo. "Look at Gertje and Buddy. She's totally devoted to him, and he totally baffles her. All that European culture and what does she get! A rampaging American capitalist."

As I drank my tea, a feeling of desolation overcame me. I had not had the opportunity to feel this way for some time. It was a way I had tried not to feel on tour, or up at the Race Music Foundation, or out in social life with Johnny. I was everywhere under false pretenses. I had no rock to stand on.

"And do you find it strange to work around so many Jews?" Leo was asking me.

"I am Jewish," I said.

"Really," Leo said. "I wouldn't have known that."

"Well, I am," I said. "In fact, I'm looking for a synagogue. I need to be educated. I mean, I've never known anyone who knows as little about things as I do."

"But you're a wonderful driver," said Leo, smiling.

"I'm a red-blooded American girl," I said. "I drive like a dream and swim like a fish. I know the words to every rock and roll song in a ten-year period. When our baby was little, the first song he ever learned was 'Rockin' Pneumonia and the Boogie Woogie Flu.' "

"Sounds good to me," said Leo.

"Oh, come on," I said. "I mean, it's nice for a kid to know the words to 'Camptown Races' and 'Shoofly Pie and Apple Pandowdy,' but, you know, where is the larger picture?"

"Are babies interested in the larger picture?" Leo said.

"You know what I mean," I said.

"I do, but here's what I mean. My mother sang me all the songs she knew as a child. When I came here, America was something to *learn*. If I had known you as a child, I would probably have wanted to be just like you."

"Oh, no," I said. "I have too many horrible qualities."

"That may well be," Leo said. "But you don't know how romantic you red-blooded Americans are to us Europeans."

At that moment I wanted to hurl myself into his arms.

"I am here under false pretenses," I said.

"Oh?"

I took a deep breath. I felt actually rather sick.

"I'm a very bad person," I said. "I wanted to kiss you."

"People often want to kiss people," Leo said.

"Yes, but I'm a wife and mother."

"Wives and mothers often want to kiss people," Leo said.

"If you kissed me, would it be because you feel sorry for me?"

Leo gave me a puzzled look. "It would be because I wanted to kiss you," he said. "I assume that you are going off to see your friend who lives in my neighborhood."

"That was a pretense," I said.

"Actually," Leo said, "we ought to think about this a little. Naturally, I'd love to kiss you, but then what?"

"You have a girlfriend," I said.

"I have a woman I have been seeing for a few years."

"Are you going to marry her?" I said.

"I'm not going to marry anyone for a long time," Leo said. "I'm going to spend a few years in Europe before I get married."

"You know," I said, "I think I should put on my hat and coat and get out of here." I stood up. He stood up too. The yellow light in his study threw a soft shadow over him. The top of my head grazed his chin. That half darkness seemed to keep us pinned to our places. We didn't speak: we breathed at one another. We moved like people under water. The tiniest gesture brought us closer.

He kissed me and kissed me. We kissed any number of times, and then we walked the few paces out of his study and across the hallway to his bedroom. I felt as if I were on fire.

When we connected, I felt a deep, inward shiver. This was not like sex for having fun or having children. It did not seem to be about falling in love, or even about having a sexual encounter, but about some ancient, primitive longing desperate to be fulfilled. Leo was more like a destination than a person. Being near him gave me access to something I needed to know.

We lay in bed and watched the big, lazy flakes spiraling down.

"We better see if it's sticking," Leo said.

"It's melting," I said. "I won't have any problems getting home."

"When the time comes, I'll drive you," Leo said.

I got into bed next to him. "I'm freezing," I said.

He warmed me up, and then he smoked a cigarette and put the ashtray on the bed between us.

"Tell me why you think you don't know anything," Leo said.

"I don't," I said. "Nothing that I know sticks together. Rock and roll. Victorian novels. How to drive. I know I'm Jewish and I wouldn't know how to give a proper Seder if my life depended on it."

"There are books devoted to that subject," Leo said.

"You don't understand," I said. "I don't want to be the sort of person who learns about a Seder from books. I want to be the sort of person who knows these things by heart."

"So this isn't about knowing. It's about being."

"It's about knowing and being as the same thing," I said. "There isn't anything *to* being an American. You don't even have to know American history. I mean, *you* know things. You're from Western Civ."

Leo put out his cigarette. "Hush," he said. He put his arms around me. "You have no idea," he said. He kissed my neck and whispered in my ear. "Oh, my America," he said. "My newfound land."

53

It was a cold afternoon. I sat in Mary Abbott's apartment helping her pin up three black skirts and a black denim jumper. These were her postulant's clothes. I had bought her five pairs of black cotton tights and she had bought herself a pair of black sneakers and a pair of plain black walking shoes (for feast days, she said). Under her bed was a tin trunk in which all these things would be packed, including white cotton underwear, cotton socks in white and black, plain white towels, washcloths and a camp blanket.

"Everything in my life is in motion except me," I said. "You're leaving me forever. Johnny's working on a big case, Little Franklin's growing up, and Leo's going to Europe any day."

"I don't get him," said Mary, her mouth full of pins.

"You'd like him," I said. "He's kind of like you."

"I don't mean him personally," Mary said. She spread a skirt over her desk and smoothed it down. "I mean, why you need him."

"My soul sort of cries out to him," I said. "If you get my drift. I don't want to run away with him. I just feel destined to know him."

"You are a pilgrim," Mary said.

"You always say that."

She sat amidst her black clothes, which lay in piles and heaps around her. She had pulled her hair back in a ponytail, which made her look very young and stark. When she took her glasses off to rub her eyes, she looked like a child.

I said, "Most people believe what makes them feel better to believe."
Mary nodded.

"Johnny is unusual in this regard," I said. "He believes what he
needs to believe because he's in the big arena, but he also knows it.
You and Leo don't have any reason to believe anything. Maybe I took
up with Leo because he reminds me of you. Oh, lucky, lucky you! To
know what your life will be like day after day, year after year. And to
think that the life you're living has been lived the exact same way for
centuries."

"I don't think that's much consolation when you're lonely and mis-
erable and thinking that you did the wrong thing."

"Really? You?"

"Everyone. Except people like your friends the Crains. It's man's
fate."

"I just don't want to be left alone surrounded by a bunch of saps."

She pinned up the hem and hung the skirt over a chair, an amazing
sight since I had never seen her sew so much as a button before. Then
she moved all her papers back onto her desk and began sorting
through them. Her dissertation was finished. She was putting in the
footnotes, and then her life would be tidily filed away. She looked
down at her notes.

"Saps," she said. "Martin Luther King, Jr. felt the same way. He said,
'The laxity of the white church in general has caused me to weep tears
of blood.' Is that the way *you* feel?"

"You shut up," I said.

"You ought to sing again," said Mary. "In fact, you should sing right
now. You don't have to go on tour with Ruby to do it. In college you
used to sing all the time. Remember that night you and I and Audrey
Stein got all dressed up and went to Mickey's Rib House and you sang
'Holy Cow'?"

"What a pretty song," I said. "Little Franklin loves it. He seems keen
on the New Orleans sound."

"You sang 'Holy Cow' and 'Nobody Home,'" said Mary. "Everyone
loved it."

"Nobody believed that a white chick had ever heard of Lee Dorsey
or Howard Tate," I said. "Good old Howard Tate."

"You were *good*," said Mary.

"I was okay," I said. "Let's have some tea or something. All this nostalgia is making me hungry."

We went into the kitchen. I sat at Mary's nasty little kitchen table, which we had found on the street and carried upstairs to her apartment one hot summer night. This had always been my second home. When Mary left, I would have only one home. There would never be another place on earth where I would feel as comfortable.

"Sing to me while I boil the water," said Mary.

"Perhaps you'd like to hear 'The Doggie Poop Song,' " I said. "Another of Little Franklin's golden gassers."

"Sing me some Otis Redding," said Mary.

I sang "Good to Me" and "I've Got Dreams to Remember." I sang "Your Feeling Is Mine." Then I sang Smokey and the Miracles' most perfect hit, "I've Been Good to You." We sat at the table and let the water boil away.

"Listen," I said. "When it's time for you to go, I want to drive you up."

"I think I have to go by myself," said Mary.

I felt my scalp tighten.

"Listen," I said. "I only want this one thing. I never asked anything like this before. You're my best friend. Don't deny me this. I'm losing you forever. Don't say no. It's unchristian."

Mary brought our teacups to the table. She put some cookies on a plate. Soon all these things, which were second nature to me, would be in the hands of William Hammerklever, who was taking over the apartment.

"There are some things I want you to have," said Mary. "I want you to take that red cashmere sweater you always liked, and the lamp with the glass globe."

"I want to drive you up," I said.

"I know you do," Mary said. "Get the tear stains off your face. Johnny and Franklin will be here to pick you up any minute."

"I mean it, Mary."

"All right! All right!" Mary said. "I think it's dangerous. You'll just cry the whole time."

"Don't you worry," I said. "I can cry and drive at the same time."

54

Inexorably it was spring. In our neighborhood the snow-drops and crocuses showed their heads. Buds burst out on the trees. From Little Franklin's window sparrows could be seen flying purposefully, their beaks streaming with urban nest-building materials: excelsior, string, shredded gum wrappers, and the papers from drinking straws.

Like an oncoming train, the day of Mary's leaving bore down on me. I sat with her while she packed up her apartment—she was leaving it mostly furnished for William Hammerklever.

"Getting a divorce, huh?" I said.

"Never," Mary said. "He's Catholic. They just won't live together, except for major holidays and the children's birthdays. In fact, they'll always be married."

"And what happens if he falls in love with someone?" I said.

"That's the price he pays."

"Pays for what?"

"Listen, Geralds. The Church has sacraments. You take the sacraments and you pays the price."

I sighed. How neat, I thought. How consoling. Even horrible emotional pain would have a reason, some terrible law one was compelled to obey.

Passover was coming, another oncoming train. I felt some primal urge to celebrate. Surrounded by my relentlessly assimilated family, I had nowhere to go. My parents had never had a Seder. Instead, we went to a series of Seders at the houses of more observant friends. The sense of spring coming, the scent of sweet renewal in the air, made me want to scream in frustration. What, as we learned in Anthropology I, were holidays if not old planting and harvest festivals? Perhaps Hanukkah and Christmas were originally about lighting up the darkest time of the year. It mattered not one jot. These were the oldest stirrings of mankind: that sense of beginning when the air turns light in the spring, or after the first chill in the fall. My deepest stirrings had no formal expression.

Pixie Lehar, whom I could never get used to calling Paulette Goldberg, had invited us for Passover, but the thought of it filled me with despair. I wanted my own.

And so I had taken Leo's advice and had begun a reading project. I read books with titles such as *What It Means to Be a Jew, How to Live a Jewish Life, The Jewish Holidays Observed, The Jewish Household, Jewish Festival Cooking, The Passover Seder, Jewish Ritual in Modern Life*.

Watching me read these night after night, Johnny gave me a funny look. "From Catholic nuns to Jewish life," he said. "What next? Chinese temple structure?"

"This is your son's true heritage," I told him. "At Passover the father of the household goes through the house with a candle and a goose feather looking for *chametz*."

"Oh, yeah?" said my heathen husband. "Does he get to wear a funny hat? And when he finds this stuff, what is it?"

"Leaven," I said. "Any bread or flour hanging around. The woman does the cleaning and the guy does the inspecting."

"How like life," Johnny said. "As you would say."

Like people plunging into swimming pools, I held my nose and plunged. Books were written about such subjects as breast-feeding, gardening and sustained prayer. Other people read them and found them useful. Now that I had done my reading project, was it a terrible presumption for me to have my own Seder?

It would be only the three of us. This was my trial run and I needed privacy. I wanted to have Passover alone in my own house.

I cleaned my kitchen, and since I was not about to sell my flour to our upstairs neighbor for a symbolic penny, I wrapped it in a cloth. Johnny found this oddly touching. While Little Franklin and Amos played with blocks at the kitchen table, I chopped up the *charoses* and gave each boy a taste.

"Yuk" said Franklin. "What's that?"

How was I supposed to tell this innocent creature, for whom the sight of a dead fly on the windowsill was unnerving, about slavery, pestilence, the slaughter of the firstborn?

"What's that stuff?" said Amos, pointing to the box of matzoh.

"It's called matzoh," I said. "It's like bread."

"It's a Saltine with no salt," Amos said.

In the fridge was a nasty-looking shank bone the butcher had given me. Obtaining this bone gave me a thrill. Here I was, a grown-up, making a Passover meal in my own house. The Italian butcher, since he only had call for shank bones once a year, wished me a happy Pesach.

I roasted a boiled egg over the burner.

"Smells," said Franklin.

The morning of Passover, I set the table with a white cloth. The matzoh was wrapped in a clean white napkin. I roasted a chicken and made eggplant caviar, since I did not think I was going to get anyone to eat gefilte fish. At Little Franklin's place I put a cordial glass and a tiny bottle of grape juice for his wine. "Oh, baby wine!" he exclaimed. All over the world people were congregating to celebrate Passover in large groups. What a pathetic table, I thought—three places set by a person who barely knew what she was doing.

I lit the candles and we sat down. It wouldn't be a proper Seder, but at least it would be an *attempt* at a Seder.

"Once upon a time," Johnny said to Franklin, "the Jewish people were slaves." I had made Johnny read the entire Haggadah the night before.

"What are slaves?" Franklin said.

"Slaves," I said helpfully, "are people who have to work all the time."

"Like Daddy," Franklin said.

"No, sweetie," Johnny said. "A slave is someone who is owned by someone else. We don't have that anymore. All men are free."

"I think this is a little over his head," I said.

Johnny was all in favor of this Seder. He liked history and he felt it gave Little Franklin a taste of ancient civilization.

"Slaves work for no money," Johnny said.

"When we do pickup at school we don't get money," Franklin said.

"It isn't the same," I said. "Many thousands of years ago these people had to work for a wicked king called Pharaoh."

This was more up Franklin's street, since he liked the idea of wicked kings.

"And then they didn't work for this guy anymore?" said Franklin.

"That's right," I said. "They had to build bricks—the stuff with the apples in it is supposed to remind us of cement, but it's really delicious. We eat the matzoh because when the Jewish people fled from slavery they didn't have time to bake real bread, so they baked flat bread. All these foods are to remind people of the story."

"Pass over a little of that eggplant, will you, Hon?" said Johnny.

"What's the chicken remind us of?" said Franklin.

"That we are now happy and free and can have a good meal," said Johnny.

"Is this because people aren't mean to each other anymore?" said Franklin.

"Yes, my darling," I said. "That's exactly it."

"Were you Jewish when this bad king made people build bricks?" Franklin asked me.

"That was thousands of years ago," I said. "Now eat your dinner."

55

Like a good former graduate student, I read up on monastic life. This project got a little out of hand since, like many Jewish girls, I seemed fascinated with nuns.

"It's because it was the first and only alternative to wifedom and motherhood," Mary said.

"I think it has more to do with clothes," I said. We were driving upstate in Mary's car. The awful day had come. I had left Franklin and Johnny eating breakfast. Later Amos Potts was coming to play. It was Saturday, and pouring rain. The rain on the roof sounded like drumming on a tin can. Mary had sold her car to William Hammerklever and used the money as her dowry.

"Dowry?" I said.

"Lots of orders have them," she said. "It's refundable if a person wants to leave."

We drove a little while in silence.

"How was it at your parents'?" I asked. She had spent a week with her family in Connecticut.

"Weird," she said. "I mean, they never expected my upbringing to backfire on them this way. They brought me up Catholic. They sent me to Catholic grammar school. They were very taken with modern intellectual Catholicism. My mother used to go down to the city to hear Dorothy Day speak. They never expected this, but they really can't say anything bad about it because it's the logical extension of everything they taught me to believe. Basically they're very bummed out. They get to come and visit in a month."

"And I don't?"

"Come on, Gerry. They're my family."

"I hate family," I said. "They're never the people you want to be connected to. When I was having Franklin I wanted to see *you*. And of course William gets to see you because his brother or something is the chaplain up there."

Mary was silent.

"Admit it," I said. "When the chips are down, I don't count."

"Please, Geraldine," Mary said. Sheets of rain fell all around us. "Watch out. That huge truck is creating a tidal wave."

"Don't worry," I said. "Your faithful servant will not get you killed, and I won't write unless I'm supposed to and I'll bring Little Franklin up to see you when I'm allowed, if I can figure out how to explain all this to him."

"Just tell him I'm a nun."

"He doesn't know anything about nuns," I said. "He doesn't know anything about God. At his age, it's a frightening concept. I know you knew all about this stuff when you were three, but he doesn't. We don't have any context for it."

"That's modern life," Mary said. "Believe me, going into a monastery can be seen as one colossal dodge."

"How interesting," I said. "Is it?"

"Sure," said Mary. "It's like a collapse or surrender. Context all the way. All the kinds of real struggles you have, I won't have. The kind of struggles you get in monasteries are like luxuries. I mean, interior stuff. I don't ever have to make up my life again, and you do."

"Great for me," I said.

"It's a noble struggle."

"Fuck it," I said. "What about my sweet little baby? I'm supposed to provide all this context for him. I can't even get a decent Seder together."

"You'll get it together," Mary said. "You always do. You'll figure it out. You're good at that."

"I'm not," I said.

"You are," Mary said. "Believe me. You second-guess and complain, but you only do what you think is right. That's a fine context for Franklin."

"I think it's much nicer when everything's laid out for you, generation after generation," I said.

We drove in silence. The rain beat furiously on the top of the car. I felt a welling desire to tell Mary everything in the world: what had I forgotten? Each inch of the road brought me closer to the fact that we would never have this sort of time together again. We would visit in the monastery parlor for an hour or so, separated by a railing. We would keep each other up to date by letter. Never again would we be two old friends in a car.

" '*I gave my heart to you, the one that I trusted,*' " Mary sang.

" '*You gave it back to me all broken and busted,*' " I sang. " '*I sold my heart to the junkman and I'll never fall in love again.*' "

"You want to stay to the right," Mary said. "It's the next exit."

We turned off the highway and onto a winding blacktop.

"There's a sign that says St. Scholastica's Abbey," Mary said. "Take this right and then the next left."

We drove down a pleasantly curving road, past an Arabian horse farm on the left and a swamp on the right. Finally we saw the beginning of a fence. The rain had let up slightly.

"That's where the Abbey land begins," Mary said. "It's big. They grow their own food and spin their own wool. Self-sufficient, just like in *The Rule of St. Benedict.*"

"How relaxing," I said.

"I haven't knitted since I was a child," Mary said. "Soon I'll be sitting around knitting scarves for the Summer Fair. You'll come, won't you?"

"Oh, sure," I said. "Me and nine hundred other people."

The fence gave way to an ornate brick wall, and the wall, finally, to an elaborate set of iron gates pulled back to let cars through. We drove down a lane of poplars, past a wide lawn on which sheep grazed, and there, around the curve, lay the monastery—a large farmhouse with wings added on, enclosed by a high wooden wall. At the top of the hill was a small chapel with a steeple.

"That's the enclosure door," Mary said, pointing to a large wooden gate. "When I get out of the car I go into the chapel. Then Mother Veronica takes me to the enclosure door. I knock and the abbess says,

'My child, what do you want?' And I say, 'The grace of God and the holy habit.' And the door opens and in I go."

I had read about this a number of times but it seemed eerie and unsettling that it was happening to someone I loved.

I stopped the car next to the chapel.

"Listen, Gerry," Mary said. "You'll always be my true friend. I've always loved you best. I'll think of you all the time, and Franklin and Johnny and the Man from Western Civ."

"The Man from Western Civ," I repeated.

"Leo," said Mary. "Now listen. After I meet all the nuns, I go to the novitiate and I'm shown my cell, and I put on that denim jumper you helped me sew and my black turtleneck. By the way, thank you for the cotton tights. I would never have found them myself." She seemed slightly out of breath. "Go find a synagogue. When you do, pray for me. I'll pray for you. Believe me, you're the best person I've ever known. You're forthright and true. I'll write in three months. Don't forget to call William about the car. He'll come and pick it up. Call my parents and tell them I'm safe."

She leaned over and got her suitcase from the back. It had begun to rain hard again. When she opened the door, the rain positively roared at us.

"Okay, goodbye," Mary said. "Be true to your school. Pray for me. Kiss Little Franklin." She swung her legs over the side. She was half out of the car. "And leave him," she said.

"Which one?" I shouted after her, but she had already dashed through the rain and into the chapel.

56

I drove straight home where my son and husband were sitting around playing with blocks. I expected my little darling to fly into my arms. Instead, he gave me a smack and told me that his truck was broken.

"He missed you," Johnny said.

I scooped Little Franklin up into my arms. "Are you angry at me because I was away all day?" I said.

"I hate you," said Little Franklin. "You're not my friend."

"I don't hate *you*," I said. "Come and help me cook dinner."

"Daddy and I cooked dinner," he said. "Daddy let me cut up the carrots. How come you don't?"

I called William Hammerklever and arranged for him to pick up the car. I called Mary's parents and told them all was well.

By dinnertime Little Franklin was sitting on my lap. "Amos came," he said. "Winnie came. We played Dog in the Bakery."

"You did?" I said. "What's that?"

"A *game*," said Little Franklin. "Can we eat now?"

We sat down to dinner. Because I could not come home empty-handed, I had stopped at our local bakery and picked up an apple pie —Little Franklin's favorite. He liked the apples and I ate the crust.

Johnny and Franklin had made beef stew from *The Joy of Cooking*.

"Mom," Franklin said. "Do you know what's in this stew?"

"I don't," I said.

He leaned over to me confidentially. *"Ingredients,"* he said. "Tell where you went with Mary, Mama."

"Well," I said, looking at Johnny beseechingly. "There is a place called a monastery. They have a big farm and sheep grazing on the lawn."

"Can we go there?"

"We can go and visit," I said. "Mary is going to be something called a nun. Next time you see her she'll have on a long black dress."

"Why will she wear a dress if she lives on a farm? Will she be a farmer?"

"Well, sort of. It's a very special kind of life. The ladies live in a big building and they sing and pray."

"What's pray?"

"It's when you ask God for something," I said.

"What's God?"

"You know, Pankie," said Johnny. "Remember we read that book about Indians and the Great Spirit? Manatu?"

Franklin did remember, and then he wanted to know if Mary would have a sheep of her very own. This will only get worse, I said to myself as I straightened up the kitchen.

Johnny gave Franklin his bath, but it was my turn to read to him. I lay down next to him and he curled up against me.

"Read," he commanded. Franklin was very fond of the *Just So Stories.* He had a long attention span for a little boy. He wanted me to read "The Cat That Walked by Himself."

" 'Hear and attend and listen,' " I began. " 'For this befell and behappened and became and was, O my Best Beloved, when the tame animals were wild.' "

"What's wild?" said Little Franklin.

"It means they live in the forest or the wilderness and are not pets or farm animals."

My son snuggled up closer and put his head on my shoulder. He smelled of soap. I could barely contain my feelings. My little boy was very tired. His eyes kept closing, and then he opened them, turned his pillow over and changed position. When he turned on his side, I believed he was almost asleep. I stopped reading.

"Read," his little voice commanded.

I read and read, and still my boy was not asleep. I kissed him and hugged him.

"No kissing," he said sleepily. "Read."

He turned over his pillow again and curled up on his side.

"Read," he said.

I read very slowly, remembering what one of the nursery teachers had said: that if we did things at a child's true pace, the world would move with incredible slowness.

" 'Out in the Wet Wild Woods all the wild animals wondered what had happened to Wild Dog,' " I continued. " 'And at last Wild Horse stamped with his wild foot and said: I will go and see and say why Wild Dog has not returned. Cat, come with me.

" ' "Nenni!" said the Cat. "I am the Cat who walks by himself, and all places are alike to me." ' "

My voice wavered and the words swam on the page, but it did not matter: my little boy had finally gone to sleep.

PART FIVE

Underwater

57

The man who swam next to me—I believed he was called Mr. Jacobowitz—lumbered in the water, a heavy, hulking walruslike presence. He was large, old, barrel-chested, and swam a steady breast-stroke. I found him the perfect person to pace myself with. Three mornings a week I swam in a pool near work, courtesy of Mrs. Hornung, for whom I had done a couple of favors. I had cheerfully photo-copied a whole sheaf of her tax papers, and after a conversation about hot chocolate, I had found the very brand of cocoa she remembered from her youth—unavailable in her neighborhood—and had given her two tins of it.

When I presented them to her she was as delighted as if I had retrieved her great-grandmother's long lost jewels. She was the widow of Caspar Hornung, the biographer of Moses Mendelssohn, and an old friend of Bernard and Gertje's: she had known Bernard's mother, the sainted Sophie Regenstein. Mrs. Hornung was small, with glowing cheeks, and white hair pulled back in a bun. One day I asked her why her hair was wet and she told me about her pool.

"A lovely place!" said Mrs. Hornung. "So soothing. Do you swim?"

I said I did.

"All American girls do, yes?" said Mrs. Hornung. "When I was a girl in Munich we had such a swimming club! And, of course, after we swam we went out to stuff ourselves with cakes. We were such gooses! You know, I am allowed one guest at my pool but I have no one to be my guest. I am the only old lady I know who swims. My granddaughters live in California. Geraldine. You know, they go *surfing.* It is so strange for me. These great big American girls in those black rubber clothes —how do you call these?"

"Wet suits," I said, looking down at her.

Mrs. Hornung clapped her hands together. "Exactly so!" she said. "Wet suits! It is quite terrifying to watch. I stand on the shore and say, This is the *Pacific* Ocean, and these big girls with blond hair are my *granddaughters.* And you know, Geraldine?" She dropped her voice. "Although they are Jewish, frankly they look exactly like those blond girls from the Nazi propaganda posters."

Her pool was in a small building owned by the Heinrich Heine Haus. A group of writers and artists had scrounged together the money to buy the building many years ago as a cultural center, and then, courtesy of a rich benefactor, had built the pool. It was Olympic-sized, tiled in black and white and overseen by a ferocious woman named Martine who checked your name against a list on a clipboard every time you came. To be a guest member cost three hundred dollars, which I paid out of my Ruby and Vernon money. I had not gone swimming in years, except to splash around in the lake at my mother-in-law's with Little Franklin.

My first time at the pool, I went with Mrs. Hornung, who wore a shapeless swimming garment. She said to me, "I look terrible, no? I am seventy-nine, but I assure you, Geraldine, that if I do not swim I look much, much worse. My poor suit, you see, has this white worm disease. The chlorine eats the material and the little white rubber threads poke their heads through, so."

After I had been introduced to Martine, handed over my check and entered my name in the guest book, Mrs. Hornung and I entered the water.

She swam an idiosyncratic backstroke, pulling both arms back at the same time and fluttering her little feet. She looked exactly like one of Franklin's bath toys, a wind-up woman who swam around in a circle.

On rainy days I was often the only person in the pool. I was always the youngest. These men and women, all elderly, seemed content in a way I could not understand. They had been uprooted from their homelands. Many of them—there were a number of people with numbers on their wrists—had been through things more terrible than I could imagine. They had had everything taken away from them: their language, their landscape, their sense of stability, and here they were, greeting each other happily in German, English and Yiddish, complaining about their hairdressers or dentists or stockbrokers, comparing the prices of shoes at Saks Fifth Avenue, and swimming up and down, up and down, in a slow, determined way.

The ceiling of the pool was blue, and often, when imitating Mrs. Hornung for a lap or two to stretch my shoulders, I felt as if I were suspended between two skies. I had not felt so effortless since my days on stage, when I often danced myself into what felt like a state of weightlessness. I could make my body do anything I wanted it to. At the best times there was no mind or body, just one flowing, sliding unit.

None of my friends except Mary had ever seen me perform. By the time I was on the road awhile my friends had faded away—except for Mary, who was not Ruby's biggest fan. She liked Ruby's early hits. When I came on the tour, Ruby was into her middle period, which was less raw and more jive. Mary often said she could hear in her mind what Ruby would eventually become: a kind of millionaire torch singer backed by a double orchestra.

The first time I sang solo, Mary was in the audience. A ring of light surrounded the Shakettes. Ruby stood in darkness on the other side of the stage. Doo-Wah stepped forward and played his riff. Then Grace and Ivy stepped back and I was alone in the light. I sang:

You don't love me like you used to do
Darling it's just, just, just not the same anymore
I'll always love you no matter what you do
Even if you don't love me like you used to do.

Then Ruby stepped into her spotlight, and Grace and Ivy joined me in mine. It was the most thrilling moment of my life.

I dipped underwater and heard myself sing it in my head. I used to sing it to Johnny, and I had sung it to Little Franklin as a lullaby when he was a baby.

As I swam my laps, one crawl, one breaststroke, I thought of Hannah Hausknecht, who had described sitting on the steps of the children's barracks at Auschwitz singing:

Was müssen das für Bäume sein
Wo die grossen Elephanten spatzieren gehen
Ohne anzustossen.

What kind of a tree is it, I asked myself, where the big elephants can take a walk or promenade without bumping their heads?

My college German was slowly coming back to me, and sometimes at night I found myself singing this very song to Franklin, always a big fan of elephants, in his bath.

58

One night while wandering around the neighborhood I stopped in front of the Neighborhood Synagogue, which I had been cruising for months, and saw that the door was open. It was a square building that looked something like a Quaker meetinghouse. A sign on the gate announced the times of services and that Rabbi Noah Pivnik would speak on the subject "What Are Jews For?" In the lobby I found an old black man wearing a skullcap and talking to a large orange cat. I was not prepared to see either of them.

"Hi," I said. "Is the synagogue open tonight?"

The man pointed at a room on the right. I poked my head in the door. There was a man—his back was to me—putting children's books onto a shelf. He was small and square. In fact he looked a little like one of those man-shaped blocks in a set called *Bill Ding*. He wore a crocheted skullcap, and when he turned to me I saw that he had a pleasant, mournful face and a shock of thick brown hair.

"Are you looking for someone?" he asked.

"Yes. I mean, no."

"I see," the man said. "Confused, right?"

"Listen," I said. "Do you teach Hebrew to grown-ups?"

The man smiled. He looked like a tired but kindly doctor.

"We call them adults," he said. "Class starts tonight. Would you like to join?"

"Oh, I couldn't," I said. "I mean, I don't know anything."

"Can that be?" the man said. "Everyone knows *something*."

"About being Jewish," I said.

"Oh, that's a different story," the man said. "But that's what education is all about. I'm Ben Cohen. I'm the head of the religious school."

"Would you take me?" I said. "Do I have to sign up?"

"There's nothing to sign," Ben Cohen said. "Just sit down. We don't charge, but you can make a donation to the synagogue if you like."

I looked at him as a starving dog might look at a steak.

"Thank you," I said. "I'm a complete moron."

"Take it easy," Ben Cohen said. "Don't be anxious. I can teach anyone. Tell me a little about yourself."

I told him a little—I felt I could have gone on all night. It seemed to me that he had heard it all before.

"Don't worry," he said. "I've turned Methodists into Jews. You at least have a head start. We also have classes for children and reluctant spouses."

I sat in my chair and waited for my classmates to appear. There was a woman my age, an elderly woman and a few older men. We were given a beginner's workbook, the kind, Ben Cohen told us, that he gave to the seven-year-olds.

For the next few minutes Ben Cohen talked to us. He swore that if we applied ourselves we would be following the prayer book within six months. "You might not know what you're reading, but you'll read," he said.

I looked down at my book. On each page was a series of Hebrew letters and a little picture of a sturdy-looking boy and girl engaged in such tasks as cooking, woodworking and greeting their father at the end of the day. The father wore a hat and the mother wore an apron. He carried a briefcase; she, a tray of cookies. I stared at the meaningless black shapes and realized that Little Franklin saw almost the same thing when I read to him. Since the letters in his books were as incomprehensible to him as the Hebrew letters to me, he was crazy about punctuation, which he could easily identify, and he knew everything from an exclamation point to an ampersand, which was his personal favorite.

Then we were asked to say who we were and why we were there. Mrs. Singer was eighty years old, a large woman with pure white hair who said she was tired of coming to services and not having a clue what she was reciting. Mr. Pizer, a businessman in his fifties, had made a five-thousand-dollar bet with his aged father that he would master the prayer book. Mr. Kapock said that if he learned Hebrew his wife had promised him a bar mitzvah—he had never had one as a boy—with a real orchestra. Erna Wilson was a serious-looking redheaded schoolteacher who was converting from Methodism to marry her Jewish sweetheart. Then it was my turn.

"I'm a kind of wandering Jew," I said. "I wander around trying to figure out how to be Jewish. It's the problem assimilated people who never had any traditional upbringing have. You know you're Jewish. You just don't know *how* to be Jewish."

"Don't worry," said Ben Cohen. "We've dealt with characters like you before."

"But you already have a Jewish identity," said Mr. Kapock. "You already *know* what you are."

"It doesn't seem to be enough," I said. "I want to know how to be what I am."

Then we got down to business. I had not studied anything in years and I was daunted by how hard I found it.

"Once you learn the vowels, you won't need them anymore," Ben Cohen said. "In newspapers they leave them out."

"They *what?*" shrieked Mr. Pizer.

"You won't need them, I swear it," Ben Cohen said.

"Oh, my God," said Mrs. Singer. "They told me the brain hardens with age. Mine is like a block of stone. They give us the vowels and then they take them away."

"Now, now," said Ben Cohen. "Really, I could teach Hebrew to this pencil."

"That pencil is smarter than I am," said Mr. Pizer.

Johnny was considerably surprised when I told him what I had done on my night out. He assumed I had gone to a movie, but I flung my beginner's Hebrew book down on the bed beside him. He looked through it. "A fiendish people, these Hebrews," he said.

"You're a Hebrew, too, and don't you forget it," I said.

The next morning Franklin seized upon my book. "What's this, Mom?" he said.

"It's Mommy's Hebrew book, Pankie," said Johnny.

"Don't call me that baby name," said my boy.

"What would you like me to call you?" Johnny said.

"Call me Mr. Franklin," said Little Franklin. "Mom, can I have your Hebrew book? Can I, Mom? Is it mine?"

"No, it's mine," I said. "But you can look at it."

"It's not fair," said Franklin. "Read it to me, Mommy."

"I can't," I said. "I'm just learning."

My son gave me a curious look. It had not occurred to him that adults ever had to learn anything. When I was a child I had been given to understand that grown-ups knew everything, and I had never heard of one studying anything.

On the way to school, my son told Amos and Ann Potts that I could read Hebrew.

"A new fact revealed," Ann said. "I didn't know you could do that."

"I can't," I said. "I was thinking of taking a class and last night I found one. It doesn't look easy."

"It's so restful to belong to a religion that requires you only to read English," Ann said. "Protestantism actually requires next to nothing. Jews and Catholics always seem to be so *busy*, what with Mass and nuns and all those holidays, and Latin or Hebrew. Being a Protestant takes up so little time, but it comes in handy for those special days like Christmas, Easter and weddings."

Little Franklin and Amos walked ahead of us. They were the same size and wore almost the same clothes: blue jeans, sneakers and T-shirts. The morning sun glinted off their hair.

I thought of all the things I would be unable to give my boy without a monumental effort: a sense of community, a sense of order in the universe. I could not imagine him at thirteen studying his Hebrew lesson while I watched. I said as much to Ann.

"Oh, don't be silly," she said. "Order in the universe—who needs it? When he's thirteen I'll give him a fountain pen and you can *say* he had a bar mitzvah."

59

Although I ought to have been used to it, I found it hard to say goodbye to Franklin in the morning. I stood in his classroom watching him and his little mates hard at work—painting, woodworking, making block buildings on the floor —for a few minutes until my beloved child made me realize that it was time for me to go.

Often as I left I felt I was crossing a physical barrier. My life was divided into four parts: school, family, work and swimming. Under the category of swimming I put Leo Rhinehart and my newly acquired Hebrew lessons. Both of these were another element, like water.

As I opened the door to the office I heard Dr. Frechtvogel coughing. I could smell him before I saw him. The very air that surrounded him was permeated with cigar smoke.

"Where is the mail?" he demanded.

"It's not here yet."

"There is no law in this country!" he barked. "This is a lawless outpost! There is no civilization where a man cannot count on routine mail delivery."

He shook his ashes at me, scattering them on his sleeves. I brushed them off.

"When I was young in Vienna," Dr. Frechtvogel said, "I hired a servant to do just this and brush the ashes away. I called this person Aschenbecker. Now you have replaced him. Ah! I hear the mail."

He tore out of the room, flung the door open and bearded the mailman by the elevator.

"What is the meaning of this outrage!" he shouted at the cowering mailman. "What have you been doing to waste time that the mail is so late! I will complain to the postal department."

The mailman, who was used to this treatment, leaned against the wall and said, "Hey, Doc. Don't beat up on me."

"The post office is a disgrace!" yelled Dr. Frechtvogel.

At this point I took him by the arm and led him back to the office, where I knew the sight of the delivered mail would pacify him. He pawed through the stack of letters, as mollified as an occupied child.

Our office was obsessed with the affair of Manfred Kirschbaum, who had retreated to Paris and spent his time sending threatening letters, or commanding his French lawyers to write to Bernard saying that they would sue him for denying Kirschbaum the right to publish what the lawyers believed to be an authentic manuscript by the great Felix Kindervater.

"It is a fraud," said Dr. Frechtvogel, smoothing out a letter. "Here is proof. Oh, I forget—you don't read German with ease. This manuscript is a sham."

"Gee, do you think Manfred wrote it?"

"We will never know," said Dr. Frechtvogel. "The world is full of such little mysteries. All his work, all ours, all yours—nothing! This matter will evaporate and we will never hear of Kirschbaum again. He will live off the Bonfiglio like a sponge."

"And will that be the end of it?"

"It will vanish as smoke," said Dr. Frechtvogel. "I am very old. The Kirschbaums of the world are very tiresome. I have seen a great many of them. Kirschbaum is a little scoundrel. There are much worse." He closed his eyes and smoked his cigar.

"I started taking Hebrew lessons," I said. Dr. Frechtvogel did not open his eyes. "I think I'm going to take a course in Jewish history. I want Franklin to have some sense of heritage." I looked at him, wondering if he had fallen asleep.

Suddenly he bounded out of his chair and began to shout. "Make him an American!" he said. "Do not confuse him with this silly business. Religion makes war! There would be no Holocaust without religion. One has it, the other hates it. Be glad your boy is a nice American.

Take him to baseball games. Let him spend his money on bubble gum."

"But what will he know?" I said. "Where will he get his sense of identity?"

Dr. Frechtvogel sat down in his chair and closed his eyes. "He will be himself. He will be himself in the cosmos," he said. "If you are worried, plant a garden. Take him to the Planetarium."

"We did plant a garden," I said. "Franklin planted a bunch of sunflower seeds and almost drove himself crazy until they sprouted. Johnny took him to the Planetarium, but it was too scary."

Dr. Frechtvogel motioned for me to relight his cigar.

"I just want him to have what I didn't have," I said.

"I will die soon," he said.

"Oh, don't do that," I said.

"I wish to die," he said. "Last week I went to visit Mrs. Weinberg. Along the way a large man came and demanded my money. He says I must give him my money or he will kill me. I said, '*Kill me at once*! I long to die. I am very old.' "

"What did he do?"

"He dropped his knife and ran away," said Dr. Frechtvogel.

His face had the sheen of parchment. He resembled one of the big cats that drowse, fully alert, with its eyes closed. His great eyebrows shot up, but he wore a faint smile, like a sleeping newborn or a Buddha.

"I don't want you to die," I said, sitting in the chair next to him. Dr. Frechtvogel took my hand. His was as soft and worn as an old kid glove. "I need you to be alive," I said. "Are you sick?"

"I have had enough of life," said Dr. Frechtvogel. "I will be happy to enter heaven, where I can smoke in peace."

"I didn't know you believed in heaven," I said. "How do you know you'll go there, anyway?"

"As I get closer," said Dr. Frechtvogel, "I believe it more. It is pleasant to think about. A quiet place, some splashing water, just like in the Heinrich Heine poem. A nice girl like you to bring lunch and some decent cigars. But I would also find eternal nothingness very agreeable."

"I need you," I said.

"And for what?"

"I need you to be in my life," I said. "You know things I don't know. Where I come from, everyone is the same. We grew up the same. Nothing terrible ever happened. We're the treacherous innocent Americans you rail about all the time."

Dr. Frechtvogel patted my hand. "You have Leo," he said. "Although he is like a library book and must be returned, yes?"

"Yes," I said. "But it isn't the same."

"You will learn, my dear child, when you get older, that it is all the same, " said Dr. Frechtvogel. "Or very near."

60

One morning I was taken aside in front of the school by Paulette Goldberg, the former Pixie Lehar.

"Oh, hey," she said. "I hope you don't mind, but I put your name in to the board as entertainment for the school fair."

I stared at her.

"It's traditional to have parents perform. Remember last year? We had Janice Bracken, who plays the fiddle. She's done it for years but her daughter is graduating, so I thought you would be perfect."

I continued to stare.

"They were thrilled and amazed," she continued. "I mean, when I said you had backed up Ruby. Nobody knew that about you. They were just overwhelmed. They want to advertise and everything."

"It's totally out of the question," I said.

"Oh, come *on*," Paulette said. "It's for the school. No one's asking you to take your clothes off. Think about it."

I thought about it. "No," I said.

"You could get Doo-Wah to back you up. He'd do it for you, right? There's a couple of musicians in the school. You could do 'You Don't Love Me Like You Used to Do,' " she said. "Or 'Hi-Heel Sneakers.' "

"That isn't really one of Ruby's songs," I said.

"She did it once at the Newark Armory. I saw her, and you were backup," Paulette said.

"It's totally out of the question," I said.

"I don't get it," Paulette said. "I mean, are you ashamed or something?"

"Why don't *you* do it?" I said.

"Because I was a dud," Paulette said. "It wasn't just drugs why Vernon fired me. I was really pretty terrible. He did some deal with Big Thing, or maybe it was Little Ed, I don't remember, and he like owed them. That's how I got hired in the first place, and then Vernon realized that I was a lousy singer and a terrible dancer, and in addition to which Spider used to come around with his neat brown heroin and that was Vernon's excuse. But you were sensational. You had it all right. I heard Vernon say that you were the best he had ever seen, so think about it, okay?"

I had plenty of time to think. That weekend we were going to Johnny's parents in the country. Each year they gave their enormous presummer party to which the entire community was invited. My parents would be there, and I was pressed into service. The lake would be open for swimming. Family photographs would be taken. I would be introduced and reintroduced to a large number of people and their accomplished offspring, who sat on plaid blankets on the beach with an air of perfect security—the product of peace and prosperity, good schools, balanced diet, high-tech dental care, up-to-the-minute immunizations, continental travel, and enough money to foster excellent sleeping habits.

As I packed for the country I told Johnny that Pixie Lehar had nominated me as entertainment for the school fair.

"Great!" Johnny said. "I think that's wonderful. You never sang enough with Ruby. I remember the first time I heard you. It was in Portland, or someplace like that. You sang the beginning of 'Love Makes Me Feel So Bad.' It was thrilling."

"It's out of the question," I said. "They want to advertise it."

My husband sat on the bed wearing his lawyer's trousers and a ruined T-shirt with a faded picture of Little Richard on it. On the back it said THE QUASAR OF ROCK. He was barefoot, and the *Wall Street Journal* was spread in front of him. His duffel bag was neatly packed: he was an organized fellow, my Johnny.

"So what if they advertise?" Johnny said. "It'll make a lot of money for the school."

"Listen," I said. "I don't want to do it. I don't want to be identified as something I can't do anymore. It only reinforces my feeling that I'm a used-to-be."

"You can still do it," Johnny said. "You can't be a backup, but you can be a front-up."

"You don't want me to let this go," I said. "You need me to keep this thing going so you can feel that the real world of adults and lawyers hasn't sealed you up. If I stop being an ex-Shakette, the last shred of your old true self is gone."

Johnny was silent. He knew this was perfectly true.

"Okay," he said. "So maybe I do need you to be an ex-Shakette. What's so horrible about that? What's so horrible about the fact that you need me to be an adult and a straight-bag so you can be marginal? If you weren't married to me you would be living in some furnished room someplace, working at some marginal job."

Now I was silent. That was quite true, too.

"It's pretty depressing," I said.

"No, it isn't," said my always optimistic husband. "The past is unde niable. You were a Shakette. You were a terrific singer. You were a great dancer. Wouldn't you like Little Franklin to see you perform?"

"Sure," I said. "And then I'll take him down to court and he can watch you argue a case."

"Listen, honey. It's the same thing. I have to wail and boogie too. That's what arguments in court are all about."

We discussed it the next morning at breakfast.

"It's out of the question," I said again.

"What's out in the question, Mommy? What is it? What did Daddy mean?" said Little Franklin.

"We were just having a family discussion," I said.

"I want to have a family discuss too!" said Franklin.

"Please eat your breakfast," I said, "and then I have to pack your clothes for the country."

"Can I take my bathing suit?" said Franklin. "I want my bathing suit. Can I take it with me, Mommy?"

"You can take it, but it may not be warm enough for swimming," I said.

"I want it to be warm. Okay, Mommy?"

He said this several thousand more times while I packed his bag, made the bed and put away the dishes.

As we walked to school he said, "Can I swim without my swimming wings, Mom? Can I go out to the float? Can I run on the dock? Will Evelyn be the lifeguard? Will Jessie give me swimming lessons? Can I go frogging? Can I go swimming all day long? Can I swim in the big people's part? Look, Mommy! There's Amos."

Ann and Amos came up alongside us.

"I'm losing my mind," I said.

"And I, mine," Ann said. "I've lost my verbs, a bad sign."

"They think I should perform at the school fair," I said.

"Hey, far out," said Ann. "Theme night! I'll wear my tie-dyed dress."

"Johnny wants me to."

"I want you to," Ann said.

"I can't stand up in front of all those people," I said.

"You used to stand up in front of thousands of people," said Ann.

"But these people are people I *know*," I said.

"So what?"

"So I'm Little Franklin's mother," I said. "I can't just throw on my dance dress and be someone else."

"You won't be," said Ann. "I mean, they're both the same person aren't they? Besides, you're not going to let a little thing like being Franklin's mother stand in your way, are you?"

61

As we pulled into the long driveway of Johnny's parents' house, a striped caterer's truck pulled up in back of us and out hopped two sleek young men dressed all in white carrying dozens of large white paper boxes. Johnny dropped his duffel bag to help bring them in; I was left with Franklin's bag, my bag and the duffel, and a child who had been transformed from a zippy, bouncing person to a dreamy infant crawling along the ground.

"Franklin, what *are* you doing?" I said.

"I'm looking for worms," said my boy, "I am a worm. I'm a worm today, Mommy. Daddy said there would be lots of worms and I could take them home in a jar. Okay?"

The Millers' summer house was a low, Japanese-looking sprawl set beautifully along a winding forest road in a clearing in the sun. In the front of it was Dolly's cutting garden, and in the back was Herbert's attempt at shrubbery, each winter eaten down to little stubs by white-tailed deer.

The Millers spent every weekend of their existence in this place, and their annual summer party was a tradition.

It was abnormally hot for May. The sky was gray and heavy. It looked as if it might eventually storm. The gnats and no-see-'ems swirled around my head like a turban. But inside Dolly's house everything was crisp. There was no surface that did not feel clean to the touch, and there was not a frill or unnecessary object anywhere.

"This party is going to be a steam bath," Johnny said.

"Well, we'll encourage everyone to go outside," Dolly said. "Herbert, get the flambeaux and the mosquito coils. We'll need them for the bugs."

In the cellar were enormous candlelike incense sticks that emitted a strong, pleasantly flavored smoke. Dolly uttered a prayer against rain, and went down to the cellar to bring up the carton of citronella candles in little tin buckets.

Down at the beach it was easy to see that by nightfall it would storm. The lavender and gray clouds hung heavily over the water. The beach was a sandy sward cut out of the forest, with a gravel path leading down to it.

It was as hot and as close as August. Dolly, who kept in excellent trim, wore a tank suit under her white ducks and sailor shirt. She brought a big plaid stadium blanket, a basket of fruit and fruit juice, and the morning paper. There was hardly a soul at the beach she did not know, and if some young couple she had never seen before— some new summer renters—appeared, she had them pegged within three days.

This comfortable beach, Dolly's comfortable house, the abundant good food, the beauty of the landscape, somehow made me feel that there was not quite enough oxygen for me. In the comfortable bedroom, from whose picture window I could see grosbeaks, juncos and chickadees perched on the bird feeder, I longed for my own home.

There was no escape. I longed to fall asleep or take a walk, but this weekend, like many of Dolly's weekends, was rigorously planned. The day after the party we would have pancakes for breakfast and then go walking to see the Devlins, and then we would have lunch at the beach, followed by a barbecue at the beach club. My one out was Little Franklin, who would, after all, have to go to bed early.

I never got over my intuition that I was not presentable enough for Dolly, and the beach always gave me a quiver of dread. At the height of the season, arrayed on towels, were her friends, their children and numerous, stunning grandchildren. These small children wore T-shirts announcing the schools they went to, all approved of by Dolly, who did not like the idea that her grandchild went to a school so few people had heard of.

Fortunately the beach was almost empty—it was too muggy, too stormy. Three white-haired ladies played cards. Two big boys—at least eight years old—horsed around by the dock. Johnny and Franklin splashed in the water, or Franklin practiced jumping off the dock, crying out *"Geronimo!"* as his father had taught him.

I heaved myself off the blanket, where Dolly and Herbert sat reading the paper. I put on my cap and goggles.

"I'm going for a swim," I said.

I stood up to my shoulders in water and closed my eyes. When I looked back at the beach it seemed the whole world had frozen—an optical trick. The next instant the color came back into everything, but in that eerie purplish light everyone seemed drained, like people in a faint.

The water was perfect: not cold, not warm. The lake spread out in front of me.

I swam a slow, easy crawl, out to the float and past the markers. I felt my body move easily through the water. I was a fish, a whale, a creature that belonged in water. There was perfect sympathy between me and the lake. When I looked back, I saw the beach had grown considerably smaller, and when I finally heard shouting, I was halfway across.

It was wonderful and terrible. I had never swum so well, I could not bear to stop. Life gives few moments of such ease—dancing on stage was one, sitting in a rocker with the infant Franklin was another. I was not going to stop. I was going to cause a hitch in this perfectly set-up day. Johnny would have to drive the car around to the other side to get me. I would drip all over the seat, even though Dolly would have remembered to send a towel.

My happiness, for the moment, was boundless. I thought of Mr. Jacobowitz—I pretended he was swimming next to me like a big, friendly seal. I savored the silver taste of lake water in my mouth and swam, arm over arm, to the destination before me.

62

Dr. Frechtvogel died in his sleep on the very morning that his cleaning lady came, which, as Gertje pointed out, was so considerate of him, rather than, for example, dying on the weekend when no one would have found him.

It turned out he had left detailed instructions for his funeral. It was to take place at a small Italian funeral parlor in the Village—his cleaning lady's husband's funeral had been held there, and Dr. Frechtvogel had found it congenial. He left his money to Gertje and his books to Bernard. To Buddy he left his gold watch. He had had few personal effects, but he had set something aside for Franklin.

"Geraldine," Gertje said. "There are a few things I must talk with you about for the funeral. And here is something for Little Franklin that Ludwig wanted him to have."

She put a heavy package in my hand, wrapped in batting.

"Now, before you open it," she said. "I must tell you that Ludwig left a letter of instructions for his funeral. No preaching, no service. He wants me to speak, and Bernard, and a few old friends. He wants no music except you to sing."

"Me to sing?" I said.

"Yes," she said. "He wants you to sing 'The Tennessee Waltz.' Do you know this song?"

I nodded my head.

"Well, will you sing it? I will introduce you and say it was Ludwig's last wish, so you will not feel strange to sing a popular song at a funeral."

There was no way out of this, I knew. "It's too corny," I said.

"Well, Ludwig was an old cornball, I believe is the expression," said Gertje.

"Why did he want this?" I said.

"Well, he loved you and you are a singer," Gertje said. "He often said it was the only American song he knew." She gave me a hard look. "I think this singing business is hard on you," she said. "Here, open Little Franklin's package."

Inside the batting was a silver elephant that had been Dr. Frechtvogel's as a child. I looked away, but Gertje put her arms around me.

"Come, come, Geraldine," said Gertje. "He knew you loved him so."

"I didn't get to know him long enough. I wanted to know him forever."

"You do know him forever," Gertje said. "He is in your memory. Come, call the florist. Ludwig would have hated flowers, but his ladies will expect them."

The little funeral parlor was like a bower. Dr. Frechtvogel's ladies had sent flowers by the tubs. They came in bunches themselves, looking like flowers. Hannah Hausknecht wore a peacock blue linen suit and wiped her eyes with a big lace handkerchief. Mrs. Gusta Klein and Mrs. Eva Klein walked in together, and behind them came Mrs. Charlotte Klein, who had married the American captain who liberated her from Buchenwald. Dr. Frechtvogel had told me that she emerged from her barracks, half dead of typhus, a walking skeleton, and said to Captain Klein, "Thank you for rescuing us. We are not so glamorous as we once were."

There was Mrs. Weinberg, who had watched all the windows of her father's department store smashed on Kristallnacht, and old Mrs. Yvanski, whose entire family had perished. The lady in purple turned out to be the waitress from the coffee shop where Dr. Frechtvogel had his morning oatmeal, and there were dozens more: people who had worked for the original Hansonia Society, old men who had come to Dr. Frechtvogel for legal advice.

Buddy, splendid in an English suit, expensive shoes and a silk scarf around his neck, performed the function of usher.

Once they were seated, everyone peered around. No one had ever been in a room like this before.

The walls were covered with silver paper flocked with fuzzy red fleurs-de-lis. In several large niches were statues of the Virgin Mary and the Infant of Prague. On either side of a small altar stood two urns containing sprays of electric roses: in the center of each rose was a tiny light bulb. In a corner candles flickered in red glasses. The room smelled of incense and candle wax.

Because I was to sing, I sat down in the front, but, turning just a little, I could see Leo with his mother and his aunt, who wore a picture hat.

When everyone was settled, Gertje stood up. She was wearing a black suit I had never seen before and carried a large, flower-printed handkerchief.

"It was Ludwig's wish to have a memorial service in this place," she began. "He had been to a funeral here and he liked it very much. Ludwig felt it was the ideal place for him. His mother was a Jew, and his father was a Catholic. All of us who knew Ludwig know how distrustful he was of religion of any kind, but he made an exception for this little funeral place. He said to me, 'When I die, let them come to this place and sit together, and let whoever wants to speak, speak. Then feed them some cakes and tell them to go home.' "

The cakes, which I had helped carry down from the Vienna Café, were waiting in their pink and white boxes on a table in the small reception room.

That morning I had left my family setting, which was often as cozy as a little den with three bears in it, and had come out into a world of which my husband and child knew nothing. An integrated person might have invited Dr. Frechtvogel home for dinner, but I never had. I did not think Johnny would get him, or he would get Johnny. Besides, Dr. Frechtvogel did not like innovation. On Mondays he had dinner with Mrs. Gusta Klein, on Tuesdays with Mrs. Weinberg. On Wednesdays he ate dinner with Bernard and Gertje. Thursday was reserved for Mrs. Mueller, and Fridays he had dinner with his sister-in-law, who now sat in the front row wearing a black veil. On Saturdays he dined with Frau Dr. Zeller, the psychoanalyst, and on Sundays he refused to go anywhere.

Suddenly, with a great volley of coughs, Bernard stood up at the podium and began his speech. He explained that Ludwig had never worked for him. Ludwig had *visited* him. He had stopped by many, many years ago and had never left. And although what he mostly did was smoke and kibitz with his lady friends, he had been an invaluable adviser and friend.

Then Buddy stood up and said more or less the same thing. Buddy had recently closed his second business deal and was on his way to achieving his childhood dream of making a million dollars before he was twenty-one. It was said he was keeping company with a much older woman who ran a small real estate empire.

After Buddy, a parade of ladies stood to speak in German, French and English. Plain and fancy handkerchiefs were taken from handbags. The men blew their noses. I wiped my eyes on my sleeve.

Then Gertje stood up again.

"Those of us who loved Ludwig knew that he had no ear for music. He came to this country and said, 'Everywhere you go they play the radio. They play music in their cars and in their coffee shops.' He said his ears were made of tin. The only song he knew was 'The Tennessee Waltz.' He could actually hum it: I have heard him. He asked that this be sung at his funeral by Geraldine Miller, who works for us and who used to be a professional singer. As for Geraldine, he loved her very much. He did not allow new people into his life but he made an exception for her. Please, Geraldine, stand up."

I stood. My knees were made of water. I had not told Johnny that I had been asked to sing. I just wanted to do it and get it over with. I took a deep breath and began.

The chapel was a perfect place to sing in. It made your voice carry —some rooms are like that. I had forgotten how wonderful it felt. When I finished, everyone was in tears. Gertje stood up and told them to come into the lobby for coffee. I wanted to slink out, but Leo caught me by the sleeve.

"Ludwig would have loved that," he said. "Please have lunch with me."

We stayed in the lobby to have coffee, and when people began to drift out in groups of three and four, Leo and I walked to a bar near Franklin's school and ordered sandwiches.

"You're going away, aren't you?" I said.

"My fellowship came through," Leo said. "I'm going to Berlin for a year."

"I'm sorry," I said. "I mean, I'm glad."

"I'm glad and sorry, too," Leo said.

"Well, everyone I know is going away. My friend Mary Abbott, who lived near you, has gone into a monastery, and now Ludwig is going to heaven. And my little boy is turning four and growing up."

Leo took off his glasses, held them to the light and squinted at them. Then he wiped them on a napkin and put them back on.

"I'll always remember the first time I saw you, dancing with Ludwig," he said. "You can't imagine the delight it would have given him to have you sing at his funeral. I'm so sorry he missed it."

"I didn't want to do it, you know," I said.

"But you did it," Leo said. "Geraldine"—he had never called me by my name before—"I want to say something . . . I'm not sure what. Being with you made me happy."

"Really?" I said.

"Oh, yes," Leo said. "Maybe we were a little bit in love with each other, and maybe we just needed to know each other."

I drank my iced tea to keep my throat from closing.

"And now we will vanish like dust," I said.

"Oh, no!" Leo said. "It's not like that at all. It is my job to go off to Berlin, and it's your job to bring up your child. We aren't meant to be together, but we're important to each other. Unless I've got this all wrong."

"You've got it all right," I said.

"But it's our job to know each other," Leo said. "Why can't we do that? I need to know you. You're a four-square, right-on American."

"Yes, and you're the Man from Western Civ," I said.

"Well, you're the Girl from Rock and Roll. I think your going on tour was a wonderful thing to do. I really admire you for it."

"Wonderful!" I said. "You speak three languages and you know European history, and you think it was wonderful that I was a rock and roll singer?"

Leo reached over and patted my hand. "Dumb girl," he said. "Think of the Regensteins. They were European history and they spent half their lives with a bunch of old bluesmen."

I looked at Leo. I liked to think about him newly arrived from China wearing Eton shorts and high gray socks. Of his mother taking him to the Kleine Café for tea, when Leo would much rather have been playing baseball with his pals. I thought of him trying to become an American boy.

"In college we used to listen to Ruby singing 'Boy Oh Bad,'" Leo said.

"That was before my time," I said. "But she liked to keep all her big hits in her repertoire, so I sang it once."

"You know," Leo said, "I would like to think we will probably always know each other."

"Why will we?" I pleaded.

"Well, we both loved Ludwig," Leo said. "And besides. You're my American. I'm your European."

63

On a cloudy spring morning I sat with my husband and son, watching my boy eat Cheerios one by one. It was my morning to observe Little Franklin's class. I would sit on a tiny blue chair hoping that my child would not pay too much attention to me.

Although I longed for this opportunity, I dreaded the idea of showing up at school. Paulette Goldberg, the former Pixie Lehar, was lying in wait for me. The school fair was drawing ever closer and I knew I had to tell her one way or the other what I intended to do.

As my husband ate his way through a stack of toast, he hectored me.

"Come on. It'll be good for you," he said.

"What will be good for Mommy?" said Little Franklin.

"Pankie," said Johnny. "Remember when Mommy swam across the lake? You didn't know she was a great swimmer. Well, she's a great dancer and a great singer. Before you were born, she used to sing on stage."

"Where was I?" said Franklin.

"You weren't born," said Johnny.

"But where *was* I?"

"You were in my tummy," I said.

"Even before you knew Daddy?"

"You were always in my tummy," I said. This was a conversation we had had thousands of times.

"Did you have a big tummy when you sang?"

"You were just an idea in my tummy," I said. "Very, very tiny."

This satisfied him, and he went back to his cereal.

"Would you like to watch your mama dance and sing?" Johnny said.

"Why, you little shitheel," I whispered. "Don't you dare!"

"What kind of dance?" said Franklin.

"Your mommy wore a beautiful green dress," said Johnny. I stared at him in disbelief. He had gotten a faraway look in his eyes, and his voice sounded misty, as if he were about to spout forth one of the *Just So Stories*. "Your mama wore a beautiful green dress and green shoes. She wore her hair fixed up on top of her head, with curls down the sides. Up on stage she looked like a tropical bird. When she sang, it was the most wonderful sound in the world."

"Shut up," I said. Franklin looked raptly at his daddy.

"She still has that beautiful green dress in her closet," Johnny said.

"You manipulative little pismire," I said.

"If you asked her, I'll bet she would go and get it," said Johnny.

"Let's see, Mommy," said Franklin. "I want to see now, Mommy, okay?"

I had never felt hatred for my husband until that moment. My child ran off like a shot to my closet, where he began pawing through my clothes.

"Get out of there, Franklin," I said.

"Is this it? Mommy, is this your bird dress?"

Since I was still in my nightgown, it was easy enough to slip on my chartreuse dress with the fringe. It actually fit. My child looked at me in perfect wonder.

"Hey, Mommy. Look at all those *strings*," he said.

"Come on, baby, let the good times roll," said Johnny. "It still looks boss."

"Aren't you a relic," I said. "It's a little tight under the arms."

"It looks wonderful," Johnny said. "Come here, Franklin. Remember that record we listened to with Amos the other day? 'Jump for Joy'? Your mommy used to sing and dance to that song."

My hatred, which had begun as a smoldering coal, turned into a veritable barbecue. So my husband had been listening to old Ruby records with my child behind my back!

He threw "Jump for Joy" on the turntable and gave me a significant look. Oh, what the hell, I thought. I could have done that routine in my sleep. My child gaped at me.

"Be the dancer! Be the dancer, Mommy," said my boy. I did my routine and then I scooped my son into my arms and danced around the room with him. He closed his eyes and smiled a smile of fright and rapture.

By the time we were dressed I had re-metamorphosed into Franklin's mother, and together we walked off to school.

At the school door Pixie Lehar, in her guise as Paulette Goldberg, was waiting for me.

"Are you going to say yes?" she said. "We really want you."

"I don't know," I said.

Because we were early, the doors were not yet open and so Little Franklin and I sat on a ledge outside. I watched the light bounce off Pixie's expensive watch, and then I looked up at the pure gray sky. That morning Leo was flying off to Berlin. He had finished his academic year and was off to begin his fellowship. I wondered what Mary was doing at her monastery, and what she would advise me to do. How lucky were people in their vocations! How sweet and easy life was for the *identified*, I thought.

In little Franklin's classroom I watched him and his friends build complicated structures out of blocks, and paint at easels, and do woodworking with real saws and hammers. My child barely acknowledged that I was in the room.

Then it was time for rhythms, a combination of movement, dance and imagination, invented by the founder of the Malcolm Sprague School. It took place in a large, gymlike room made of polished wood. On a small stage was a grand piano at which a woman in a white sweater sat.

I sat on the stage and watched Little Franklin and his classmates file in. Then the music began, a jaunty kind of march. The children knew exactly what to do: they pranced and skipped.

"Hello," said the rhythms teacher. "Now that you've all marched in so nicely, maybe we should have a little gentle gallop."

At this the music picked up. The children galloped and skipped in a circle, and jumped in the air.

"Now," said the teacher. "Once more around, and then trot up to the front."

When they were assembled in front of her she said; "You know, it's such a cloudy day, I thought it might be nice to have some color."

"Scarves!" shouted my son.

From a large cloth bag the teacher took a number of long crepe de chine scarves of brilliant colors. "I dye them myself," she said to me. "It's the only way I can get the colors I want Now, let's see who wants which color. Franklin, is your favorite color still green? Yes? Then have your mommy tie this one around your waist."

I tied his scarf and the scarves of several of his pals.

The music began again, and the children were asked to imagine that they were birds. They swooped and glided, and picked up the ends of their scarves and used them for wings.

I sat on the stage and watched my boy. He had forgotten I was there. He twirled and danced and then he and his classmates settled into their nests and draped their scarves around them. When the music changed, they got up and stretched, and little by little they flew again.

I could not take my eyes off these beautiful children. Their skin gleamed in the dark light, and the whites of their eyes were blue. They moved as easily and happily as leaves in the wind, like fish, like birds. That space was theirs to dance and glide through, like water to a swimmer.

I followed my boy, whose coppery hair flopped into his eyes. I thought of what he would be, what I had been, of the old man he would turn into whom I would never know. The journey seemed impossibly strange, amazingly long, and over in a flash.

They were in their element, as free as shooting stars or dragonflies. My boy danced around and waved his crepe de chine wings at me.

I thought to myself that I might as well say yes to Pixie Lehar. Why not? It was an undeniable fact of my life that long ago I had been a singer and a dancer and, in the end, it was certainly something I still knew how to do.

Penn blvd
19 s
around 2 miles

O clean ave MAKE left   on to

Go   1 traffic — merrick rd
make Right

HOT SKATES
Then